Peter Temple is the most acclaimed crime and thriller
writer in Australia, with a legion of fans around the world.
He has won the Ned Kelly Award for crime fiction an
unprecedented five times, most recently for *The Broken
Shore*, and was awarded Australia's premier literary award,
the Miles Franklin Prize, for *Truth*. He is also the author
of *An Iron Rose*, *Shooting Star*, *In the Evil Day* and three
other novels featuring Jack Irish: *Black Tide*, *Dead Point*,
and *White Dog*.

Praise for Peter Temple

'A towering achievement that brings alive a ferocious
landscape and a motley assortment of clashing characters.
The sense of place is stifling in its intensity, and seldom
has a waltz of the damned proven so hypnotic.
Indispensable' *Guardian*

'Peter Temple's prose is brusque and tender, according
to need, his characterisation subtle yet strong, and his
themes urgent and universal. Put simply, Peter Temple is
a master' John Harvey

'Temple is a master of the complex plot and his
characters leap from the page fully realised in a taut,
action-packed thriller' *Sunday Telegraph*

'Great locations, hard-nosed dialogue and a twisting plot
combine to create superb entertainment'
Evening Standard

'This is crime writing at its very best and discovering
Peter Temple has been the highlight of my year'
Mark Billingham

PETER TEMPLE

Bad Debts

Quercus

First published in Australia 1996 by HarperCollins

Published in Great Britain 2007 by Quercus
This edition published 2013 by

Quercus
55 Baker Street
7th Floor South Block
London
W1U 8EW

A CIP catalogue reference for this book is available
from the British Library

ISBN 978 1 78206 480 0
EBOOK ISBN 978 1 84916 432 0

10 9 8 7 6 5 4 3 2 1

Printed and bound in Great Britain by Clays Ltd, St Ives plc.

For Anita and Nicholas: true believers

I found Edward Dollery, age forty-seven, defrocked accountant, big spender and dishonest person, living in a house rented in the name of Carol Pick. It was in a new brick-veneer suburb built on cow pasture east of the city, one of those strangely silent developments where the average age is twelve and you can feel the pressure of the mortgages on your skin.

Eddie Dollery's skin wasn't looking good. He'd cut himself several times shaving and each nick was wearing a little red-centred rosette of toilet paper. The rest of Eddie, short, bloated, was wearing yesterday's superfine cotton business shirt, striped, and scarlet pyjama pants, silk. The overall effect was not fetching.

'Yes?' he said in the clipped tone of a man interrupted while on the line to Tokyo or Zurich or Milan. He had both hands behind his back, apparently holding up his pants.

'Marinara, right?' I said, pointing to a small piece of hardened food attached to the pocket of his shirt.

Eddie Dollery looked at my finger, and he looked in my eyes, and he knew. A small greyish probe of tongue came out to inspect his upper lip, disapproved and withdrew.

'Come in,' he said in a less commanding tone. He

took a step backwards. His right hand came around from behind his back and pointed a small pistol at my fly. 'Come in or I'll shoot your balls off.'

I looked at the pistol with concern. It had a distinctly Albanian cast to it. These things go off for motives of their own.

'Mr Sabbatini,' I said. 'You're Mr Michael Sabbatini? I'm only here about your credit card payment.'

'Inside,' he said, wagging the firearm.

He backed in, I followed. We went through a barren hallway into a sitting room containing pastel-coloured leather furniture of the kind that appears to have been squashed.

Eddie stopped in the middle of the room. I stopped. We looked at each other.

I said, 'Mr Sabbatini, it's only money. You're pointing a gun at a debt collector. From an agency. You can go to jail for that. If it's not convenient to discuss new arrangements for repayments now, I'm happy to tell my agency that.'

Eddie shook his head slowly. 'How'd you find me?' he said.

I blinked at him. 'Find you? We've got your address, Mr Sabbatini. We send your accounts here. The company sends your accounts here.'

Eddie moved aside a big piece of hair to scratch his scalp, revealing a small plantation of transplanted hairs. 'I've got to lock you up,' he said. 'Put your hands on your head.'

I complied. Eddie got around behind me and said, 'Straight ahead. March.'

He kept his distance. He was a good metre and a half behind me when I went through the doorway into the kitchen. There were about a dozen empty champagne bottles on various surfaces around the room – Perrier Jouet, Moët et Chandon, Pol Roger, Krug. No brand loyalty here, no concern for the country's balance of payments. The one on the counter to my right was Piper.

'Turn right,' Eddie said.

I turned right very smartly. When Eddie came into the doorway, the Piper bottle, swung backhand, caught him on the jawbone. The Albanian time-bomb in his hand went off, no more than a door slam, the slug going Christ knows where. Eddie dropped the gun to nurse his face. I pulled him into the room by his shirt, spun him around and kicked him in the back of the right knee with an instep while wrenching him backwards by his hair. He hit the ground hard. I was about to give him a kick when a semblance of calm descended upon me. I spared him the grace note.

Eddie was moaning a great deal but he wasn't going to die from the impact of the Piper. I dragged him off by the heels and locked him in the lavatory along the passage.

'Mate,' he said in a thick voice from behind the door, 'mate, what's your name?'

I said, 'Mr Dollery, that was a very silly thing to do. Where's the money?'

'Mate, mate, just hold it, just one second...'

The freezer had been stocked for a two- or three-week stay, but all the recent catering had been by Colonel Sanders, McDonald's and Dial-a-Dino.

Dessert was from Colombia. There were dirty shirts and underpants all over the main bedroom and its bathroom. The mirror-fronted wall of cupboards held three suits, two tweedy sports jackets and several pairs of trousers on one side. On the other hung a nurse's uniform, a Salvation Army Sally's uniform, a meter maid's uniform, and what appeared to be the parade dress of a female officer in the Waffen SS. With these went black underwear, some of it leather, and red suspender belts. My respect for Mrs Pick, florist and signatory to the house's lease, deepened. By all accounts, she had a way with flowers too.

I was passing the lavatory on my way back from looking over the laundry when Eddie Dollery said, 'Listen, mate, you want to be rich?'

He had excellent hearing. I stopped. 'Mr Dollery,' I said, 'meeting people like you is riches enough for me.'

'Cut that smart shit. Are you going to do it?'

'Do what?'

'Knock me.'

His was not a proper vocabulary for someone who had been an accountant. 'Don't be paranoid,' I said. 'It's that marching powder you're putting up your nose.'

'Oh, Jesus,' said Eddie. 'Give me a chance, will you?'

I went into the sitting room and telephoned Belvedere Investments, my temporary employer. Mr Wootton would return my call, said Mrs Davenport. She'd had twenty years as the receptionist for a specialist in sexually transmitted diseases before joining Wootton. J. Edgar Hoover knew fewer secrets.

I looked around some more while I waited. Then I

sat down next to the phone and studied what I could see of Mabberley Court. Nothing moved except a curtain in the house opposite, a building so sterile and with surroundings so perfectly tended that it could have been the Tomb of the Unknown Suburbanites.

The phone rang.

'Jack, my boy. Good news, I hope. Speak freely, old sausage.' Wootton was in a pub.

I said, 'Dollery thinks I'm here to kill him.'

'Got him, have you? Bloody spot on.'

'I expect to be warned about the armed and desperate, Cyril. There'll be an extra five per cent deduction to cover my shock and horror at having a firearm pointed at me.'

Wootton laughed his snorting laugh. 'Listen, Jack, Eddie's a disloyal little bugger with lots of bad habits but he wouldn't actually harm anyone. People like that think the worst about everything. It's the guilt. And eating icing sugar with their noses. What's on the premises?'

'Ladies' uniforms,' I said.

Wootton laughed again. 'That's one of the habits. He's got the stuff on him, hasn't he?'

It was starting to rain on Mabberley Court. Across the road, an impossibly white cat had appeared on the porch of the Tomb.

On my way out, I stopped to speak to Eddie. You can't help admiring a man who can get the local florist to dress up in Ilse Koch's old uniform over crotchless leather panties.

'Mr Dollery,' I said outside the lavatory, 'you're going to have to be more cooperative with people whose money you have stolen. Pointing a firearm at their representatives is not the way.'

Eddie said, 'Listen, listen. Don't go. Give me the gun back and I'll tell you where to find ten grand. Go round the back and put the gun through the window. Ten grand. Notes. Old notes.'

'I know where to find ten grand,' I said. 'Everybody keeps ten grand in the dishwasher. And everybody keeps seventy grand in the airconditioner. Wootton reckons you're short twenty. I'm pushing a receipt for eighty grand and a pen under the door. I want you to sign it.'

There was a moment's silence.

'Mate,' Eddie said, 'every cent. Tell him every cent.'

'You tell him. Just sign,' I said.

The receipt came back, signed.

'The pen, please.'

The pen appeared. 'Thank you. Goodbye, Mr Dollery.'

Eddie was shouting something when I closed the front door, but he'd stopped by the time I reached the car. Across the road, the white cat was watching. I drove out of Mabberley Court. Two hours later, I was at Pakenham racecourse watching a horse called New Ninevah run seventh in a maiden.

The next day, I went to Sydney to talk to a possible witness to a near-fatal dispute in the carpark of the Melton shopping centre. It was supposed to be a six-hour quickie. It took two days, and a man hit me on the upper left arm with a full swing of a baseball bat. It was an aluminium baseball bat made in Japan. This would never have happened in the old days. He would have hit me with a Stewart Surridge cricket bat with black insulation tape around the middle. Except in the old days I didn't do this kind of work.

It was 5.30 p.m. on Saturday before I got back. I listened to a summary of the football on the radio on the way from the airport. 'Fitzroy started in a blaze of glory...' said the announcer. I felt like switching off. The only question left was: By how much? By 114 to 78 was the answer.

I turned off at Royal Park and drove around the university and through Carlton to the Prince of Prussia. It was one of the few pubs left in Fitzroy that still made a living out of selling beer. Most of the proud names had been turned into Thai–Italian bistros with art prints in their lavatories.

I parked a block away, two wheels on the kerb in a one-way street, and made a run for the Prince. I could have found it by smell: a hundred-odd years of spilt beer. My grandfather used to drink there. So did my father. His dark, intense face is in the faded photographs of the Fitzroy Football Club sides of the late 1940s on the wall near the door marked GENTS.

There are only a few dozen Fitzroy supporters left who remember my father; to them I represent a genetic melt down. Three of these veterans were sitting at the bar nursing glasses of beer and old grievances. As I stood brushing rain off my sleeves, they looked at me as if I were personally responsible for Fitzroy's 36-point loss to despised Carlton on Saturday.

'Three in a row, Jack,' said Eric Tanner, the one nearest the door. 'Played like girls. Where the hell were you?'

'Sorry, men,' I said. 'Business.'

Three sets of eyes with a combined age of around 220 examined me. They all held the same look. It was the one the boy in the gang gets when he is the first to put talking to a girl ahead of kicking the football in the street.

'I had to go to Sydney,' I said. 'Work.' I might as well have said I had to go to Perigord for truffles for all the exculpatory power this statement carried.

'Should've taken the team with you,' said Wilbur Ong.

'What kind of work does a man have in Sydney on Satdee arvo?' said Norm O'Neill in a tone of amazement. These men would no more consider being away from Melbourne on a Saturday in the football season than they would consider enrolling in personal development courses.

I caught the eye of Stan the publican. He was talking in undertones to his wife, Liz, at the serving hatch to the kitchen. Only half of her face was visible, her mouth a perfect Ctesiphon curve of disgust. Stan said a last word and floated over, a big man, thinning head of pubic hair, small nose like an afterthought pinched out by the divine sculptor. His eighty-six-year-old father, Morris, owned the pub and wouldn't sell it. To Liz's disgust, he also wouldn't die.

'The boys missed you today,' he said.

'They told me how much,' I said. 'Cleaned these pipes yet?' The beer had been tasting funny for weeks.

Stan looked at me pityingly. 'Jack, you could give a baby milk through these pipes. I had the bloke in. Nothing come out 'cept clean steam. Clean steam in, clean steam out. Chucking my dough away, he reckons.'

He put the first full glass on the counter. 'Your Mr Pommy Wootton's been ringing. The old bat said to give him a tinkle when you came in, quick smart.'

'He's about as pommy as you are,' I said. 'His old man taught welding at Preston Tech.'

'Wish my old man'd taught welding at Preston Tech,' Stan said with controlled venom. 'Then I wouldn't be standin here till all hours listenin to old buggers fartin on about footie games sixty years ago.'

I rang Wootton from what Stan called his office, a midden of old bills, junk mail, newspapers, telephone directories. Under the telephone was a Carlton & United Breweries page-a-day diary. The year was 1954.

'Mr Wootton has made a number of attempts to contact you,' said Mrs Davenport. 'Please wait while I see whether he's free.'

'Free, free, like a bird in a tree,' I said. I don't know why.

'I beg your pardon?' said Mrs Davenport, not startled.

'It's a line from an American poet, E. A. Presley.'

There was a silence of precise duration. It told me my flippancy had been noted. Then Wootton came on the line, querulous.

'What's the point of having an answering machine if you don't plan to respond to messages? I even resorted to ringing that filthy hole you drink in.'

'Even as we speak I am in that hole.'

'Well, see if you can get out of it by Monday to do a small task for me.'

'Cyril,' I said, 'do I detect a hint of the master-servant relationship creeping in here? Let's start with a nice thank you for the parcel I dropped off on Thursday. And then we can talk about the possibility of future dealings.'

'Thank you,' he said ungratefully. 'I notice that you remunerated yourself rather lavishly in excess of the agreed fee.'

'The agreed fee didn't cover uniform fetishists armed with dodgy guns. I explained that on the phone.'

'Perfectly harmless little turd.'

'There's no such thing as an armed harmless little turd.'

We went on like this for a while. Then I went back to the bar, drank a beer with the lads, ate a toasted cheese sandwich crafted out of recycled sawdust and polyvinyl by the reluctant hands of Liz. I was at the door when Stan said, 'Another bloke looking for you. Thursday, I think it was. Said he'd been round your office.'

'Name?'

'Didn't say. Didn't ask. Said he'd come back.'

'What'd he look like?'

Stan thought for a while, squinting slightly. 'Short,' he said. 'Dangerous.'

'That's half the people I know.'

I went home. The flat smelled of musty books. It took me back to the start of my legal career, searching through document boxes stacked like tin coffins in a crypt. I put my bag in the bedroom and opened the sitting room windows. The cold came in like a presence. At the end of the lane cars flicked by. The rain held in the streetlight's cone seemed to rise from the sharkskin pavement.

I made a drink of whisky, ice and tap water and slumped on the sofa beside the telephone. In the gloom, the little red light on the answering machine blinked nervously. I went to push the button and thought, bugger it. Tomorrow.

I finished the whisky, made some Milo and took it to bed, feeling tired and lonely. It took six pages of a Bolivian novelist to put me away.

On Sunday I fiddled around, doing nothing, restless, vaguely sorry for myself. I spent an hour writing a letter to my daughter in Queensland. Claire was cooking on a fishing boat out of Port Douglas. In my mind, I saw her, a beautiful stick with wrists the size of some men's knuckle-bones. She was circled by large males, blond men with permanent sunburn and the eyes of dead sharks. I thought about the first time I saw Claire's mother, on Bells Beach. She had been surrounded by testosterone-crazed surfers, all lying belly down to hide their erections.

I reread Claire's most recent letter. It made too many mentions of the boat's skipper, a man called Eric. I ended my letter with some delicately phrased warnings about the distorting effects of propinquity on judgment. Still, at least Eric had a job.

I walked to the corner to post the letter. The sky was low, the colour of misery, wind whipping the naked trees. There was no-one in the park except a man and a small boy sitting at a table near the playground. The boy was eating something out of a styrofoam box, his eyes on the table. The man was smoking a cigarette. He put out a helpless hand and touched the boy's hair.

I went home and the winking light on the answering machine caught my eye as I came in the door. I pressed the button and slumped on the couch.

Jack, Andrew. Thought you'd be back by now. Listen, I've pushed a little lease thing your way. Bloke called Andropolous. I just got his cousin off a couple of obtaining-by-deceptions. Andy's all right. Cash in hand. Pause. By the way, Helen's fucked off. Give me a ring when you get back. Cheers. Oh, my secretary says a guy called McKillop was around here today looking for you. Ex-client, I gather. See you.

The machine's deep voice said: *Thursday, July 23, 6.20 p.m.* Andrew Greer, former law partner.

Jack. Mate, it's Danny McKillop. Pause. Danny, y'know, the hit-and-run? In '84? I'm out. You said ring you, like if there was something? I'm in a bit of strife, mate. You reckon you can give me a ring? It's 9419 8432. Tonight if you can. Cheers.

The machine said: *Thursday, July 23, 7.47 p.m.*

I stopped the machine. Danny McKillop. *Y'know, the hit-and-run?* It meant nothing. A former client? A client who went to jail. Plenty of those around. I pressed the button again.

Jack, Laurie Baranek. Look, this agreement needs a bit extra, know what I mean? Can we stick in a coupla other penalties? I just want it so he understands he don't deliver, he's in big shit. Get my meaning? Ring me. Not at work, I'm on the mobile.

Friday, July 24, 2.28 p.m. Laurence Baranek, vegetable merchant and property speculator.

Jack, it's Danny. McKillop. Get my message? Listen, ring any time, doesn't matter what time. Pause. Jack,

I'm in deep shit. Can you meet me in the carpark of the Hero of Trafalgar in Brunswick? It's off Sydney Road. Seven o'clock tonight? I wouldn't ask only I'm shitting myself, okay? Cheers.

The man said it was Saturday, 25 July, 3.46 p.m.

There were no more messages, just a lot of silences and disconnections. Danny McKillop? The name still meant nothing. I rang the number. No answer. I put on Mahler, made a beef stew, opened a bottle of wine, rang my sister and listened for half an hour. The day passed.

On Monday, Cameron Delray, the small man's enigmatic footsoldier, picked me up at Taub's Cabinetmaking in Fitzroy. It's in Carrigan's Lane, a grubby one-way that runs down to Smith Street, Collingwood. Cam blocked the street with his Kingswood. I was at the back of the shop making myself useful, ripping some ash for a bureau carcass. I switched off the machine with my knee and took off my helmet.

Cam gave me a nod and walked over to where Charlie Taub was fine-tuning some clamps on a George III writing table.

'G'day, boss,' Cam said. 'How's the apprentice coming on?'

'Not bad,' said Charlie, taking the long-dead cheroot out of his mouth and looking at it. 'Five, six years, he'll make a joint that fits. Then I'll sell him the business and retire.'

I was taking off my leather apron. 'Retire at ninety?' I said. 'Premature, that's what they'll say. Best work still ahead of him.'

Cam said, 'Get along without the boy for a bit?'

'I'll try,' Charlie said. 'Fifty years on my own, if I'm ready yet I don't know.' He gave me his appraising look from under the exploding grey eyebrows. 'I blame myself,' he said. 'Introducing you to Harry Strang.'

I said, 'Don't torture yourself, Charlie. People have introduced me to a lot worse than Harry Strang. By a factor of about three thousand.'

'Horse business,' Charlie said. 'Never met a man it didn't ruin.'

'I should be so lucky to be ruined like Harry Strang,' I said. 'I'm scared Harry'll die before he ruins me.'

'Material possessions,' Charlie said. He lit the cheroot with a kitchen match and coughed for a while, waving the smoke away with a hand the size of a tennis racquet. 'Material possessions he's got. Otherwise, a ruined man. Ruined.'

Cam's Kingswood smelt faintly of expensive perfume. The radio was on. An ABC voice, rich with authority, was saying:

The Premier, Dr Marcia Saunders, today defended the six hundred million dollar Yarra Cove project.

Approving the project, which will transform a large section of the west bank of the Yarra, was one of the new government's first acts.

Dr Saunders said she and her party had for years in opposition called for a number of large Melbourne developments to be given the go ahead.

The Premier's voice, hoarse, slightly too loud, the voice of someone you interrupt at your peril, followed.

The previous government was so obsessed by its hatred of anyone who made a profit and created jobs that it allowed this State to stagnate. Well, the people of Victoria have had enough of social engineering. This government is trying to get this State moving again. We're unashamedly pro-development and so are the people who voted us into office.

The announcer came back.

Opposition leader David Kerr said the Yarra Cove project had no merit whatsoever.

David Kerr's gravelly voice said, *This government would like to hand the whole State over to their pals the developers. Yarra Cove is bad enough, but it's just the beginning...*

'Yarra Cove?' said Cam. 'What the hell is Yarra Cove?'

'Sounds tropical,' I said. 'Topless girls in grass skirts swaying by the banks of the Yarra, that sort of thing.'

'In this climate,' Cam said, 'they start topless, they'll end titless.'

We were on Johnston Street. I closed my eyes as Cam aimed the Kingswood at a gap between two vehicles that had to grow about two metres before he reached it. It obviously grew. I opened my eyes. Cam punched over to 3MP Easy Music. They were playing 'The Way We Were', probably for the fifth time since breakfast. He screamed and punched over to a man talking about public transport.

Harry Strang lived in Parkville, in a huge Victorian house behind high red-brick walls. Cam spoke into the voicebox in the studded street door and the door unlocked itself. The house was fifty metres away, at the end of a stone path that wound through a two-gardener garden.

Lyn Strang let us in. Harry's wife was in her forties, sexy in a bush-hospital nurse way: short hair, snub nose, legs-apart stance. She had a generous mouth, big knowing hands and broad calf muscles. Lyn had been married to a small-time country trainer called Ronnie Braudel. Ronnie lucked on to a horse called Fiery Continent, a little thing with no more breeding than the average can of dog food. But the horse was more than the sum of his parents. He was an equine freak, a once-in-a-lifetime horse.

Ronnie Braudel was just smart enough to keep his mouth shut and look for help with the horse. His old man knew Harry Strang, and Harry knew what to do with Fiery Continent.

It took just under twelve months to set it up, but it was the mother of all paydays for Ronnie. He transferred his operations to Queensland, taking with him a new friend, eighteen-year-old Valma, a highly qualified nail technician from Wangaratta. Harry extended his sympathies to the deserted wife and Lyn Braudel ended up the fourth Mrs Harry Strang. She gave Harry about thirty years' start and he conceded two hands in height but there was an electricity between them.

Harry was waiting in the study. The room was the idea of a study that is stored up in heaven. It had a full wall of mahogany bookshelves, probably five metres high and ten metres wide, opposite the windows. The upper shelves were reached by four teak and brass ladders that moved on rails. On the shelves was what seemed to be every book ever written on horse racing.

The other walls displayed a collection of racing paintings and prints. Between the windows hung a set of photographs in walnut frames of Harry Strang winning English and French races in the late 1940s and early 1950s: the English and Irish Derbies, the King Edward VII Stakes, the Queen Alexandra Stakes, the Prix de l'Arc de Triomphe, the Grand Prix de Deauville, the Prix de Diane, the Grand Prix de Saint Cloud.

Harry could ride at about the same weight now as when he was in the photographs. He was tall by jockey standards and looked taller because of his shoulders-back, chin-up carriage. He had a full head of short hair, dark with some unscented oil, a small-featured face barely lined. Today he was wearing a Donegal tweed suit, dark-green silk tie on a creamy shirt, russet brogues. I could never help staring at his feet. You can't buy handmade brogues to fit ten-year-olds in the shops, so Lobb's in London made Harry's shoes: $400 a shoe.

'Jack, Cam,' he said. 'Sit.'

Harry liked to get on with it.

We sat down in leather club armchairs. Harry went behind the desk, a classic piece in the style of Eugene Harvill made by Charlie Taub. Almost everything in the apartment was made or restored by Charlie.

Harry put his hands on the desk. They were the hands of someone half his age and twice his size: square-tipped, tanned, strong-looking. There was nothing wrong with his eyes, either.

'Crook arm, Jack?' he said.

I hadn't been aware of touching it. 'Just a strain,' I said.

Harry cocked his head. 'Give it the balsam three times a day. Now. Business. A bloke I've done some transactin with across the years, he reckons he's got somethin for us.'

The years spent in Europe had done nothing to take small-town Victoria out of Harry's voice.

There was a knock at the door and ancient Mrs Aldridge, Harry's housekeeper for thirty-odd years, came in, followed by Lyn Strang carrying a tray of coffee things. At the table, Mrs Aldridge took command, shooing Lyn out of the room. When we had each been served a cup of hell-dark brew from the silver pot, plus a chocolate biscuit, business resumed.

'This fella's name is Tie. Rex Tie,' Harry said. 'Trains a few cattle out in the bush.'

Cam said, 'Time Urgent.'

'That's the one,' Harry said.

'You do that Time Urgent thing?' Cam asked.

'What's past is past,' Harry said. 'I want to have a little look, see if Rex Tie's brain's still workin. We'll have to get on the Drizas, motor out to the bush next week. Suit, Jack?'

I nodded.

'Good. Cam, let's step over and look at the movin pictures.'

We went across the passage into Harry's wood-panelled cinema and sank into the plush armchair seats. Cam plugged in the video cassette I'd given him, pressed some buttons on a remote control, and moist Pakenham appeared on the wraparound screen. Harry had been at Pakenham. I'd seen him up near the back of the stand, on his own as always, grey felt hat, undistinguished raincoat, eyes stuck to the X15 binoculars. You never went near Harry on a racetrack, that was the rule. You didn't talk to Cam either if you saw him. My job had been to video New Ninevah's run with about twenty thousand dollars' worth of small video camera. For this and a bit of legal work, I got paid a retainer.

'Take the start in slow, Cam,' said Harry.

We watched in silence.

'Again,' Harry said. And so it went on. It took nearly ten minutes to watch a race that was over in 1 minute 24.20 seconds. When Cam put the lights on, Harry looked at me and said, 'Did he or didn't he?'

I shrugged. 'Looked like he was trying to to me. Didn't miss the start this time.'

'No,' Harry said. 'No, he came out fightin. Cam?'

'Clean, I'd say,' Cam said. He was putting a label on the video cassette. 'Reckon he just don't like the wet.'

Harry got out of his chair. 'Course we could be pissin on the wrong campfire again.' He walked over and looked out the window, hands in his jacket pockets. 'Doubt it though.' He sighed. 'Well, that's it for today, gentlemen. Ballarat on Wednesday. Freeze our arses off as usual. Come round nine for a bit of sustenance. Suit? Jack, Cam'll drop you back. Then he's got some computin to do. That and clean the gutterin and prune the roses.'

'After that I'm going to put on my burglar suit and give the dogs savaging practice,' said Cam.

'I forgot,' Harry said. 'They're getting rusty.'

Cam dropped me at my office, which is down the lane from Taub's Cabinetmaking. The sign outside said 'John Irish, Barrister & Solicitor' but I didn't do much that resembled law from the place. Apart from the odd lease or conveyance for Harry Strang, most of my income came from collecting serious debts or finding witnesses. It was something I'd drifted into doing when I stopped being a criminal lawyer.

The office was just one large room on the street, with a small room and a toilet behind it. It had once housed a tailor, and I used the large table he'd left behind as my desk. The man at the corner shop told me the tailor used to sit cross-legged on the table to do his handstitching. I sat down and switched on my Mac, got out my notebook and started work on the statement I'd got from the witness in Sydney.

When I'd finished, I got a salad sandwich from the corner shop and ate it at my table. Then I drove around to the offices of Andrew Greer – my old offices – at the city end of Drummond Street, Carlton. You could walk to the magistrate's courts from there, that was why we'd bought the old terrace house and spent months fixing it up ourselves.

Andrew's filthy old Saab was outside.

There was no sign of his secretary. I was walking down the passage when he appeared at his door.

'Nice bit of cloth,' I said. Drew was wearing a navy-blue suit.

He looked down at himself. 'Bought it with the tip Mrs De Lillo gave me,' he said. 'From Buck's. Nine hundred dollars.' He pointed at a lapel. 'There's a puke stain here you can barely see.'

'Nearly invisible,' I said. 'From about a hundred metres in bad light. I got Mrs Brierley.'

'You beauty. What does she say?'

'She puts your bloke about five metres from the deceased at the vital moment. She says she knows him by sight. Used to buy fish and chips at the shop.'

A smile grew on the long face. He shook his head. 'Lord,' he said, 'thou art merciful, even unto him who hath sinned. Let's have a drink on this.'

'It's 3 p.m., Andrew.'

'Pre-dinner drink. We in the law eat early.'

'Her boyfriend hit me with a baseball bat.'

'What? Didn't break anything? No?'

I shook my head.

'Good, good. Your suffering won't be in vain. I'll get you something for pain and suffering. This bloke's loaded. Dudded plenty of insurance companies.'

I followed him down the passage into the kitchen at the back of the building. We sat at the formica-topped table. Drew opened two bottles of Coghills Creek lager. I had a sip, put the bottle down and put my hands in my pockets. Reformed binge drinkers know how things start.

'What's this about Helen?'

Andy drank about a third of his bottle, held it up to the light and gave a little laugh. 'Gone, mate. Gone to live in Eltham with a painter. Left me with the kids.'

'House?'

'She doesn't get the house. Not if I can help it.'

'The painter. Does he paint houses?'

'Oh. No fucking way. This is a romance. With a serious artist. Though no-one's ever heard of the cunt. Bruce Seal. You ever heard of Bruce Seal?'

'I hate to say this, but yes.'

'You're not supposed to say that. You're supposed to say never heard of the cunt.' He drank more beer and wiped his moustache. 'What have you heard about him, anyway?'

'Just your normal Eltham bloke. Hugely talented artist. Speaks five languages. Plays classical piano. Two-handicap golfer. Fourteenth dan in karate. Twelve-inch dick. Why?'

'Forget it. I don't think I'm going to get the sympathy I'm looking for.' He drained his beer and opened another one.

'How's Lorna?'

Drew looked at me suspiciously. Lorna was a public prosecutor he'd been having a desultory affair with for a long time. 'Lorna's fine. This has got nothing to do with Lorna. Helen doesn't know about Lorna.'

'What do the kids think?'

He held up his hands, palms outward. 'I don't know what Michael thinks. Only five billion people on the Internet know what Michael thinks. Vicky thinks it's cool. She was probably the only girl in her class living with both her parents.'

I had a small sip. 'What's Helen say?'

Drew looked at the ceiling. 'She says she's fallen in love with a wonderful man and it wouldn't have happened if I'd found a little more time for her over the last twenty years. Does she think I've enjoyed working my arse off?'

I said, 'She might. Everyone else does.'

'You prick. This is what I get in my hour of need.'

'Sounds like that's what Helen got in hers. If it's a consolation, it probably won't last. They say Bruce is more of a hunter than a farmer.'

'They say that, do they? Your artistic friends.'

'You've got to broaden your social horizons, mate,' I said. 'There are people out there who aren't lawyers, cops or crims. Listen, what did you do with my old files?' I had a final swig of beer, got up and poured what was left into the sink.

It took me about twenty minutes to find Daniel Patrick McKillop's file. He'd pleaded guilty in the County Court on 22 November 1984 to a charge of culpable driving. The victim was a twenty-year-old woman called Anne Elspeth Jeppeson, knocked down in Ardenne Street, Richmond, at 11.40 p.m. on 18 June 1984. She died instantly. The Crown called a witness who saw McKillop driving the car minutes after the collision and later picked him out of a line-up. McKillop was found asleep at the wheel of the vehicle about an hour after the collision. He had a blood alcohol count of 0.1. Blood and clothing fragments on the vehicle matched those of Anne Jeppeson.

The headline on a clipping dated 23 November 1984 said: WITNESS SAW JEPPESON DEATH CAR.

The story read:

The car that knocked down and fatally injured public housing campaigner Anne Jeppeson was seen swerving almost out of control three blocks from the scene, a court was told yesterday. The driver, Daniel Patrick McKillop, had a blood alcohol reading of 0.1 more than two hours later, according to evidence.

Mr McKillop, 24, of Zinsser Street, Richmond, pleaded guilty in the County Court to a charge of culpable driving on 18 June.

Anne Elspeth Jeppeson, 27, of Ardenne Street, Richmond, was killed instantly when she was struck by a vehicle outside her home on 18 June.

Mr Ronald Bishop said he was driving along Freeman Street, Richmond, at 11.40 p.m. on 18 June when a yellow car came weaving towards him.

'It almost hit the parked cars on my side of the street then it swerved across in front of me over to the other side and almost crashed into the cars there. The driver had to brake to avoid hitting them. It was almost out of control.'

Mr Bishop said he saw the driver's face clearly. He noted part of the car's registration number and telephoned the police when he got home.

Senior Constable Ivor Wilkins said Mr McKillop was found asleep behind the wheel of a yellow Ford Falcon belonging to him in the garage of his home. Mr Bishop later identified Mr McKillop as the driver of the vehicle he saw in Freeman Street.

Senior Constable Lauro Martines, of the traffic alcohol section, said Mr McKillop's blood-alcohol content was 0.1 per cent more than two hours after the accident.

Dr Alfred Hone, of the police forensic laboratories, said blood and fragments of cloth found on Mr McKillop's vehicle matched those of Miss Jeppeson.

Mr McKillop was remanded for sentencing until 4 December.

I found the clipping on 5 December under the headline: JEPPESON DEATH: DRIVER GETS TEN YEARS.

The story said that Daniel McKillop had a previous conviction for driving under the influence and had just emerged from his licence suspension at the time of the accident. He had been drinking in two hotels earlier that evening and had no recollection of the accident. The judge said some harsh things about drunken drivers, expressed regret at the loss of a 'courageous young woman with her life ahead of her' and complimented Mr Ronald Bishop on his public-spirited behaviour. McKillop got ten years in spite of his lawyer's plea that he was as much a victim as Anne Jeppeson: 'an unloved boy who has drifted into multiple addictions'.

I looked for his previous convictions. They took up half a page, mostly juvenile stuff. He had two convictions for drunken driving and was on a two-year suspension at the time of the accident. Somehow he'd never been to jail. The judge made up for that: McKillop got a non-parole period of eight years.

All of this was complete news to me. I looked at the date again: November 1984. It was at the beginning of the forgotten zone, the year or so I spent drunk and semi-drunk after my wife's death.

I looked through the other files for 1984 and early '85. There were only five or six after McKillop. I didn't remember any of them either.

I went back to Drew's office. He was reading something, beer on the desk.

'When I went off the rails back then,' I said, 'after Isabel's death...Did you try to keep me out of court?'

He took off his glasses and rubbed his eyes. 'I think you could say that,' he said. 'If it's worrying you, I hijacked all the defended matters between that day and the day you quit. I don't think you did any damage. Except to yourself.'

'And the firm,' I said. I felt a rush of gratitude towards this gangling, unemotional man.

He put his glasses back on and reached for the beer. 'Nothing permanent,' he said. 'We had a fair bit of goodwill to live off.'

'This McKillop who was looking for me. Remember him?' I offered him the file.

He took a minute to look it over. 'No, not him. The woman was a bit of a name on the left. Used to drink at the Standard with the free housing push.' He handed the file back. 'Danny got what was coming to him, Jack. Probably just in the shit again.'

At the front door, Drew said, 'I think I might take up seriously with Lorna.'

I put my hand on his shoulder. 'Mate, first look up "holiday" in the dictionary. It's an experience you might want to try. Want to come to the football on Saturday?'

He screwed up his face. 'We haven't been to the football for a bit, have we?'

'No,' I said. 'A lot of the same names still around though. Only it's the sons.'

'Fuck off. We'll go. Have a steak afterwards. At Vlado's.' He paused. 'Or Vlado's son's.'

Why did Danny McKillop want to see me so badly? I'd again put off ringing the number he'd left on the machine until I had him placed. The phone rang for a long time before a woman answered. I asked for Danny. There was a long silence. I could hear heavy traffic.

'Danny's not here.' The phone went down. I dialled the number again. The woman picked it up straight away.

I spoke quickly. 'Danny rang me. Left this number. Can you give him a message?'

Again, I listened to the traffic for a while before she spoke. 'Danny's dead,' she said. 'There's no point in ringing here.' Click.

I went to the window and watched the women from the pressing sweatshop across the lane on their smoko. They leant against the wall, laughing a lot, taking deep drags on their cigarettes. Then I looked up McKillop in the phonebook. There was a D. P. McKillop in Windermere Street, Northcote. I put my hand out to dial several times and withdrew it. Danny McKillop comes out of a black hole in my past, looks for me everywhere, and a few days later is dead. I opened the file I'd brought from Drew's. Danny would have been in his late thirties. Died of what?

When I finally dialled the number, a child answered, a girl, four or five perhaps.

'This is Kirsty McKillop speaking,' she said in precise tones. 'Mum's hanging up the washing.'

'Could I speak to her please, Kirsty,' I said.

'Hold on. I'll call her.'

I heard her shouting, 'Mum, a man's on the phone, a man's on the phone…'

When she came on, the woman was out of breath. 'Hello, Sue McKillop.'

I said, 'Mrs McKillop, sorry to bother you. Is that the home of Daniel Patrick McKillop?'

I could hear her breathing. 'Danny died, was killed on Friday night.' Her voice was flat, slightly hoarse.

'I'm terribly sorry,' I said. 'My name's Jack Irish. I was his lawyer once. He was trying to get hold of me last week, but I was away…'

'Yes, well, thank you for ringing, Mr Irish.'

'Forgive me asking, but how…'

She didn't let me finish. 'A policeman shot him. Murdered him.' She was making a statement of fact.

'Where did it happen?' I asked the question without thinking, and as I did a chill came over me.

'In a pub carpark. In Brunswick.'

'What pub was—'

'The Hero of Trafalgar.'

I never blamed myself for my wife's death. Not then or now. A client of mine, Wayne Waylon Milovich, shot and killed Isabel in a parking garage in La Trobe Street. When he'd done that, he taped a letter addressed to me to her forehead and went back to his car, a 1974 Ford Falcon with one hundred and thirteen unpaid parking tickets against its number. He then detonated two or three sticks of gelignite on his lap. The letter went: 'Mr Judas Lawyer Did You Now My Wife Run Away And Took My Kids While I Rotted In Jail Were You Sent Me Because You Wood Not Listen To What I Was Telling You As Your Clynt You Bastard.'

Deranged clients. It's a risk you run. Isabel knew that. She practised family law, where practically all the clients are deranged to some degree. I didn't blame myself. I just raged against fate. I couldn't get that through to people. They kept telling me to stop torturing myself. They *wanted* me to blame myself. I wasn't walking around drunk, crying in pubs, getting into fights with strangers because I was blaming myself. I was in a state of incoherent rage. I had lost someone who had cast a glow into every corner of my life. I was entitled to my feelings. Loss. Hate. Hopelessness. Worthlessness. Only the return of Isabel would have been enough.

Isabel and I were very different. Her childhood was the opposite of mine: she grew up in a fierce tribe of children, all lovingly neglected by their parents, a musician and a painter. She had emerged from the chaos clever, funny, diligent, dreamy, sensuous, and with an affection and concern for other people that descended indiscriminately like warm summer rain. She came into my habitual gloom and dispelled it, dissolved it, with one endless, helpless laugh.

After her death, I lost control for months. I would have put Wayne together again fragment by fragment just to tear him apart with my hands and teeth. I could not be still. I could hardly bear to sit down. I could not listen to music, read, exchange more than a few words with anyone. I slept only when hopelessly drunk; I woke within minutes, slick with cold sweat. All food tasted like dry oats and I did not eat for days on end. After I walked out on Andrew Greer, I drifted for months, driving without aim, drinking all day in sour little country pubs, lapsing into unconsciousness in the car or in some paper-walled motel room. I got arrested eventually in a sodden town in Queensland called Everton. Someone went through my wallet and got word to Andrew Greer. He pulled strings with a relative, a Cabinet Minister in the Queensland government, to get me off a variety of charges without a conviction. My car had vanished. We flew home together. I'd been in the cells for six days, hadn't had a drink, was over the worst. I stayed at home for weeks, going out only to buy food, and then I began slowly to resume some sort of normal life.

Sitting in my office, elbows on the tailor's table,

thinking about Danny McKillop brought the darkness of those times back to me. I wasn't over Isabel. I would never be over Isabel. She had made things complete, and they would never be complete again without her. I felt the pang of her absence every day, and at those moments I sometimes uttered an involuntary groan and shook my head like a dog.

Danny McKillop had been shot dead outside the pub where he was hoping I would come to meet him. I couldn't just leave the matter there. I knew I *should* leave it there, but I couldn't. At the worst time in his life, Danny had needed a sober lawyer. He had got me. Years later, he had turned to me again. And I didn't show up. I must have got home around 6.45 p.m. Would I have gone to the Hero of Trafalgar if I'd listened to the messages on the answering machine instead of going to bed? Probably. I'd have cursed a lot, but I'd have got there by 7 p.m. Sydney Road was only minutes away at that time on a Saturday night.

The phone rang. It was Drew.

'Seen the *Herald*?'

'No.'

'Daniel McKillop's on page three.'

I got the paper at the corner shop. A small item on page three said:

Police have identified the man shot dead by police in the carpark of the Hero of Trafalgar hotel in Brunswick on Saturday night as Daniel Patrick McKillop, 34, of Northcote.

Assistant commissioner Martin Doyle said the fatal shots were fired after Mr McKillop pointed a pistol at policemen who saw him behaving suspiciously in the hotel carpark shortly after 7 p.m.

'A full inquiry into the circumstances of Mr McKillop's death is in progress, but we have no reason to believe that the officers acted improperly,' Assistant Commissioner Doyle said. 'They feared for their safety.'

Mr McKillop was released from prison several years ago after serving eight years for killing a woman in a hit-and-run accident.

There wasn't anything to do except see Danny's widow.

Sue McKillop was on the plump side, with short dark hair and an open face made to smile. Her eyes were red. She was wearing a green tracksuit.

'You mind coming in the kitchen?' she said. 'I'm in the middle of Kirsty's tea.'

We went down the passage into a large, warm room that had a kitchen on one side and lounge chairs and a television on the other. The girl was in pyjamas with small roses on them in front of the television, watching a game show.

'Kirsty, this is Mr Irish. Say how do you do.'

Kirsty said it.

I sat at a pine kitchen table and watched Sue McKillop cut toast into squares and pile on scrambled eggs from a pan.

She found a small fork in a drawer.

'You can eat in front of the TV tonight, darling,' she

said, taking the plate over to the girl and kissing her quickly on the forehead.

When she came back, she sat down opposite me. 'My dad's coming from Queensland tonight,' she said. 'He's nearly eighty. I told him not to. We'll be all right.'

I said, 'What about Danny's family?'

She smiled, a wan lip movement. 'We're it. He was brought up by his nanna. She died while he was inside. There's just a cousin.'

'Danny left a message for me to meet him at the Trafalgar on Saturday night,' I said. 'I didn't get it until Sunday. Why did he want to see me?'

She moistened her lips. 'He was scared. They waited for him outside here on Thursday night, but he parked around the corner and when he was walking towards the house he saw them.'

'Who?'

'I don't know. Men. It's from the accident. Something, I don't know.'

'The accident Danny went to jail for?'

'Yes. He didn't do that.'

'Why do you say that?'

She shrugged. 'Someone told him he was fitted up. Someone who knew.'

'Do you know who the person was?'

'No. It was a woman. Danny said something about her husband dying.'

'When was that?'

'About a month ago. He changed all of a sudden. Got upset easily. Why do you want to know?'

I hesitated. 'I may be able to do something.'

She hugged herself. 'You can't do anything. You can't bring Danny back.'

'You said the police murdered him.'

'Danny never had a gun. And if he'd had one, why would he threaten the police?'

'Perhaps he didn't know they were police.'

She ran a hand through her short hair. 'The policeman who came here said the men identified themselves to Danny as police.'

'Danny been okay since he came out?'

She looked me in the eyes. 'Danny wasn't a crim. He finished school in jail. He worked with a friend of mine at Marston's. That's how I met him. It's a car part company in Essendon.'

'He used to be on smack.'

She shook her head. 'In another life. He wouldn't even drink more than two stubbies.'

I believed her. One thing practising law gives you is a feeling for some kinds of truth.

'When he saw the people waiting for him outside,' I said, 'what did he do?'

'He went to a callbox and rang Col Mullens next door and Col came over and called me to the phone.'

'Why didn't he ring here?'

'I don't know.'

'What did he say?'

'He said he couldn't come home because the house was being watched and he'd stay somewhere else for the night and sort it out on Friday. He was scared. I could hear it.'

'Why didn't he go to the police?'

She shook her head and took a tissue out of her

sleeve. 'Danny reckoned the cops were in on it.' She blew her nose. 'Had to be the cops fixed him up for the accident, didn't it? Did you know they gave him pills and stuff to take every day before the trial? Danny said he didn't hardly know where he was.'

'No, I didn't know that. So the men outside could have been cops?'

'Suppose so.'

'He didn't say they were cops?'

'No.'

'Have you told all this to the cops?'

'Yes. Friday night when they come around here.'

The girl came over with her plate. 'Cream, please,' she said, eyes fixed on me. Sue got up, took a tub of ice cream out of the fridge, put two scoops in a bowl and handed it to her daughter.

'Would you like some?' the girl said, showing me the bowl.

'No thanks, Kirsty,' I said. 'I haven't had my tea yet.'

She nodded and went back to the television.

Sue said, 'I'm sorry. I haven't offered you anything...'

I shook my head. 'That's fine. What did Danny do after this woman phoned him about being fixed up for the hit and run?'

'He said he was going to get the case opened again. The person who told him said there was evidence.'

'And did he find any?'

'I don't think so. I don't know. He wasn't a big talker, Danny. He'd sort of plan things in his head for weeks, just sit thinking, and then one day he'd just start doing something and he wouldn't stop until it was finished.' She looked around in pride and wonder. 'Like this room. Danny built the whole thing in two weeks in his holidays. I didn't even know he could knock a nail in.'

'Great piece of work,' I said. 'Does this phone number mean anything to you?' I read out the number Danny had left on the answering machine.

'No. I don't know that number.'

I had other questions but suddenly I wanted to be out of the snug room that Danny McKillop had built for his little family and out in the cold, streaming evening. I gave Sue my card and left. The child came to the front door and waved at me.

'I should've taken the fucken package, Jack,' Senior Sergeant Barry Tregear said.

We were sitting in my car in the carpark of the Kensington McDonald's, eating Big Macs. Barry Tregear also had two large French fries and a large Coke. He was a big man with a pear-shaped head, its summit and three upper slopes thinly covered in greying blond stubble. He always looked two slabs of beer away from fat, even when I'd first met him in Vietnam, but nothing moved when he walked.

'You could've gone back to Hay,' I said.

Barry grew up somewhere out on the endless plains around a town called Hay in New South Wales. His father hadn't come back from World War II, along with half of the other fathers of the kids in his school.

'Fuck Hay,' said Barry. 'Bloke offered me half a motel outside Lismore. Was in Licensing with me. Turned it down like a stupid prick. He sells out a couple of months ago, doubles his money. And I'm still driving around in the fucken rain, member of an elite group. Number eight on the new Commissioner's Top Ten shit list. Is that judgment or fucken what?'

He took a savage bite of his Big Mac.

A lot of work had drifted my way in the old days

because of Barry. He'd been in Consorting and then Major Crimes, squads closed down now but once home for hard men all but indistinguishable from the criminals they spent most of their time with. I'd had plenty of clients who'd come in and said variations on 'Barry Tregear reckons y'might get me a fair shake'.

I said, 'You've got an ex-cop for a Police Minister now. He'll see you old blokes right, won't he?'

Barry took in about eight chips and chewed thoughtfully. 'Garth Bruce is a cunt. And he's got selective amnesia. You hear him sprouting all that shit about getting rid of the old culture in the force? Mate, I'm part of the old culture and fucking proud of it,' he said around the potato.

'What exactly is the old culture?'

'The dinosaurs left over from when it didn't count if you took an extra ten bucks for the drinks when you put in for sweet for your dogs. When you had to load some cockroach to get it off the street. Public fucken service. We're the ancient pricks think it's okay to punch out slime who dob in a bloke who's walked out on the wire for them to fucking Internal Affairs. That's us. That's the old culture.'

I said, 'They got all of you on armed robbery now?'

Barry finished the chips, drained the Coke, put everything away neatly in the recyclable brown paper bag, opened his window and threw the bag out into the carpark. 'The ones they're hoping will take a bullet,' he said. 'We're out there doing the in-progresses. When I done this line of work years ago, only the mad dogs fired on you. Now it's all fucken mad dogs. They all fire on you. Chemical war's going on inside their heads. The stuff come in the nose is fighting with the stuff come up the arm. Cause for concern, I can tell you.'

He looked at his watch. 'Shit. I've gotta get moving. What's your interest in this McKillop?'

'Ex-client of mine. Wife reckons he thought someone wanted to kill him.'

Barry sighed. It triggered off a burp. 'Jesus,' he said, 'I'm all wind. Listen, short story is this Quinn, drug squad, he got a call just before seven Saturday night, there's a handover set for the yard of the Trafalgar, 7 p.m. There was a bit of stuffing around, they didn't get there till quarter past.'

He burped again and patted his pockets. 'Never got a bloody Quikeze when you need one. Anyway, they hang around for a bit, no-one in sight, reckon they've missed the boat. Then they take a stroll through the cars, one from each end, and this cunt pops up with a .38 pointing at Martin, Quinn's offsider. So Quinn, who's behind this guy, puts four in him. Dead on arrival. There's about five hundred bucks' worth of smack in his car. End of story.'

'And McKillop?'

'Form.'

'Not since.'

'Well shit's shit.'

'Wife can't believe it. Kid, job. Says he's been absolutely straight.'

Barry gave a snort. 'That's what Mrs Eichmann said.' He rubbed his stomach.

'What if Quinn went out, knocked him and planted the gun and the shit?' I said.

Barry gave me a long look, shaking his head. His eyes were light green, with little dark flecks. 'Jack,' he said. 'Jack, he's an officer with sixteen years' service. You take my meaning?'

'No.'

He got out of the car and leaned in. 'He'd have knocked him somewhere less public. Mate, I got to go. I'm further up shit creek if I don't get to town in about five minutes.'

'I'll be in touch. Buy you a drink,' I said.

Barry put his head back in the window. 'Drinks, mate, drinks. You're dealing with the old culture here.'

'Danny's dead,' the old woman said through the small opening. 'Who're you?'

I was standing on the leaking porch of a weatherboard house in Richmond. I'd got the address from a prison officer I knew from the days when I visited clients in Pentridge. The prison records had Mrs Mary McKillop, aunt, as Danny McKillop's next of kin. I looked her up in the phone book: it was the number Danny had left on the machine. Sue McKillop hadn't known the aunt was alive and had no idea how to find the cousin she'd mentioned.

'Mrs Mary McKillop?' I said.

'He's dead,' she repeated. 'Whad'ya want?'

'I'm a lawyer. I'd like to talk about Danny.'

'Danny's dead. Bugger off.'

The two-inch opening closed with a crack. I stared at the door's peeling green paint for a while, thinking about trying again. I could still smell the ancient fumes of boiled cabbage and cat piss and decaying ceilings that had leaked out when the door opened. That decided the issue. But as I turned the door opened a sliver.

'Try next door.'

The door closed again.

I tried the house to the right. A thin woman in her forties with lank, dead hair answered my knock. She blinked at me as if unaccustomed to light.

'I'm making inquiries about Danny McKillop,' I said.

She looked at me for a long time, then she put her hands in the pockets of her pink housecoat. 'He's dead. Was in the paper.' Her voice was toneless.

'It's his cousin I'd like to talk to.'

She looked at me in silence.

'It's about the accident Danny went to jail for. It's possible he didn't do it.'

She waited.

'There might be some compensation.'

She cleared her throat. 'You'd better talk to Vin. He's Danny's cousin. He's not here.'

'Is he Vin McKillop?' I said.

She nodded.

'Do you know where I could find him?'

She thought for a while, then said, 'Suppose he's working. Only time he gets up before twelve. Dennis Shanahan in Edge Street'll know.'

I found Dennis Shanahan in the phone book. A woman said he was demolishing a building in Abbotsford, Joseph Street.

There were three middle-aged men, a teenage boy and a lean brindle dog with a studded collar on the

49

site. I could see them all from across the road. One man was sitting in the cab of a truck behind the shell of the single-storey building, the second was prising out a window with a crowbar, the third was feeding a fire of old timbers in the back corner. The teenager was cleaning bricks with a hammer and chisel. The dog was watching him. A portable radio somewhere in the ruin was putting out 'Bridge over Troubled Water' at full volume.

I crossed the road and walked along a plank bridging the exposed floor beams to the first doorway in the passage. A smell of poor lives hung over the place: cooking fat, yellow feet, burnt ironing boards and blocked drains.

'I'm looking for Vin,' I shouted to the window remover. He made a gesture with his thumb without looking around.

I guessed the man in the truck would be the boss, so I tried the man at the fire. I couldn't get close: the heat was intense. It didn't seem to bother the man feeding it. He was short, heavyset, with dark curly hair and sideburns, probably in place since Elvis. The same could be said for his jeans and the grime on his hands and under his nails. His nose was flattened and slightly askew and a big piece of right eyebrow was gone.

'Vin McKillop?' I said.

He had a length of two-by-four hardwood in his right hand, poking the fire. He looked up at me without expression. Boxer's eyes. 'Who wants him?'

'I'm a lawyer,' I said. 'It's about Danny McKillop. I know he's dead but I need to talk to someone who knew him.'

The man threw his two-by-four into the flames.

'What about him?' he said.

'It's about the accident. The woman's death.'

He picked up another splintered piece of wood. 'He done the time,' he said flatly.

'I'm trying to find out if he done the crime.'

The man spat into the flames. 'What's it to you if he done it or not done it?'

'It's complicated,' I said. 'Can you spare me a bit of time? There's an interview fee.'

'I'm on the job.'

'Take half an hour unpaid. I'll pay you for that too.'

Vin McKillop positioned the wood carefully on the fire and rubbed under his nose with a forefinger. 'There's a pub around the corner,' he said. 'Cost you twenty bucks.'

The pub was empty except for two old men sitting at a formica table in a corner looking at nothing. The place smelt of stale beer and carbolic. I got two beers and sat at a table near the door. Vin came in and went straight through the door marked GENTS. When he came back, he stood at the bar. He was making some kind of point. I picked up the beers and went over to him.

'Cheers,' I said.

Vin didn't say anything. He just picked up the glass and drank three-quarters of the beer. 'So,' he said, 'what's the fee?'

I had a fifty-dollar note ready. I put it on the bar. Then I put a twenty on top of it.

Vin put the money in his top pocket. He took a cigarette out of the same pocket without revealing the pack and lit it with a plastic lighter. He took a deep drag and let the smoke run out his nostrils. I felt like asking him for one. 'You a Jack?' he said.

'No.' I took out a card and held it up for him to read. He looked at it.

'Need glasses,' he said. 'What's it say?'

'It says I'm a lawyer.' Vin couldn't read.

'Danny don't need a lawyer now.'

'There's his wife and child,' I said. 'Had you seen him recently?'

'Seen him when he come out. Didn't know him. Lost about a hundred pounds.'

'What kind of work did he do before he went in?'

'Nothin.' Vin drained his beer and signalled the barman with a big, dirty finger.

'Surprise you when he hit the woman that night?'

Vin flicked his cigarette stub into the trough at our feet. It lay there smoking. He lit another one. 'Yeah, surprised me.' He held his cigarette hand just above the counter and drummed with his thumb.

'Why's that?'

'What's it matter? Cunt's wormfood now.'

Vin's beer arrived. I paid.

'It matters. Why were you surprised?'

He drank half the beer and wiped his mouth on his cuff. 'Hadn't been near the car for months. He was on a year suspended for pissed driving. Fat prick was shit-scared of doing time.'

'But he could've forgotten all that, he was so pissed.'

Vin scratched an armpit. 'Yeah, well, that could be right if you can work out how a bloke that's so legless he's passed out in Punt Road about quarter past eleven can get sober enough to go home and get his car and drive about thirty blocks to cream some bitch at twenty to twelve.'

'Danny didn't mention that before the trial.'

'Fucking right.'

'How do you know where he was at quarter past eleven?'

'Mate of mine saw him.'

'You didn't tell the cops?'

'Didn't hear about it till after Danny was inside.'

'Why didn't your mate tell the cops at the time?'

Vin blew two flat streams of smoke out of his nostrils. 'Cause he was hoping Danny'd get about fifty years. Danny was a dog. There's lots of people hoped they'd throw the fucking key away.'

'Dog for who?'

'Drug squad. He'd dob anyone, every little twat he heard big-noting himself in a pub. Jacks'd pay him off with a couple've hits.'

'He was on smack?'

'On anything.'

Two men in donkey jackets and woollen caps came in from the street. Vin looked them over carefully while draining his glass.

I signalled for two more beers.

'One of his Jack mates was talking to him near the pub that night,' Vin said.

'How do you know that?'

'Same way. My mate. Saw Danny with this cunt Scullin in a car down the road. Danny come in, full of dough, drinking Jim Beam, in and out of the pisshouse, gets off his face. They kicked him out round eleven. Then my mate sees him lying behind a bench, he's drunk another half of JB.'

'That was a quarter past eleven?

'Thereabouts.'

'You reckon your mate would talk to me? For a fee?'

'No.'

'Why's that?'

'Dead. OD'd on smack.'

'The cop's name's Scullin?'

'I forget.'

'Where did Danny keep his car?'

'Garage behind his nanna's house.'

'That's in Collett Street?'

'Yeah.'

'Fair way from Clifton Hill.'

'Fucking A.' He finished his beer. 'Got to go.'

I said, 'Thanks for your help.'

'You got nothing from me, mate. Is that right?'

'It's right.'

Vin McKillop looked back at me before he went out the door. There was still nothing showing in those boxer's eyes but he wasn't going to forget my face.

We went to Ballarat in the big BMW, Harry driving through Royal Park and on to the Tullamarine Freeway like the late James Hunt on cocaine. The day was fine, thin cloud running west. In ten minutes we were passing through Keilor, the beginning of a huge sprawl of brick veneers nominally divided into suburbs with names like Manna Gum Heights and Bellevue Hill. These were the places where teenage dreams came to die.

'Heights,' said Harry in wonder. 'Flat as the paper under the lino.'

I was in the back, reading the *Age*. Cam was in front, fiddling with the laptop.

'Wootton tells me you put the squirrel grip on one of his commissioners, Jack,' Harry said.

'Not without difficulty,' I said. Harry knew Wootton well. He used him for big jobs.

'More buggers doin a runner these days, seems to me. Probably time for another Happy Henry.' Harry turned to look at me while accelerating past a tradesman's ute with two cattle dogs on the back, barking into the wind. I paled.

'You know about Happy Henry, Jack?'

'No.'

'Hidden history of the turf,' Harry said. 'Commissioner called Happy Henry Carmody. Happy shot through on a big punter, Baby Martinez, came from Manila, Hawaii, somewhere like that, got into a few duels with the books. Silly bugger, really. Happy did a bit of work for him, came highly recommended too. Then one Satdee Happy had a kitbag of notes owed to Baby, thought bugger it, Baby's just some dago'll cop it sweet, go home and weep under the palm trees.'

Harry looked around again.

'Baby's friends come on Happy up in Brisbane. The dickhead, it took so long to get there in his Falcon, he thinks he must be in a foreign country. He's tossin Baby's dough around, whores, cards, buyin drinks for the cops and politicians and the like.'

There was a pause while Harry groped for the Smarties box. In the interests of self-preservation, Cam found it for him.

'Anyway, next thing Happy's up in the little hills they got there, nailed to a blue gum. Five feet off the ground, they say. Six-inch nails. Like Jesus Christ.'

'Fuck,' said Cam.

'Not again either,' Harry said. 'Cut it off, put it in his shirt pocket like a little cigar. Was a while before any of your commissioners' minds went wanderin again, can tell ya.'

Harry chuckled to himself for a while. Then he said, 'Give us a rundown on the field in this Topspin bugger's race, Cam.'

While Cam talked, consulting the laptop, Harry kept a steady thirty kilometres over the speed limit and we covered the 110 kilometres in sixty-five minutes. It wasn't raining in Ballarat and the locals were standing out on the pavements, looking at the sky in amazement. Many of them had the pale, staring look of people newly pushed out of institutions. Someone once said that nobody went to live in Ballarat; you had to be committed by a magistrate.

Dowling Forest is on the other side of town, at the foot of a round, bald hill. By the time we got there, thin and steady rain was falling.

'That's more like it,' said Harry. He'd said nothing since the Happy Henry story, listening to Cam in silence. He parked well back from the gate and took over my newspaper.

Cam locked the laptop into its housing under the dashboard.

'Well?' he asked, big hands on his thighs.

Harry reached into his Donegal tweed jacket with his right hand and came out with an envelope about a centimetre thick. 'I'll give you the nod,' he said. 'Yokels lined up, I take it.'

'Better be,' Cam said. He put the envelope in the inside pocket of his trenchcoat and set off briskly.

I got the Sakura Pro FS100 out of the boot, loaded it, hung it around my neck, put on my Drizabone and followed. Harry was on the car phone.

We were in Ballarat for two reasons. The first was a three-year-old filly called Topspin Winder running in the third. She had started five times and her best run was a seventh place at her first outing. After four runs, she'd been given an eight-week rest. When she'd reappeared at Pakenham the week before, she'd run eighth.

I bought a race card and wandered into the huge barn of a betting ring. Most of the city bookmakers were fielding, trying to keep afloat until the Spring Carnival could rescue them. It was five minutes before the second race and there was a fair amount of action by country standards. I went out onto the grandstand. Over to the right, the members were snug behind glass. Out here it was all streaming eyes and snuffling noses.

The second looked a mediocre affair on paper and it proved to be one of those races where it's a pity something has to win. Or come second. Or third.

'Not much pace in that,' said the caller.

'Putting it bloody mildly,' said the man next to me. 'First time I've seen the whole field trying to throw a race.'

I went back through the betting ring to the mounting yard.

Cam was near the hot dog vendor, eating something wrapped in paper. As I looked around, Harry rounded the corner of the stalls. The small man stopped and patted his raincoat pockets, looking down.

When he looked up, he nodded briskly to himself, as if he'd found what he was looking for. Then he set off in the direction of the carpark.

Cam crumpled up the greaseproof paper and shot the ball into a bin a good three metres away. He set off for the betting ring. As he entered the large opening, he patted a thickset man in a greasy anorak on the arm.

I didn't waste any time checking the odds. Topspin Winder was showing 40-1 with the book nearest the entrance and I took it. I invested a modest $50, not enough to scare anybody. By the time I'd finished my circuit, Cam's team of punters had struck terror into the numbers men: Topspin was down to 15-1.

Then the second wave hit the bookies – a panic rush of Topspin's connections, caught napping by Cam's troops and now jostling with the dumb money that was always on the alert for a plunge. The market went into freefall, ending up on 6-1.

On my way to have a look at the beast concerned, I passed Cam, leaning against the mounting yard fence. He was smoking a little cigar and reading the card. Nothing in that Aboriginal/Scottish/Italian face suggested anything other than mild boredom.

Topspin was equally impassive. I'd seen her at her previous three appearances and had grown rather fond of her. She was small, calm, unprepossessing. Her form to date had not prepossessed the racing press either; in the *Age* that morning, Ron Pevsner assessed her odds at 50-1 and Bart Grantley gave her a rating of two out of ten.

Topspin Winder had come to Harry's attention in her first outing, over 1600 metres in pouring rain at Moe. The small horse missed the start completely, then appeared to stumble about ten metres out. By the time the jockey got things organised, the closest horse was twelve lengths away, vanishing into the mist. Cam was out on the fence and for some reason he put the watch on Topspin at the 200-metre mark. About 500 metres out, there was a bad fall, two horses going down in the mud. Topspin was too far back to be affected and ran seventh out of the remaining thirteen, about eight lengths behind the winner. What interested Harry was

Cam's estimate that she took under 60 seconds to cover the 1000 metres to the 1200 mark. And that in the excitement over the fall, no-one said anything about it.

We hadn't seen that speed again. In her next three races, all 1600s, Topspin was ridden by another jockey, a leather-faced veteran of the inland circuit called Marty Bacquie. The horse seemed to be trying but she kept getting caught in the middle of the herd, boxed in half a dozen lengths off the pace, and flagging badly over the last two hundred or so. At her last appearance, at Pakenham, I filmed Bacquie talking to the trainer after the race and Harry brought in his trusted lip-reader to look at the video. The trainer was saying nice things to Marty. And that was why we were in Ballarat.

There were twelve horses in race three, 1200 metres. The best performed, Quigley's Pride, had one win and nine places from nineteen starts. Second best was Extension Date with one win from five. After that it was winter. There were no more than a hundred people on the grandstand. I took my usual place out on the eastern edge. Harry was down in the front row, undistinguished in his elderly raincoat and hat. No sign of Cam.

They came out of the gate in a good line. Topspin had a new jockey today, Lance Wallace, a New Zealander in his second season in the big time, rider of several upsets in the past year.

A horse called Denaderise took the front and opened up a two-length lead. I knew Denaderise. This was her role in life. She had about 500 metres in her.

At the 600, Quigley's Pride, specialist placegetter, was a length off Denaderise. There was no pace in it. Topspin was lying well back, perhaps eighth or ninth, nothing outside her.

At the 700, Wallace moved the horse further out, almost to the centre of the track. Denaderise was gone, slipping backwards. Extension Date took over the lead, on the rails, moving well. Quigley's tucked in behind, losing a little ground as they approached the 800. Outside them a horse called Under the Gun, a 15-1 shot, came into contention.

With 200 metres to go, Under the Gun's jockey used the whip and the animal surged past Extension Date, seeming to draw Quigley's Pride along. At the 150, Under the Gun was the winner, stride lengthening, towing Quigley's Pride away from Extension Date.

The race caller was saying, 'It's Under the Gun now coming away, Quigley's Pride hasn't got the finish to stay with him, Extension Date being left…'

Something had gone badly wrong in our calculations. And, presumably, in the connections' calculations, too.

And then, very smoothly, no whip, hands and heels, Lance Wallace and Topspin Winder began their run down the outside. The little horse gave no great impression of speed; the other horses seemed to slow down.

The caller went into overdrive, 'Down the outside Topspin Winder, she's mowed down Extension Date, fifty metres to go she goes up to Quigley's Pride, no resistance there for the plunge horse. It's Under the Gun and Topspin Winder, Under the Gun Topspin

Winder, metres to go it's Topspin Winder pulling away, Topspin Winder by three-quarters of a length...'

I looked across at Harry. He was having a little swig of Glenmorangie from the flat silver flask he took to the races on cold days.

I filmed the fourth race, a Class 1 handicap over 1600 metres. This was the second reason we were in Ballarat. My attention was on Red Line Value, a new object of Harry's attention. It went well early, weakened and finished in the middle of the field, making a little ground in the closing stages.

Cam and Harry were in the BMW when I got there. Harry gave me a small smile. 'I think we might have a look at the Dom when we get home,' he said.

We parked a block away from the Peter Lalor Hotel in the middle of Ballarat. Cam went off. He had a date with the commission agent who had organised the team of punters.

'Collectin' can be the hardest part,' Harry said. 'Still, the boy's got a look about him keeps the buggers honest. They know a bare-knuckle man when they see one. What'd ya make of that Red Line?'

Cam was back inside fifteen minutes. On Harry's orders, we stopped at McDonald's on the way out. Harry ordered two Big Macs.

'Take over the helm,' he said to Cam. 'Got to get outside these snacks. Man gets weak up here in the glaciers.'

The second hamburger didn't make it to the city limits. 'Now that's what I call food,' Harry said. 'Not a word to the wife. She reckons you eat the stuff, you end up needin one of them coronary overpasses or whatever.'

He found a Willie Nelson tape and pushed it into the system. 'Give us the sums, Cam,' he said, tilting his seat back. 'Moonlight in Vermont' flooded the car.

'Well,' Cam said, 'we unloaded it, but it's no great average. Round 10-1. Some of these books see a go coming if you put down fifty bucks. It's getting hard to find someone in the bush'll take a decent-size whack.'

'Tens are fine,' Harry said. 'Thing didn't require millions. You don't want to nuke the bastards. We want 'em there next time.'

I had no idea how much money they were talking about. I'd been part of five betting plunges with Harry and Cam and I had no idea of the sums involved. I was happy that way too.

Harry's head peeped around the side of his seat. 'Get that fifty on at something decent, Jack?' He set the figure for personal bets.

'At the top,' I said.

'Goodonya.'

In Parkville, joined by Lyn Strang in a black dress, not small but rippable, we drank two bottles of Dom Perignon. Harry excused himself for a while early on and when he came back said, 'Fair bit of satisfaction in the combinations.' This meant he had done well in the coupling of Topspin Winder with other horses in other races.

Cam and I left at 7.45 p.m. At the door, Harry shook hands with both of us and slid an envelope into my jacket pocket. I opened it at home: $6000 in fifties. I went downstairs in search of company. Dom Perignon excites the blood.

The next day wasn't productive. I did a lease for a landlord who had come in off the street and put a couple of extra penalty clauses in Laurie Baranek's agreement. At home, I slumped on the old leather sofa in the everything room with the Danny McKillop file and a bottle of Huon Falls Lager. I lived in half of the top of a small converted boot factory near Edinburgh Gardens. I'd owned the whole building in the good times and had managed to hold on to a quarter. No, to be accurate, a suburban lawyer, the fittingly named Prudence Webb, of Moloney, Hassan & Webb, had held on to a quarter for me when I was bent on liquidating all my assets, including myself, after Isabel's death.

The answering machine played two clicks from callers who didn't want to speak, a message from a lawyer about a witness, and my sister, Rosa, twice. She is the only woman named for a communist heroine ever to live in the old-money belt of Toorak. Impregnating my mother with her was one of the last things my father did on earth. What Bill Irish, stonemason, footballer, socialist, would make of Rosa is hard to say. She grew up in total privilege in my mother's parents' mansion in Toorak, doted on by four adults, one of them my mother's nanny, recalled to service at sixty-five.

I read the whole file again. What was clear was that the evidence against Danny at his trial was overwhelming. A witness put him about three blocks from the scene within minutes of the collision. He was found asleep behind the wheel of the car that killed Anne Jeppeson: there were blood and clothing fragments on it belonging to Anne Jeppeson. The witness had taken the registration and the police had identified it as belonging to Danny and gone to his house. The witness had later picked Danny out of a line-up.

In his statement to the police, Danny said he had started drinking at around 3 p.m. on the day. He remembered nothing after about 10 p.m., when he was still in the Glengarry Arms in Punt Road. He had no idea how the evidence of the collision came to be on his car. He said the same in his interview with me at Pentridge.

I put the file down and stared at the shadows on the ceiling. From my notes, it appeared that I'd had no hesitation in advising Danny to plead guilty. I'd certainly made no effort to establish whether there was any other possible explanation for the circumstances. Why should I have? Danny didn't offer any alternative account, his record was terrible and the police case was a prosecutor's dream.

I was fetching another beer when the phone rang. It was my sister.

'Aren't you ever at home?' Rosa said. 'Doesn't that machine of yours work? I need your advice. Phillip wants to marry me.'

'Who?'

'Phillip. Phillip? How many men do you think I'm seeing?'

'It's not a question of number,' I said, 'it's a question of sequence. Which one is Phillip?'

She sighed. 'Jack, you met him at dinner. The investor. With the sexy mouth. You brought that Sydney tart.'

'She speaks warmly of you too. What sort of advice were you after?'

There was a pause. 'Do you think I should?'

'Marry him?'

'Yes. Marry him.'

'No.'

'Why on earth not?'

'I think you should hold out for a less than one hundred per cent shit. What happened to Kevin? He seemed to have a lot of decent Catholic guilt. For a currency speculator, that is.'

She sighed again. 'Jack, Jack, Kevin is a two hundred per cent shit. He's got a little computer thing, you can see what's happening to the dollar and the yen and the fucking zloty. He goes to the toilet in restaurants and looks at it. Can you believe that? I know it for a fact. The rest of them are in there snorting and admiring each other's cocks and Kevin's drooling over his little money meter. His wife left him for a nightclub bouncer, all of twenty-two, I believe. Can you blame her?'

'I can't find it in my heart to, no,' I said.

'The men I meet,' she said, 'if they're not married and on the prowl, they're gay or they're going to a group to come to terms with their female side or they can't shut up about their inner child. I suppose that's why Phillip looks like such a find.'

I said, 'It's Phillip's inner shark that worries me.'

I gave her some more excellent advice and we arranged to meet for lunch. Then I made some grilled ham and tomato sandwiches and got back on the couch. I clicked on the box and caught the end of the last segment on 'This Day'. An ABC-type person with fair hair, spots and little round glasses was standing in front of a high diamond-mesh fence with a suave-looking man in a dark suit. Behind them you could see what looked like the beginnings of a vast gravel pit and beyond that an expanse of greasy water and the city skyline.

'Mr Pitman,' the spotty man said, 'as the Minister responsible for seeing the Yarra Cove development through the Cabinet, how do you react to some people's unease over a six hundred million dollar development being approved without public consultation?'

The Minister smiled. He had a thin, sly face with high cheekbones. Something about it said cosmetic surgery. His full head of dark hair was the kind that doesn't move in the wind. 'Well, Andrew,' he said, 'I don't know who these people are you're referring to. Perhaps your colleagues at the ABC. Or at the *Age*. There are always some people who want to knock anything the government does. But they're not the people who elected us to government.'

'But—' said Andrew.

'The people who elected the Saunders government to power,' Pitman went on, 'want this State to come back to life. They lived in the Gulag created by the previous government quite long enough. It's projects like this they want to see come to pass. Projects like this that inject huge amounts of capital and energy into this State.'

Andrew made a few other feeble attempts to put Pitman on the defensive. Pitman ignored them and kept to his line about what the people wanted.

Finally, Andrew gave up and said, 'Within twelve months, this,' he pointed at the gravel pit, 'will be Yarra Cove, a huge six hundred million dollar marina, waterfront shopping and entertainment precinct and, arguably, Melbourne's smartest new address. But will the Saunders government's lack of concern for public consultation over projects that change the face of the city set a precedent for future developments? Andrew Leonard for "This Day".'

After that I had a choice between television entertainment on the themes of a) child abuse, b) parent abuse, and c) tree abuse. Failing these, there was a documentary on the drinking problem in Lapland. I failed all of these, killed the telly and fell asleep over chapter three of Eugene Marasco's *In the Absence of War*.

Some time in the small hours, startled by something in a dream, I awoke and staggered to the bed proper. But sleep had fled. I lay and thought about Danny, one-time police informer, addict, convicted hit-and-run killer, born-again model employee, husband and father. If his cousin's mate, dead of smack, had told the truth, a policeman could have given him an alibi. And therefore the star witness was lying. The witness's name was Ronald Bishop.

I put on the light, got the file from the lounge, and read Ronald Bishop's statement again. It was a model of its kind: Ronnie Bishop didn't have any doubts about what he saw. I put off the light and fell asleep with the strange career of Danny McKillop turning in my mind.

In the morning, I rang Barry Tregear at home to catch him before he left for work. A woman said he'd left but she would pass on a message. I gave her my name. About ten minutes later, he rang. From the noise, he was on a mobile phone.

'Ronald Bishop?' he said. 'Morton Street, Clifton Hill. I'll see what I can do.'

I had breakfast at Meaker's on Brunswick Street, a street which boasted trams and, at each end, a church spire. Sometimes, when a freak wind lifted the pollution, you could see the one from the other. Brunswick Street had been a grand thoroughfare once and a long passage between rundown buildings and hopeless shops for a long time after that. In the eighties, the street changed again. Youth culture happened to it. The old businesses – clothes-pressing sweatshops, drycleaners, printeries, cheap shoe shops, the gunsmith, dim central European coffee and snooker cafes – closed down. In their place, restaurants, coffee shops, delicatessens, galleries and bookshops opened. Suddenly it was a smart place to be.

Meaker's had been in Brunswick Street since before it was smart. It had changed hands several times and moved once but nothing had really changed. Well, nothing except the appearance of the customers. And the staff. There was a new waitress today. She was probably in her late twenties, tall and raw-boned with scraped back hair and an amused, intelligent look.

'I'm Sharon,' she said when she put down the tray holding the Cholesterol Supercharge: eggs, bacon, sausages, fried tomato. 'The cook says you're Jack.'

'So what do you do?' I asked her when she brought the coffee. It was assumed in Brunswick Street that waiting on table was not one's vocation.

'I'm an actor,' she said. 'In the theatre. Don't you recognise me?'

'No,' I said, 'but I don't get to the theatre much these days.'

'What about you?' she said, wiping the table.

'I'm a bishop.'

'Right,' she said. 'Is that a crook you've got in your pocket or are you just pleased to see me?'

I could see she was going to be an asset to the place. Not as religious as one would have liked, but an asset.

I didn't have anything in the legal line to do, so I put in five hours at Taub's. Charlie was making the boardroom furniture for a Perth mining company's new Melbourne office. It was what the business pages call an 'emerging miner'. Usually, your emerging miner wants a table shaped like Australia minus Tasmania, chairs like breaking waves. This outfit hired a decorator who convinced them that big business in Melbourne favoured a more traditional look. A Charlie Taub look, in fact. The decorator was married to Charlie's grandson: the extended family has its uses.

I spent the early part of the day trying to get Charlie to tell me what I was doing. He'd got out of the habit of doing drawings. 'What for do I need drawings?' he said. 'I don't make anything I haven't made before.'

'Charlie,' I said, 'I haven't made this table before. All I've got is some measurements on this piece of paper torn off the side of the *Age*. I'd like to have some idea of how what I'm doing fits into the plan you've got in your head. That's a lot to ask?'

He went off grumbling to the office and came back in ten minutes with several school exercise book pages. On them were detailed working drawings of an armoire designed to contain bottles, glasses and television and video equipment, a boardroom table, very severe, and a chair, equally spare.

'You want drawings, I give you drawings,' he said.

I went around the corner to Flash Advanced Telecommunications, prop. G. Bertoli, former telephone-repair person, and made two copies.

Barry Tregear rang at noon while I was reading the *Age* and eating the corned beef and gherkin on rye sandwich I'd brought from home. He couldn't find any trace of a Ronald Bishop.

I knocked off at 1.30 p.m. and drove around to the address in Clifton Hill, no more than a few kilometres away. Morton Street was close enough to Collingwood Football Ground to hear the sobbing when Carlton beat them. Fitzroy used to beat them once upon a time but it would take divine intervention these days.

The bourgeoisie had long since occupied most of this once deeply working class area pinched between two main roads and a freeway. Morton Street, however, had the unloved look of a trench fallen to the rentiers.

Ronald Bishop had once lived at number 17. But not even the house still lived at number 17. It had been extracted like a tooth, its earthly remains some blackened broken bricks where a fireplace had stood and a mound of damp ashes that had saved the demolishers the trips to the tip. I knocked at number 19. No-one was home or admitting to it. I trudged off to number 15.

The bell didn't work. I tried tapping and then gave the door a couple of thumps. The door was wrenched open and a large red-faced man in his sixties glowered at me. He was wearing a dirty blue nylon anorak zipped up to the neck and black tracksuit pants with a stripe, possibly white once, up the side.

'Don't fucken hammer my door,' he said. 'Whaddafuck d'ya want?'

I apologised and gave him my card.

'So?' he said, not noticeably impressed.

'I'm trying to find out about someone who used to live next door,' I said. 'About twelve years ago. Were you living here then?'

'Depends,' he said. He ran both hands through his long, greasy grey hair.

'We have a standard fee of twenty dollars for useful information,' I said.

'Who's the someone?'

'Ronald Bishop.'

'Come inside,' he said.

I followed him down a passage dark as a mineshaft into a kitchen that smelled of sour milk and burnt fat. All surfaces were covered in dirty plates, open tins, takeaway containers, empty cigarette packets. The gas stove had a baked and blistered topping of spilt food.

'Garn!' the man shouted at a huge tabby cat walking on tiptoe across the littered table. It floated its flabby body across to an impossibly small perch on the sink.

'Wanna beer?' he asked.

'That'd be good.' There was no knowing how he would take a refusal.

He took two cans of Melbourne Bitter out of an old fat-bodied fridge. The light inside wasn't working. We sat down at the table. I couldn't find anywhere to put my can down so I held it on my lap.

'So what, he's inherited some dough?' he said. He gave the can the suck of a man who measures out his days in tinnies.

'Not that I know of,' I said. 'His family's trying to get in touch with him. Did you know him when he lived next door?'

'Fucking poof,' he said. 'Bloody lucky he got outta here alive. We was just about to give him a hammer-drill up the arse when he pissed off.' He wiped spit from his lower lip with his thumb and took a packet of Long Beach Lites out of the anorak. 'Smoke?'

'No thanks. What made you like him so much?'

He gave me a suspicious look over the flame of the plastic lighter. 'Bloody house was fulla kids. Sleepin all over the place. He used to come back here in the bloody middle the night, half a dozen kids in the car. Street kids they call 'em now. Bloody drug addicts. Should lock 'em away. You wouldn't believe the bloody racket they made.'

'So Ronald was trying to help them, was he?'

He looked at me with utter scorn. 'Where the hell've you been? He was tryin to root 'em. Tryin and bloody succeedin. Half of them's so off their faces they wouldn't know if a gorilla rooted 'em.'

He took another measure of beer, dragged on the cigarette and tapped ash into a catfood can.

'And how long was he here?'

'Would've been about a year. Been a bloody lot shorter if I hadn't been...' He scratched his neck. 'I only come back a coupla weeks before he pissed off. Bloody Moira put up with him, Christ only knows women. Used to talk to the little cunt over the fence.'

'He just left, did he?'

'Showed up one day in a white Triumph sports. Y'know the kind? They don't make 'em any more. TR something. Just packed his case, buggered off. Left the old Renault standin out there. Coupla them kids took off in it. Never come back, neither.'

'He didn't leave because of you?'

He shook his head. 'I hadn't got round to him yet. He just pissed off. Reckon the cops were on him.'

'Why's that?'

'Two come round there a couple times.'

'What, uniform cops?'

'No. Plain clothes.'

'You sure?'

He had another suck on the can. 'I know the one,' he said.

'You know his name?' I had a big swig of my beer.

'Scullin. His name's Scullin. He grew up round Abbotsford.'

'So the cops came around twice and then he left?'

He nodded. 'More than twice. Coupla times. Told Moira before he pissed off some bullshit about he'd won some money, something like that. I reckon it was drugs.'

'Anyone else around here know him?'

He thought about it, smoke seeping out of his nostrils. 'No,' he said. 'Bloke on the other side's dead.'

I drained the can. 'This is helpful,' I said, getting up. 'Much obliged.' I took out my wallet, found a twenty and offered it. He took it and put it under the catfood can.

At the front door, I said, 'Well, thanks again.' He gave me a little wave.

I was at the gate when he said, 'I'm just thinkin. Remember the bloke on the other side, Greek he was, tellin me one day he read where Ronnie dobbed in some hit-and-run bloke.'

I paused. 'When was that?'

He spat on to the path. 'Dunno.'

'Was it while he was living here?'

'Must've been. Bloke said he remembered Ronnie gettin in a car all smartened up. Then he read where he dobbed this other fella. That's what the Greek said. Don't get time to read the paper myself.'

'That's useful,' I said. 'Thanks.'

I went back to my office, made some black tea and sat in the client's chair. Where was Ronnie Bishop now? Last seen tooling off in his Triumph, fresh from doing his civic duty in the matter of *R. v. McKillop*. And where was a policeman called Scullin, whose circle included the accused and the star witness?

Barry Tregear didn't need to think about the name Scullin.

'Martin Scullin. I know Scull,' he said. 'What's the problem?'

'No problem. He might be able to help me with something.'

'You still farting around with that McKillop business?'

'On and off.'

'You've missed Scull today. By about six years. He took the package. Gone fishing.'

'What about a number or an address?'

'Big ask. I'll have to talk to the man. What do you want to see him about?'

I thought for a moment. 'Tell him it's about an old dog of his, Danny McKillop.'

'Where'd you get that?' Tregear asked.

'Widely known at the time.'

'I'll get back to you. Where are you?'

I gave him the number.

I gave the R. Bishops in the phone book a quick run-through. There were only two Ronalds and neither of them had ever lived in Morton Street. I rang an estate agent called Millie Vincent I'd had dealings with and asked her to check the Landlords' database for Ronald Bishop. She rang back in twenty minutes.

'They'll drum me out of the trade for doing this,' she said. 'A Ronald Arthur Bishop rented a house in Prahran in 1984–85. Then a Perth agent ran a check on him for a property in Fremantle in late '85.'

She gave me the name of the agent.

I got through to a man called Michael Brooke. He got the impression I was a fellow real estate agent and told me a Ronald Bishop had been the tenant of a house in Walpole Street, Fremantle. 'Then he bought it at auction in, oh, '86 or '87. Paid a bit over the odds then but it's turned out to be a smart buy. By the way, he calls himself Ronnie Burdett-Bishop now. Moved upmarket.'

R. A. Burdett-Bishop was in the Perth phonebook.

No-one answered at the first two attempts. The phone rang for a long time before a low-voiced male answered on the third try.

'Could I speak to Ronnie, please,' I said.

'Who is that?'

'An old acquaintance suggested I call him.'

There was a pause. 'Ronnie's in Melbourne.'

'That's where I'm calling from. Is there some way I can get in touch with him here?'

There was another pause. 'Who did you say you were?'

'My name's Jack Irish,' I said. 'I'm a lawyer. You'll find me in the Melbourne phone book.' For some reason, this statement sometimes had a reassuring effect on people.

'Well, I'd like to help you,' the man said. 'My name's Charles Lee. I'm a friend of Ronnie's. I'm keeping an eye on his house. No-one seems to know where Ronnie is at the moment...'

'You don't have a Melbourne address for him?'

'Um, you could try his mother. Would you like her number?'

I wrote it down, said thanks and goodbye, then dialled it. No-one at home.

It's nice that there's a special occupation for the anal retentive. It's called librarianship. The thin man with the silly little cornsilk moustache gave me a smile of pure dislike and went away. I was sitting at a table in the *Age* library on the fourth floor of the paper's hideous building on Spencer Street. A message from Steve Phillips, the assistant editor, had preceded me but that had only made me more unwelcome. I went back some distance with Phillips. In the early '80s I'd got his teenage son off a drugs charge. I'd been recommended by a reporter called Gavin Legge for whom I'd obtained extremely lucky verdicts on a bunch of charges arising from his birthday party at a fashionable restaurant called Melitta's.

Mr Silly Moustache took all of ten minutes to produce the file. I slid the fiche onto the platen, switched on and, as always, found that it was upside down. When I'd corrected this, I zoomed across to the end and worked backwards.

The last clipping was a short item from 1986 about the setting up by her parents of the Anne Jeppeson Memorial Scholarship at Monash University. It was to go to a student studying politics. Before that came the court reports I'd already seen in my file on Danny, then the report on Anne's death. It was a page three story, with a picture of the scene and an inset photograph of her. She had short hair and a snub nose and she looked smart and formidable. A quick look at the headlines on the rest of the clippings suggested that this was the case. I wrote down the bylines on those stories that had them.

Anne Jeppeson had been a campaigner for public housing and public housing tenants. At the time she was killed she was involved in trying to prevent the closing down of a public housing estate called Hoagland in Yarrabank.

I leaned back in the upright chair and closed my eyes. Ronnie Bishop had helped send to jail the man accused of killing a woman campaigning against the closing of a public housing estate. Why would he lie to do that? Public-spiritedness? It didn't sound like Ronnie Bishop.

I asked SM whether I could get the Jeppeson file photocopied. He looked at me as if I'd asked for a colonic irrigation.

'Would it help if I went through Steve Phillips?' I said sweetly.

'It'll take half an hour,' he said. 'There isn't anyone to do it now.'

I said I'd come back and went looking for a caffeine jolt.

I came upon the drinks machine without warning, which made it impossible to avoid my former client Gavin Legge. He looked up from stirring his styrofoam cup. The smile of a professional greeter appeared on his face.

'Jack Irish,' he said. He put down the cup and stuck out a small hand. 'Great to see you. Who's in the shit this time?'

Legge was in his early forties, with greying curly hair and small features being overwhelmed by pudge. Behind thick-lensed designer glasses his eyes were slitty. All his stories in the paper seemed to involve free travel and free eating and drinking. He also dropped a lot of names. At the time I was defending him, one of his mercifully unneeded character witnesses said of him, 'For a free sausage roll and a couple of glasses of plonk, Gavin Legge will get six mentions of anything you're selling into the paper.'

'Using the library,' I said. 'Maybe you can help.'

'My pleasure.' He was eager to please. As well he might be, given that it had taken me a year to get any money out of him.

I put the coins in the machine and pressed for white coffee. I got out my notebook and found the three bylines on the Jeppeson stories. 'These people still around? Sally Chan? Matthew Lunt?'

'Jeez, you're going back a bit. Chan went to Sydney about ten years ago and Lunt's dead.'

'Linda Hillier?'

'Return of the starfucker. Came back to Melbourne

a few months ago. She works for PRN, Pacific Rim News, it's a financial news outfit. Just around the corner. Want to meet her?'

'Wouldn't mind. I saw your byline on a story about Yarra Cove.'

Legge whistled. 'Now those boys know how to treat the media,' he said. 'Nothing but the French at the launch. Non-vintage but the French. Like the good old days. It's been local pissfizz at these things for years.'

'Only the fittest have come through,' I said. The machine started spitting out my drink.

Legge took a sip of his coffee and pulled a face. 'This stuff tastes like piss too. Bloody machines. Christ knows why we put up with it. Fucking useless union. Follow me.'

We left the building and walked up two blocks towards the city centre. Pacific Rim News had the fourth floor of a small office block. A security man gave us labels and we went into a huge room full of formica desks and computer terminals.

Legge said, 'I still owe you that lunch. What about tomorrow? It's on the paper. I'm reviewing a new restaurant. They fall over themselves.'

'Don't you do these things incognito?'

'Certainly do. But I gave them an anonymous tip-off.' He laughed, an unpleasant gurgling sound.

'Thanks,' I said, 'but I'm out of town tomorrow. Some other time would be nice.'

Linda Hillier was in a corner of the room where several desks seemed to have formed a huddle. She had been alerted and watched us coming, a pencil cross-wise in her mouth between toothpaste-commercial teeth. When we got to her, Legge said, 'Linda Hillier, I want you to meet Jack Irish, the lawyer who kept me out of jail for punching that food bitch.'

Linda Hillier removed the pencil from her mouth. She was in her mid-thirties, shiny brown hair, a full mouth, dark eyes and a scattering of faded freckles. She wasn't good-looking but she was handsome.

'Hello,' she said. 'Next time tell us what you'll take to throw the case.'

'Jack's interested in something you covered when you were a young groupie,' Legge said.

'That far back?' Linda said. 'When you were still married to that nice plump girl from Accounts? The one who was sweet enough to blow all the *Age* copyboys at the Christmas party?'

'Touché,' said Legge. 'I can't stand around all day talking about old times. Jack, I'll ring you about lunch.'

We watched Legge walk off. I noticed that all the men in the room were frozen into poses suggesting deep concentration while all the women seemed to be typing. Could it be that the men were transmitting thoughts to the women, who were typing them up? I suggested this to Linda Hillier. She looked at me speculatively.

'Thoughts?' she said. 'Most of these guys couldn't transmit herpes. What's your interest in history?'

'I'm interested in the Anne Jeppeson hit-and-run,' I said. 'Remember her?'

She nodded.

'I saw your byline on some stories in her file.'

She said, 'Is this a legal matter?'

'No. I don't practise much anymore.'

'What do you do?'

'Live off my wits,' I said. 'Gamble. Drink.'

She smiled, an attractive downturning. 'Then you'll be keeping much the same company as before. Well, what can I tell you about Anne Jeppeson?'

'Did it cross anyone's mind at the time that she might have been deliberately run down?'

'By that drunk? Was he capable of forming an intention?'

'What I mean is, did anyone think he might have been used to kill Anne Jeppeson?'

She shrugged. 'I've never heard anyone suggest that.' She paused and looked at me intently. 'Hang on a minute. It's just come back to me. Didn't you appear for the driver?'

I nodded. 'Not with any distinction. He came out of jail a few years ago. New person, good job, wife and kid. Then a cop shot him dead in Brunswick last Friday.'

'Jesus,' she said. 'I read that the bloke'd done time for hit-and-run. I didn't make the connection.'

The phone on her desk rang. She talked to someone in monosyllables for a while, then put the phone down. 'Look,' she said, 'I'm under the gun here for a while. I've got to file a story for Hong Kong in about eight minutes.'

I took a chance. 'Can we talk outside hours?'

She gave me a questioning look. 'You mean tonight?'

I hadn't had a date in two years. 'If you're free,' I said.

There was a pause. We looked at each other in a new way.

She said, 'Ring me here at seven. We can fix something.'

It was raining outside. I didn't mind much.

Linda Hillier said she'd be finished by eight. We agreed to meet at Donelli's in Smith Street, Collingwood. It was owned by Patrick Donelly, an Irishman who wanted to be an Italian and who owed me money.

Linda was wearing a tailored navy jacket. I watched her hanging up her raincoat. She was taller than I remembered. Then I remembered I'd never seen her standing up. She felt my eyes on her and turned her head to look straight at me across the crowded room. For some reason, I felt embarrassed, as if I'd been caught looking down her dress. She came across and I stood up and pulled out a chair.

'Thanks,' she said. 'This is a nice way to end a real pain of a day.'

I poured her some of the house white, the menus came and we inspected them for a while. When we'd ordered the same things, she said, 'Gavin Legge rang up and told me about your wife. I'm sorry.'

'Thank you,' I said.

'Well,' she said, 'what else can I tell you about Anne Jeppeson? I've been thinking about her since you left. I talked to her the morning before she was killed. She was like a happy attack dog. "I'm going to get the bastards," she kept saying.'

'You weren't one of her admirers?'

She thought for a moment. 'There were things about her I admired. But, no, I wasn't one of her admirers. She had this deep contempt for the media and this equally deep need to be the subject of its attention.'

'You had dealings with her before the Hoagland business?'

'Long before. She cultivated me when she was trying to market herself as a barefoot paralegal in Footscray. It wasn't enough for justice to be done. Anne Jeppeson had to be seen to be doing it.' Linda drank half her glass. 'Hoagland was her chance for real fame.'

I said, 'My memory's pretty vague about that period. I read the clippings today. It's not clear how she got into the limelight.'

'She was a natural for the part from the moment it leaked out that the government was going to knock down the Hoagland Housing Commission flats. Do you know Yarrabank?'

'Vaguely. I had a client from there once. Stabbed someone in a park. His best friend, I think it was.'

'That's what Yarrabank friends are for,' said Linda. 'It's shitsville. Maybe it's going to be Venice when the Premier's mates are finished with it, but it was darkest shitsville then.'

I suddenly connected. Yarra Cove – the new development I'd seen the sly-faced Planning Minister, Lance Pitman, and the spotty ABC reporter going on about on TV – was on the site of the old Hoagland housing estate. There was a freeway on one side and once there'd been collapsing warehouses on the riverbank, filthy docks all around. There was a munitions factory there in the forties, a battery factory burnt down there in the early sixties. Christ knows what the soil pollution level was.

'How did a Housing Commission block ever get there?' I asked.

'One of the great mysteries of our time. They've shredded the files and composted the bits. People say the land was bought from a mate of the then Housing Minister for about ten times its value and the buildings were put up by another mate for about five times the going rate. The story goes the three of them bought half of Merimbula with the proceeds.'

'How did they get anybody to live there?'

'No choice for some people,' she said. 'That or under a bridge. And the Commission shunted in their problem cases from all over. Move to Hoagland and we'll forget about the three years' rent owing and the fire and the explosion and the missing hot water system. That sort of thing. It was a hellhole. The cops called it the Leper Colony, LC for short.'

'Small, though?'

'Couple of hundred inmates. Small by Housing Commission standards, fifty flats, three three-storey walk-ups. When it leaked out that the government planned to close it, the Ministry said the place was so wrecked it was cheaper to build new flats than to fix it. But Yarrabank was not the place to build them. The place to build them was on land the Commission had bought on the outskirts of Sunshine.'

'Not from the same mate?' I said.

'One day we'll know.'

'What did the residents think?'

'Well, you'd have thought that even Sunshine would look like Surfers Paradise from Hoagland. But we don't actually know what the residents thought because Anne Jeppeson came on the scene like Batwoman and after that all we knew was what the Fight for Hoagland action committee thought. Well, what Anne Jeppeson said the committee thought. All the media attention was on her. It was the Anne Jeppeson Show.'

'What was her background?'

'Strictly middle class. Deep suburbia. Volvo in every drive. Private school. Did politics at Monash. Worked for the Footscray Legal Service for a while. Tried to organise pieceworkers in the rag trade, then she got together a bunch of leftier-than-thou people and founded Right to a Roof. She organised a lot of squats in empty mansions in Toorak, that sort of thing. Great TV pictures.'

Linda finished her drink. I poured some more. 'Anyway, when Hoagland turned up, she stitched together a big coalition of left groups. Christ knows how. They were people who hated one another. She got about five thousand people out for a demonstration, got the Building Workers' Alliance to black-ban the Sunshine site, talked the public service unions into running stop-works. She was all over the papers, TV. The camera liked her. Joan of Arc come back in tight jeans and boots.'

'And then she got killed.'

Linda nodded. 'Without her, the whole Hoagland

protest fell apart. Fight for Hoagland didn't actually exist without her. No-one really gave a shit about Hoagland, least of all the tenants. They came out and said: "Please God, can we move somewhere else?" Suddenly the Housing Commission discovered it had empty flats all over the place. Hoagland got flattened inside a month.'

I said, 'So it wouldn't be likely that she was killed to stop her obstructing Hoagland's closure?'

Her eyes flicked around the room and came back to me. A little smile. 'Bit of an extreme step for the Housing Commission to take, don't you think?'

I told her how the witness against Danny had abandoned his old Renault and taken off in a sports car for a new life in Perth after the trial.

She listened with her chin on her hand. 'What does that suggest to you?'

'I don't know. I'm told Danny was unconscious near a pub miles from his car about half an hour before the car hit Anne Jeppeson. I'm groping around.'

'Why would anyone pay Ronnie Bishop to tell the lies that sent McKillop to jail?'

'Well, maybe it was the only way they could get the verdict,' I said.

'Are we talking about the cops?'

I poured some more wine. You don't get much waiter-pouring at Donelli's. 'It's possible. A drug squad cop called Scullin knew both Danny McKillop and Ronnie Bishop.'

Linda said, 'Let me get this straight. Someone wants a conviction for Anne Jeppeson's death. They use Bishop to frame McKillop. Is that right?'

'That's my extremely vague line of thought.'

'Let's move over to the "How". As I recall, Ronnie gave the cops the car rego that night and they ran the number and went to McKillop's place and found him asleep in the car. Blood all over the front.'

'That's right.'

'And then Ronnie identified McKillop in a line-up.'

'Yes.'

'So if McKillop is innocent, someone else drove the car? And planted him in it later?'

Our first course arrived: honey-cured salmon with a mild peppercorn sauce. This was very fast for the establishment. People had eaten their shoe-leather while waiting for their first courses at Donelli's. Donelly was obviously feeling some remorse about his outstanding debt and had given our order priority.

We talked about other things as we ate. Television, newspapers, the law. Linda had a sharp eye for a target and a spare, funny delivery, but she didn't give away much about herself.

There was no pause between dishes. Donelly himself, head like a sculpture in Virginia ham draped with seaweed, white jacket tight as a bandage on his fat torso, came out of the kitchen with the main course.

'If I may say so, Irish, it's impeccable taste you're showing dining with this lady, and she with you,' he said, eyes never leaving Linda. 'Not to mention your choice of establishment.'

'It chooses itself, Patrick,' I said. 'For many reasons.'

'All of them sound,' he replied. 'And you'll do me

the honour of accepting a little libation I'll be sending over with the young fella.'

It was an old-fashioned Italian dish, chicken and veal risotto, the kind of thing you might cook yourself on a Sunday if you had someone to eat it with. Donelly's libation arrived, a bottle of Barolo by Giuseppe Contratio, ten years old.

Linda tasted it. 'Wow,' she said. 'They know you here.'

'Carnal knowledge,' I said. 'In a manner of speaking.'

We got back to Ronnie Bishop over coffee. Linda came back from the women's room, slid into her seat and said, 'Listen, Jack, let's say that the driver, let's say that McKillop was the target. Someone wanted him in jail and they framed him. So Anne was just unlucky.'

'Chosen at random, you mean?' I said.

'Yes. They had to knock someone down at a certain time of night, in a certain area. And she was there. Could've been anybody.'

'It's hard to see why anyone would go to that trouble to put Danny inside. Easier to knock him off.'

She nodded. Tips of hair slipped around and touched the corner of her mouth. She was faintly flushed from the wine. I found her very attractive and she knew it. 'Maybe the Hoagland tenants saw their chances of escaping from the ghastly place slipping away and put out a contract on Anne Jeppeson,' she said. 'And whoever did the job decided to give Danny the credit.'

We laughed. I poured the last of the wine. 'Can we do this again?' I said. 'Are you free to do this kind of thing?'

She looked at me with a half-smile still on her face. 'You mean eat and drink?'

'That or whatever else takes your fancy.'

'You're asking me if I'm involved with someone else?'

'In my awkward and out-of-practice way.'

'I'm free to do this kind of thing but I don't think I've been much use to you,' she said. 'Can I ask you something?'

'Sure.'

'Why are you going over all this ancient stuff?'

It was the question I'd been putting off thinking about. 'I'm not sure,' I said after a pause. 'Part of it's guilt. I'm not sure that I gave Danny a fair shake when I represented him. I was either drunk or monumentally hungover for all that time. It was just after my wife's death. That's not an excuse. That's just the way it was. I didn't ask any questions about the evidence against Danny. The cops got the bloke to trial in an amazingly short time, jumped all the queues. His wife tells me he told her they fed him pills from his arrest onwards. I didn't know that. But I wouldn't have noticed at the time.'

I stopped talking. I could have gone on for a bit but I was just thinking aloud.

Linda smiled at me. 'Sounds like a good enough reason,' she said. 'I've got to go. I've got a running engagement at 6 a.m. Call me next week. I'll think about Anne Jeppeson.'

'Noise? I'm in Hoddle Street. In the mother of all fucken jams, that's the noise. What's the name of that fucken street you're in?'

I told Senior Sergeant Tregear.

'Be there in, I don't fucken know. I'll hoot for you. Gimme a word outside.'

Ten minutes later, he hooted. I went outside. He was in a blue Falcon fifty metres down the street, half on the kerb. When I got close I saw his eyes in the rear-view mirror. He raised his left arm and pointed to the passenger side. I got in. The car was warm and smelt of cigarette smoke and Chinese food.

'Jack,' Barry Tregear said. He was wearing a blue suit, a green shirt and a violet tie, all tired looking. 'What's with the fucken overalls? Joined the working class now?'

'Helping out,' I said. I didn't feel like explaining.

Barry took a packet of Newport off the dash and extracted a cigarette with his teeth. He lit it with a throw-away lighter.

'I got two minutes,' he said. 'Jack, listen, this McKillop business. Can I give you a word of advice?'

'Everyone else does.'

He took a deep draw, puckered his lips and blew a

thin jet of smoke up past his nose. 'I'd give it a miss if I were you.'

'Why's that?'

'I don't think it's something you want to get mixed up in now. Sensitive business these days, cops shooting people. Wait for the inquest.'

'That doesn't answer the question,' I said.

'Trust me, mate. I've got your interests at heart.'

'I'll think about it. Did you get hold of Scullin?'

Barry nodded. 'Not easy. He's a busy man.'

'I thought you said he'd gone fishing.'

'Just a manner of speaking. He's a smart fella. Runs some kind of security business now. Makes big bucks.'

'What did he say about McKillop?'

'He says he never talks about police business.' Barry wound down his window and flicked the cigarette stub out. It landed on the bonnet of a car on the other side of the street.

'That's all?'

'That's all.'

'You drove around here to tell me that?'

'No. I wanted to tell you something else.'

'What's that?'

'Jack,' he said, 'don't ask me any more questions about McKillop. Okay?'

Ronnie Bishop's mother lived deep in working-class Brunswick. But even here the first seeker after capital gains had appeared. Right next door. The humble weatherboard dwelling had been given a picket fence, brick paving, two silver birches, a paint job and a brass ship's bell. Mrs Bishop's cottage appeared to be trying to lean on the newly straightened frame of its facelifted neighbour.

Mrs Bishop looked at me long and hard from behind a security gate after I introduced myself. Behind her the house was dark. She was probably in her seventies, small, sharp-featured, well-preserved and dressed like someone going out.

'I rang about Ronnie,' I said.

She held up a hand. 'Sorry to stare. You look like my sister's late boyfriend. Now there was a devil. Come in.'

We went down a dark passage, two doors on each side. She opened a door at the end and light flooded in. Beyond was a large new section, the width of the house, with full-length windows looking on to a paved terrace crammed with greenery.

'This is nice,' I said, looking at the glossy sealed floorboards, the newish upholstered chairs and sofa. Next door wasn't the only place on the street that had been smartened up.

'Ronnie paid for it,' she said. 'Sent me to Noosa for two weeks, rained all the time, never mind that. Came back, I nearly fell over, I can tell you. Opened the door and there it was, new furniture, everything. Like a dream, really. Sit down. I've just made some tea.'

There were biscuits too, bought biscuits but nice, on an EPNS server in the shape of a giant leaf.

'Nice and warm, isn't it,' Mrs Bishop said. We were both sitting on the sofa. 'Ronnie put in the central heating. Before that I used to sit on a hot water bottle with my feet on another one some days. Cold as a mother-in-law's kiss, my late husband used to say.'

'You said on the phone that Ronnie was depressed...'

Mrs Bishop looked away and when she answered all the cheerfulness had gone out of her voice. 'Ronnie has AIDS, Mr Irish.' Tears began to run down her powdery cheek, turning pink in the clear light from outside. I felt deeply helpless. I cleared my throat.

'Do you think that had something to do with his disappearance?'

She turned back to me, shaking her head. 'I don't know. When I went to the police, they didn't seem interested after I told them Ronnie was...was sick.'

'How long was he going to stay in Melbourne, Mrs Bishop?'

'Only a few days. Then he said he had to see someone and he'd be back soon. And he didn't come back. And I've heard nothing. He wouldn't do that.'

'Why did he come to Melbourne?'

'To see someone. And to see his mum, of course. He's a lovely boy, Mr Irish. There's no harm in him.'

'Yes, I'm sure. Did he see the person?'

Mrs Bishop tidied her hair. 'I don't know, Mr Irish. But he said something to me a few days before he disappeared.'

I nodded helpfully.

'He said, "Mum, if anything happens to me I'm insured for two hundred thousand dollars and most of it goes to you." And then he said something else.'

She put both hands on my sleeve. 'He said, my blood went cold, Mr Irish, he said, "Mum, if I turn up dead somewhere don't ever believe it was my own fault." That's what he said. He was standing over there by the window. He'd been walking around the house for hours. Just smoking cigarettes and walking around.'

'You told the police this?'

'Of course. I told the lady policeman, Miss Ryan. She wrote it all down.'

'Mrs Bishop, do you know any reason why anyone would want to harm Ronnie?'

She looked out of the window again. 'No.'

'And you don't know who the person was he came to see?'

'No, I don't. Ronnie never talked about himself, Mr Irish. Doug always said Ronnie would make a good spy.'

'Did he take anything with him that day?'

'No. Nothing. Everything he brought is here. I even found a CD he'd brought for me. Didn't say a word, just slipped it into my rack. Just like him. He gave me a kiss and said he was going out for a while and he didn't come back. I wanted to put a bandaid on the scratch on his cheek but he didn't want me to.'

'He had a scratch on his cheek?'

She nodded. 'He said he scratched it on a hedge on his way to the corner shop to buy cigarettes.' She looked at me as if something had just occurred to her. 'You're not a policeman yourself are you, Mr Irish? Two policemen came and had a really good look around. I'm not sure what they were looking for.'

'No, Mrs Bishop. I'm a lawyer. I was involved in a trial years ago where Ronnie was a witness. There's been some new developments lately and I thought Ronnie might be able to help with some information.'

'I'm sure he'd be delighted to help,' she said. 'Did

97

you know he was a social worker once? Helping the poor homeless children on the streets. Of course, what he really wanted to do was make films. Ronnie loved films. He saved up to buy a movie camera. He was always filming things.'

'Was he a trained social worker, Mrs Bishop?'

'Well, not really. He was a clever boy and he started at Melbourne University but he didn't really settle down. Doug and I were living in Queensland then, for Doug's health. Not that it improved. He missed the football so much, you know, I think it lowered his resistance.'

'So Ronnie was a paid social worker, was he?'

'Oh yes. He worked for the Safe Hands Foundation. They help the homeless.'

I'd never heard of the foundation but that didn't mean anything. 'Why did Ronnie move to Perth, Mrs Bishop?'

She pondered this for a moment. 'I don't know, really. Just wanted to go somewhere else, I suppose. Young people are like that, today, aren't they?'

Ronnie was always going to be a young person to his mum. 'He bought a new car before he left. That must have been expensive.'

She smiled. 'He won some money on the Lotto. He took me to Georges to buy a winter coat. I've still got it. Beautiful. He's such a generous boy.'

It was time to go. Mrs Bishop came to the front gate with me. In front of the house next door, a man in a dark double-breasted suit was leaning against a BMW, talking into a mobile phone. He gave Mrs Bishop a wave: five stiff fingers moved from side to side. He'd be making her an offer for the house any day now. I said I was sure Ronnie would be in touch soon, gave her my card, shook her small hand, and left.

I went back to my office and brooded for a while. Ronnie Bishop came to Melbourne a worried man. Perhaps his friend Charles Lee, the man who'd answered his telephone, could tell me why. He certainly wasn't going to tell me on the phone. That meant going to Perth. I didn't want to go to Perth. Did I owe it to Danny? What did I owe Danny, anyway? Bloody something. I phoned Veneto Travel.

'Perth?' said Shane DiSanto. He had recently inherited the business from his uncle Carlo. It was a big change from panel beating.

'Put Denise on, Shane,' I said.

'Jack, Jack, Jack, I'm the boss here now. You're talking to the owner. I can handle this. What you want to go to Perth for? You don't go to Perth in winter. I can do you Hamilton Island. You can't live at home and eat McDonald's for what I can do it. Dirt, Jack, dirt. Are you listening?'

Shane eventually agreed to let me go to Perth and made the booking. I rang Linda Hillier and left a message on her machine. Then I considered ringing Charles Lee and decided against it.

When I went to pick up the ticket at the airport, they'd never heard of me. I rang Veneto and got Denise.

'You're lucky it's only Perth,' she said. 'He made all the bookings for Frank La Bianca's daughter's honeymoon. High season in Florence. Lucky couple had to have sanctified root numero uno in the back seat of the Hertz car.'

I hired a Corolla in midair from a steward called David. He thought a person like me would be happier with a BMW. So did I.

It takes hours to get to Perth, flying over the huge shark-infested dent in the continent called the Great Australian Bight. And when you get there, you're two hours in the past. I didn't know Perth; it was just an airport on the way to Europe. They tell me the locals have secessionist tendencies. I can understand that. Judging by the accents, they'll probably have a fight over whether to rename the State Manchester or Birmingham.

It was a sunny day in Perth, insignificant wisps of cloud decorating a sky the colour of old blue jeans. I studied the map book for about ten minutes and set off for Fremantle. On paper, getting there was a matter of keeping to the highroads. On land, however, the Corolla had a tendency to wander off the beaten track. On my second sighting of the same pub I stopped for lunch and directions. I sat out in the beer garden with a bottle of Swan Lager and a big piece of charred West Australian steer. Around me the locals, mostly Britons with flaking skins wearing towelling hats, were being enthusiastic about the chances of the West Coast Eagles against Carlton. I thought it would be nice if they both lost but this wasn't the place to say it.

After lunch, I took some counsel from one of the

Poms and went off driving again. By the time I found Fremantle I had a fair idea of Perth. It was a huge suburb built on sand dunes around a shallow estuary. The upmarket bits had more dark-green vegetation and more trees. I went through the city centre with its standard collection of glass towers and roughly followed the course of the Swan River to its mouth, which is the port of Fremantle.

Fremantle looked like an English Channel port transported to the Mediterranean; handsome Victorian stone buildings looking slightly uneasy in the hard light. There were plenty of signs of the tourist trappings that had made the place so dangerous during the America's Cup challenge, but it also felt like a working harbour.

I had a good cup of coffee in a place full of voluble Italians and people with time to read a book in the middle of the day, walked around the fishing harbour, visited the maritime museum, browsed in a bookshop, had another cup of coffee.

Ronnie Bishop's house was two or three blocks back from the waterfront, a sandstone dwelling in a street of smart revamped houses. It had two young palms in front, high walls blocking off the neighbours and a severe wrought-iron fence with spear tops. Morton Street, Clifton Hill, this was not.

The front door was a nice piece of woodwork, a rich, dark jarrah frame with panels of pine oiled to a dark honey colour. I pressed a brass button in a brass plate and heard the chime. No-one came. I took a walk up the street. The house next door bore a brass plate saying Souter & Whale, Architects. I was back in the car reading a novel I'd bought called *The Means of Grace* when a white Honda Civic drew up outside Ronnie's address and a man in jeans and white golf shirt got out. He checked Ronnie's mailbox, unlocked the front door and went inside, leaving it open. He was out again in minutes and set about watering the garden.

I got out of the Corolla and went over to the fence. He caught sight of me approaching.

'You must be Charles,' I said.

He was a tall man, early forties, light tan, thin and fit-looking. What remained of his hair was close-cropped. He looked like the mature outdoor male in an advertisement.

'Yes,' he said, warily. He held the hose as if ready to water me.

'I'm Jack Irish, the lawyer from Melbourne. I rang you about Ronnie.'

His face relaxed.

'You've come a long way,' he said. 'Let's go inside.'

I followed him through a small hallway with a highly polished floor into a sitting room furnished in a dark masculine style. He opened the curtains and we sat down in Morris chairs.

'Well,' he said, 'I'm very worried. I didn't know anything until I rang his mum about the break-in.'

'The break-in?'

'Last Wednesday. We've cleaned up, but my God, the mess.'

'What did they get?'

'My dear, they walked off with the weirdest stuff. And they took housekeeping money as far as I can tell.

Ronnie told me he'd left it in the usual place, which is under the breakfast cereals. Not a lot. I think it's a hundred dollars. Mrs G says it's not there.'

'They gave the place a going over, did they?'

'Certainly did, my God! The study you would not believe. A shambles. All Ronnie's business papers on the floor, all the books off the shelves, all the drawers out of the desk.'

I said, 'Charles, why would Ronnie disappear?'

He shook his head. 'Jack—may I call you Jack?—I can't think of any reason why. He's been very, very depressed, of course, but...' He looked away into the middle distance.

'Why was that?'

'Well, business has been terrible, for one thing.'

'What business is that?'

'Ronnie's in video. It's suffered with the rest of the economy. And he put a lot of capital into some compact disc venture. CD-ROM. Very high tech. A mystery to me.' He put his right hand to his mouth. 'I haven't even offered you a drinky. I generally have a G and T around this time.'

I accepted a gin and tonic. It came large, with a smudge of bitters. Charles folded a leg under him as he sat down.

'Ronnie's mother says he has AIDS, Charles.'

He sighed. 'The dear old girl. That's simply not true. Ronnie is HIV-positive. There's a big difference, you know. He'll probably outlive us all.'

'Did he think that way?'

He eyed me like a dog show judge. After a while, he said, 'I'm not sure that I understand what's going on.'

'Going on?'

'Going on. Something's going on and I'm the poor bunny in the middle of it.'

'Well, as I said on the phone, I'm interested in talking to Ronnie about evidence he gave in a trial in Melbourne years ago.'

'You must be very interested to come to Perth to ask me questions.'

I shrugged. 'I'm feeling a bit driven. And Ronnie's the only person who can help me. If I knew a bit more about him, I might be able to find him.'

Charles looked at his nails. Clean, pink, blunt nails. 'Well,' he said, 'ask away.'

'Why did he go to Melbourne?'

'He said he had to see someone.'

'Do you know what about?'

'I'd only be guessing.'

'Even a guess might help.'

'There were phone calls from Melbourne.'

I waited. Charles sipped his drink. There was a beautiful sunset going on outside. I could see a coral glow on the wall of the neighbour's house. You don't see sunsets in Melbourne in winter. It isn't even clear to me that the sun rises in Melbourne in winter.

'A man rang twice.'

'Was that unusual?'

'Yes. To ring here, that was unusual. I stop in on my way from work every day and give the garden a sprinkle, that sort of thing. It'd die if it was left to Ronnie. He doesn't come home until all hours, so I listen to the answering machine and I ring him at the shop if it's anything he needs to know about. The only person who calls from Melbourne is his mum and she generally rings on Sunday mornings.'

'What did the man say?'

'He said he needed to speak to Ronnie urgently. I rang Ronnie and gave him the message. Twice.'

'Did he say anything?'

Charles was silent again for a while. He was still at war with himself about answering my questions.

'The first time he said something like, "Oh, Christ, no". Something like that.'

'The man gave a name and a number to ring?'

'Yes.'

'Can you remember the name?'

'I'm afraid not. I'm hopeless about names. It'd be on the tape.'

I felt a small flush of excitement. 'You've got the answering machine tape?'

'No. The burglars took all the tapes. They took all the CDs too, but you can understand that. Ronnie didn't wipe any answering machine tapes. He just put in a new tape. Some of them have got messages that go on for half an hour or more, my dear. He's got these weird girlfriends. They don't seem to want to talk to him. They just pour out all this drivel about men and shopping and films to the machine.'

'But all the tapes were here?'

'Yes. They were all in the phone table drawer. The burglars dumped the drawer on the floor, my dear. Gave it a kick too, by the look of things. Pens and stuff everywhere. They took the tape out of the machine, too.'

I tried the name Danny McKillop on him.

'I can't say yes and I can't say no,' he said. 'I think it *was* an Irish sort of name. But I can't be sure.'

'Did Ronnie ever talk about his past?'

'Never. The man was like the Sphinx. Could've been born yesterday.'

What had Ronnie's mother said? *Doug always said he would make a good spy.*

'He never mentioned any names?'

Charles picked up his glass and stuck the tip of his tongue into the liquid. He looked at me over the rim. 'Not ever. I've been over all this before. I told the detectives that. They asked these questions. I told them the same thing. Ronnie simply did not talk about himself except in the vaguest way.'

'These were the detectives about the break-in?'

'Oh, absolutely not. That was PC Plod from the local station. These were men in plain clothes. Rather grubby plain clothes in the case of one of them.' He laughed, a light laugh, verging on the nervous.

'And they identified themselves as policemen?'

He didn't answer for a few seconds, turning a gold band with a single red stone in it on the little finger of his right hand. 'No,' he said. 'They didn't. They came to the door at home. It's just around the corner. My unit. About nine at night. Smelling, reeking of drink, if you don't mind. One expects more.'

'You assumed they were detectives?'

'Yes. I did. They were, I think. They had that manner. The smaller one took out some sort of notebook. He wasn't small, mind you. The opposite. Just small*er*. He said something like: "It's in connection with the disappearance of someone you know. Ronald Bishop. We'd like to ask you some questions."'

I savoured the last of my drink. 'Can I get the timing sorted out?' I said. 'This visit was after the break-in?'

'Two days after. Mrs G and I had spent hours cleaning up and then I came home, utterly drained I can tell you, and I'd had a shower and slipped into a gown and there they were pounding on the door.'

'What did they want to know?'

'Refill time,' Charles said. His drink was hardly touched but he took both glasses away. I took out my notebook, full of horse observations, and made a few entries. When he came back, Charles sat on the edge of his chair, glass held in both hands.

'All they were interested in, Jack, was what Ronnie had told me about going to Melbourne,' he said. 'Names. They wanted to know any names he'd mentioned. And they wanted to know what he'd told me about his life in Melbourne before he came to Perth.' He leaned towards me. 'They were very crude, Jack. It upset me. I'm not used to that sort of thing. Not at all. I'd have complained if I'd thought it would do any good.'

'Crude in what way?'

Charles made sure we had strong eye contact. 'The smaller one said: "You poofs tell each other everything, don't you? What did your boyfriend tell you about Melbourne?" Those were his words, Jack. Chock full of hatred, I can tell you. Almost spitting. And that is not the nature of our relationship at all. It is not physical.'

I nodded. 'How did you respond?'

He shrugged. 'I said Ronnie was a good friend and that he told me nothing about his early life and never mentioned names. And I said I'd like to have my lawyer present.'

'And then?'

'He became quite chummy in a nauseating sort of way and said they didn't have any more questions. Then he asked if Ronnie had given me anything to look after for him. I said I didn't want to answer any more questions and he said: "Answer me, cockbreath." Those were his words. I felt scared. I said no he had not and would they please leave. And they did. Just walked out without another word.'

'They never said anything about a court case long ago, in Melbourne?'

'No. Nothing like that.'

'Did Ronnie ever speak of giving evidence against someone?'

Charles was looking into his drink. 'No. You don't think they were policemen, do you, Jack?'

'It's hard to tell, Charles. If they come around again, don't let them in. Say you have to get dressed, something's on the stove, anything, and phone the police emergency number and say you're being attacked. Then phone your lawyer.'

'I don't really have a lawyer,' he said.

'Get one.'

I finished my drink, gave him my telephone numbers, and he gave me his.

At the front gate, I asked, 'Charles, would you call Ronnie a trustworthy person?'

He clicked the gate closed behind me. Another sigh,

this one much deeper. He put his hands in his pockets and looked at the gatepost.

'No,' he said sadly. 'He didn't tell you much, but what he did was almost all lies. Even when it didn't matter a fig. Variety. That's all he wanted. New bodies, new sensations. Boys. Girls. Didn't matter to him. He got beaten up quite often. Once in this house by some little thug he was tying up. Face swollen like a pumpkin. Kicked in the head, all the money in the house taken, VCR, CDs. I had to take him to casualty. I thought that was what had happened when his mum rang me. That he was probably lying in some public toilet.'

'Did he need money?'

'I think so. He'd borrowed nearly five thousand dollars from me. They refused his American Express card at Latino's the day before he went. I paid for the meal with my card. And there's trouble about this house. It's going to be sold by the bank.'

'How did he get that way?'

Charles shook his head. He looked much older now, less firm of face. 'I honestly don't know, Jack,' he said. 'He didn't tell me and I wouldn't have dreamed of asking.'

We shook hands. I liked him. He clearly deserved better than Ronnie Bishop. Burdett-Bishop.

'Why did he stick the Burdett on his name?' I asked.

Charles sighed and looked heavenwards. 'He was thinking of going into real estate and he thought it sounded impressive.'

I went in search of lodgings, thankful that I'd bought a book.

A weak sun was shining on Melbourne, but to compensate a marrow-chilling wind was blowing. I rang the security parking garage and they sent their little bus to collect me.

'Jetsetting again,' the driver said. 'You joined that Mile High Club yet?'

He was an ex-cop called Col Boon, pensioned off the force for extreme hypertension after shooting another cop during a raid on an indoor dope plantation in Coburg. A tragic mistake, the coroner said. I suppose in some ways it's always a tragic mistake to shoot the man who's rooting your wife every time you're on nightshift and he's not.

'The club reckons I couldn't stand the excitement of high-altitude copulation,' I said.

Col made an animal noise. 'Tell 'em you'll do it sitting down. You growing a beard?'

I felt my two-day growth. 'Stewies like a bit of hair,' I said.

He shook his head. 'Bit? Seen less hair on pussies.' He took a corner with a squeal of balding tyres. 'Talking pussies, you want to pick your stewie. Mate of mine put his hand in the golden triangle, found a big cock. Qantas I think it was.'

I pondered the significance of this story. My maternal grandmother apparently addressed stewardesses as 'waitress'. She would not have taken well to the idea that some of them were, in fact, waiters.

At the parking garage, Col said, 'There's a bit of a problem with your car. That grease monkey rang. Says he took your motor to pieces and he can't put it together again till he can find parts. Two weeks, minimum.'

I groaned. This was what happened when you left your ancient Lark for a service with a backyard mechanic who was a Studebaker fanatic.

'Now you tell me. What am I supposed to do?' I said. 'Walk?'

'He says he's got an old Chevy you can use.'

'I hate old Chevies.'

'Well,' Col said, 'we've got a special on unclaimed vehicles this week. Nice Celica. Say two weeks, hundred and fifty.'

'You work this out together?'

He looked hurt.

I said, 'Throw in a full tank.'

'Give us a break. There's a good bit in it.' He gave me an appraising look. 'Had a call if your car was here.'

I waited.

'Your office. A girl.'

I shook my head.

'No. Well, this isn't the lost and found either. Told her you hadn't parked here for a while.'

'You give a complete service here, Col,' I said.

He handed me the keys. 'I'd say look after it like your own,' he said, 'but that's the last thing we want.'

*

I thought about Ronnie all the way to Fitzroy. I'd got the addresses from Charles and visited Ronnie's two video rental shops in the Perth suburbs. One was closed. The other was in a small shopping mall and it didn't look healthy. From behind a partition of grey tin shelves came the sobbing breaths, grunts, yells and urgings of a pornographic video and the jeers and cheers of a teenage audience. After a while, a sallow youth with a pigtail emerged and said, 'Yep?' It turned out he didn't know Ronnie but was standing in for his friend's friend, who sometimes worked in the shop.

At the workshop, Charlie was finishing up for the day, pottering around endlessly as usual – a dab of oil here, a wipe of a surface there, here a gentle opening and closing of a cabinet door, there a pull–push of a drawer. I gradually worked him through the front doors like a sheepdog with a particularly difficult sheep. We drove around to the Prince of Prussia. Usually we walked, but Charlie's hip was hurting. I parked the Celica around the corner in a loading zone.

'No respect for the law,' Charlie said. 'That's where it all begins. *Und du bist rechtsgelehrt.*'

'Have a heart,' I said. 'It's only a little municipal regulation, shouldn't apply after 5 p.m.' When we were alone, Charlie often expressed his doubts and disappointments about me in German, language of my great-grandfather.

Wilbur Ong and Norm O'Neill were in position, beers, pies, *Herald Sun* form guides on the counter. They gave us the briefest acknowledgment.

'My feelin is we're lookin at a rerun of Kyneton twenty months ago,' said Norm. The peak of his flat cap rested on his spectacles, which rested on a nose of heroic size.

'Well, I've always loved yer feeling, darlin,' said Wilbur, 'but there's a lotta wishful here. He's bin five, seven, five first-up since then.'

''Course he has,' said Norm. 'That's why we're lookin at bloody forties here. Know it in my bones.'

'Relied on your bones,' Wilbur said, 'we'd be round the Salvos eatin rabbit stew.'

'Given these pies, that's not a frightenin thought,' said Norm. He turned to me. 'Jack, prepared to divulge yer thoughts on the gallops at Geelong?'

'People in the know treat my tips as scratchings,' I said. 'However, since it's you lot.'

Charlie Taub gave a snort and went off to talk football to a retired tram driver called Wally Pollard. Wally's only son, Bantam Pollard, ruined a promising career with Collingwood through bad timing. On a Friday night in 1975, the club president took six guests into the committee box to show them the ground's new floodlights. They came on, casting a cold white light on the playing field and on Bantam Pollard's spotty bottom. It was dead centre of the field, bracketed by the fleshy thighs of the president's sixteen-year-old daughter.

We were on race four when a man came in the street door. He was about fifty, bald, of below medium height, with a heavy body. RayBans sat on a darkly tanned bull-terrier face. He'd spent about three grand on his gear, most of it on gold chains and a golden brown leather jacket that fitted him like a condom. The style said Sydney or the Gold Coast; the walk, as if he were rolling a tennis ball between his upper thighs, said cop, probably vice squad.

Stan the barman was at the far end of the counter. He exchanged a few words with Mr Gold Coast and then came down to our end of the bar.

'Bloke's asking for Jack,' he said, looking at Wilbur. 'What'll I tell him?'

'Tell him I'll be along in a minute,' I said. I lingered for a minute or two and then walked down the bar.

Stan had served Mr Gold Coast something with tonic. At my approach, he smiled at me, a lip lift to show lavatory-white capped teeth. It conveyed no more sentiment than a facial tic. He put out a hand.

'Jack. Tony Baker.' The hand exerted no pressure; a hand that felt to be made of one-inch brass plumbing fittings didn't need to do anything other than Be.

'What can I do for you?' I said.

'Have a drink with me.'

'I've got one waiting.'

'You do work among the elderly. That's nice.' He swallowed the contents of his glass and rapped it on the counter several times. Stan responded to the summons by leaving the room.

Tony Baker edged closer to me. The top of his head came up to my chin. This gave me all the physical confidence the giraffe feels when it meets the rhino. He showed me his teeth again.

'Clubby here, am I right? No risk of anyone wanting to join though, mate. Well, this isn't a social occasion. I'm here to straighten a coupla things out.'

'Such as?'

'Such as your getting in the way of an official investigation.'

'Of what?'

'Of a number of matters, one of which touches Mr Ronald Bishop.'

'What do you mean, touches?'

Tony Baker put his hand to his muscular sausage of a neck and turned his head a few centimetres to each side. 'Jack,' he said, speaking softly, 'you don't want to know, right? If you get in the way of this investigation you'll get squashed so fucken flat they'll post you.'

'Who'll squash me?' I asked.

His eyes went hard. I noticed a small gold fleck in the right iris. 'You're not listening, Jack. I'm telling you to back off, drop it. This matter is at a very high level, a national level. I've said too much now.'

'Have you got some identification?' I realised I should have asked earlier.

Tony Baker closed his eyes and sighed. 'Can I get this across to you without a map? You don't want to know anything about me. Take it as gospel: you are obstructing an official operation. Pull your head in, forget about Mr Bishop, or you'll wish it was you that cunt blew up in the carpark. Just fucken butt out.'

He left. I went back to the form but couldn't concentrate. At six-thirty, Charlie's granddaughter, the lovely Augustine, hooted outside. I went out with him. It was intensely cold after the warmth of the pub and the air had the burnt petrol smell of winter cities everywhere.

Charlie got into the car and wound down the

window. 'Eat some proper food,' he said. 'You need someone to look after you.'

I put my hand on his shoulder. 'Maybe you can talk your driver here into marrying me. It's all indoor work.'

'Let's talk pay and conditions,' Gus said. She was a trade union official.

Charlie snorted. 'Go,' he said to Gus. 'Some men you don't want in your family.'

I stood in the street and considered whether to go back into the pub and settle down or to go home. I decided to go home. I've learned to take the hard decisions.

The apartment was cold, the bulb in the bathroom had fused and the fridge smelled of five-day-old fish. Cam, Wootton and my daughter were on the answering machine. Claire said: *Listen, Jack, I'm just ringing to say I miss you and I'll be down for a visit soon. I might bring Eric to set your mind at rest. Your letter sounds glum. Don't be. Love you. Bye.*

I made a stiff Jameson's and soda and rang Linda Hillier. She wasn't in the office.

Hardhills was a shop, a garage and a weatherboard pub at a churned-up crossroads. The nearest town of any size was thirty kilometres away. In between, it was all low sky, wet sheep and ponds in every hollow.

There were three utes outside the pub. Harry Strang eased the BMW to a stop beside the shop and switched off. He looked at his watch.

We sat in silence for five minutes. I was thinking about Ronnie Bishop. Cam was reading the *Sporting Globe*. Harry had his eyes closed, head back on the rest. Then he said, 'Now this fella Rex Tie, supposed to meet us out here twelve sharp, he's sittin in the pub over there with this other fella we've come to see. Talkin horses. Couple of the yokels no doubt waterin the tonsils. Publican's hangin about. Rex's takin the view that we'll come in, have a few gargles first.'

'Sounds reasonable,' I said.

'Not in this line of work,' Harry said. 'Thought I'd schooled Rex the last time. Easier to train a horse.'

At 12.15, two men came out of the pub. One of them, a gangling figure in a battered half-length Drizabone, came over to the car. At his approach, Harry pressed the button and his window slid down.

The man bent down to look in. He had a long, sad, middle-aged face, much of it nose.

'Sorry, Harry,' he said. 'Thought you might come in for a quick one.'

Harry looked at him. 'Rex, you've forgotten.'

Rex straightened up and then he came down again. 'Jeez, Harry, have a heart. This is bloody Hardhills. There's only about four people.'

'That's four too many, Rex. Drive. We'll follow.'

Rex and the other man got into their utes and drove off, the other man in front. We followed at a distance.

'Harry, why do you need a lawyer for driving around the Western District?' I asked. The question had been on my mind for some time.

He gave me a quick look. 'The yokels've got a lot of respect for lawyers, Jack. Doesn't hurt to show them one. That bloke up front, he's got a horse called Dakota Dreaming, five years old, hasn't run for two years. Not that it ran much before that either. What's the 'rithmetic, Cam?'

'Seven, one, one,' said Cam. He was studying the landscape out of the side window.

'Five-year-old. Seven races. Now that's what I call lightly raced,' Harry said. 'And the reason is, Jack, the animal's got a horrible record, truly horrible. Lucky he's not in the pet's mince or got a big copper's bum on him. The fella up there, he's owner number four, and number three made him a gift of the horse. Gratis and for nothing. He's put two years into patchin up the beast and he reckons it's got one or two big runs in it. Tell Jack the history, Cam.'

Cam looked around. 'He's bred for staying. Third

highest price for a yearling in New Zealand in his year. Won his first race by seven lengths. Then Edgar Charlton bought him for a fair bit for a dentists' syndicate. First time out he ran seventh against a good field, pulled up lame. Out for seventeen weeks. Came back at Sandown in December, second in a bunch of spring leftovers. Tendon trouble, twenty weeks off. March at Caulfield. Ninth out of thirteen. Ballarat three weeks later. Stone last. Bleeding. Took the compulsory count. The dentists spit the dummy, sold him. Turned out twice for the third owner for one sixth and one last.'

'Fella trains over near Colac,' Harry said. 'John Nisbet. Gave our friend up ahead the horse with a bowed tendon on his near side and bone chips in both front legs. A dead loss.'

'With respect, this outing doesn't look like an investment to me,' I said.

'Shake,' said Cam.

'Won't hurt to have a look,' Harry said. 'Old Rex's no Rhodes Scholar but he's not Curly Joe.'

The front vehicle turned right. A rutted track ran around the gentle eastern slope of a round-topped hill. At the foot of the northern slope were a farmhouse, stables, assorted sheds, a round yard. Horses in rugs were standing around looking bored in half a dozen paddocks. About a hundred metres from the buildings, the front driver pulled half off the track, got out and opened a gate. He waved us through.

Rex parked next to a shed and Harry pulled up beside him. We all got out and put on our coats. The north wind had ice in it.

'Christ, Harry,' said Cam, 'can't we do this in the summer? Bloody nun's nipple.'

The lead driver parked next to the farmhouse. All the buildings except the stables were old but the place was kept up; fresh paint, taut wire, raked gravel. As we got out of the ute, a boy of about fourteen appeared at the front door of the house.

Harry introduced us to Rex and when the other man came over, Rex said, 'Tony Ericson, this is Harry Strang, Cam Delray, and Harry's lawyer, Jack Irish.'

We shook hands. Tony was jockey size but too heavy, lined face, thick dark hair cut short, big ears.

'Never thought I'd meet you,' he said to Harry. 'Me dad used to say, "Think you're Harry Strang?" when we tried some flash riding.'

'How's your dad?' asked Harry.

Tony Ericson cocked his head. 'You remember me dad? He always said he knew you.'

'Ray Ericson,' Harry said. 'Still goin?'

Tony Ericson shook his head.

Harry patted his arm briskly. 'Sorry to hear it. Ray could get a camel to jump. Now what's the story?'

Tony Ericson looked at Rex Tie. 'You want to, Rex...'

'You go,' Rex Tie said.

'Let's get down the stables,' Tony said. 'I brung the horse in. Lives outside normal. Bugger's had enough soft in his life.'

We went down a gravel path, through a gate and round the corner of a long cinderblock stable building. There were eight stalls but only one horse. It was waiting for us, brown head turned our way, nostrils steaming.

Tony said, 'Rex tell you his name's Dakota Dreamin? We call him Slim.'

The horse snickered as we approached. Tony stroked his nose and fed him something.

'They say he was a deadset mongrel, kickin, bitin, but we never seen it. Like a lamb. Me girl looks after him, ten-year-old.' He looked behind us and said, 'Tom, shake hands with the gentlemen. This is me boy Tom, waggin school. He'll give the horse a little hit out.'

The boy from the front door came up and shook hands awkwardly. Someone other than a barber had given him a recent haircut. He was going to be too big for a jockey.

We walked down a road between paddocks and over a small rise. Below us, invisible from the stables, was a training track. You could smell the watermelon scent of new-mown grass before you saw it.

'Two thousand four hundred metres,' said Tony Ericson. 'Got a twelve hundred metre chute over there.' He pointed to the left. 'Starting gate. Same grass as Flemington. Bloke done it in the sixties. Went bang here. Used to have rails and all. Had sheep on it for twenty years but we mowed it and rolled it and it come up good.'

I looked at Harry. He had his hands in the jacket pockets of his leather-trimmed loden jacket and a faraway expression on his face.

He took a hand out and rubbed his chin. 'Very nice,' he said. 'Pride of the district, I imagine.'

'Don't follow,' said Tony.

'Other people use this?'

Tony shook his head. 'No trainers around here. We only cleaned it up bout a year ago. Whole thing, that is.'

We all turned at the sound of hoofs. The boy, Tom, walked Dakota Dreaming up to us. The horse shone like glass, groomed to a standard only achievable by ten-year-old girls. It had pristine bandages on all legs. I knew enough about condition to know this creature was well advanced in his preparation to race.

Tony held the horse's head. 'Remember what I said. Take him out to the seven furlong. I'll give you a bang. Don't push him. If he's feelin strong at the three hundred, let him go.'

The boy nodded and took the horse off. On the track, they went into an easy canter.

We walked along to where a big tin lollipop painted red marked the finish. Cam lit a cigarette, held it in the corner of his mouth while he fiddled with his stopwatch. Harry took out a small pair of binoculars and hung them around his neck. Tony Ericson put a blank into a starting pistol.

'Don't he mind the gun?' asked Rex Tie.

'Can't hardly hear it over there,' said Tony. 'He's ready. Light's flashin.' He raised the pistol above his head, waved it. The boy's right arm went up and down. Tony fired, a flat smack.

Tom set a nice pace, about what you'd expect for a frontrunner over 1400 or 1600 metres on a country track. The straight was about 350 metres. When they came around the turn, you could see that the going was soft and that the horse was not entirely happy.

But the going wasn't going to stop Slim putting on

a show. At the 300-metre mark, you could see Tom urge the horse with hands and heels. It didn't require much. With every appearance of enjoyment, the horse opened its stride, lowered its head and accelerated home. They went past the post flat out.

We stood in silence watching the boy, standing upright in the stirrups, slow the horse down.

Harry took off his hat and scratched his head. Cam was looking for a cigarette. Their eyes locked for a good three seconds.

'What's it say?' asked Harry.

Cam found a cigarette and lit it with his Zippo.

'For a stayer,' he said, 'smokin.'

Drew poured some red wine into our glasses, leant back and put his stockinged feet on the coffee table. 'You want my advice?'

Harry and Cam had dropped me off at home but I didn't go in. I'd been brooding all the way back from Hardhills and I felt the urge to talk to Drew. Once upon a time we'd talked to each other about all our problems.

I found him eating takeaway pizza over a pile of files in front of the fire in his house in Kew. The children were nowhere to be seen.

I said, 'Well. Yes.'

'Drop it. Forget Danny ever left the message. Take the gorilla's advice about this Bishop too. You've touched a nerve somewhere.'

'If I hadn't been three-quarters pissed years ago I'd have tried to find out more about Danny's movements the night of the hit-and-run,' I said. 'I might have kept him out of jail.'

Drew chewed for a while, studying the flames. Finally he said, 'Bullshit, mate. Even if you'd been stone-cold sober and at the top of your form, it would never have occurred to you. You'd have pleaded him. You had to plead him. Since when do lawyers go looking for other explanations when the Crown's got

125

a case like that? Don't kid yourself. There was no negligence there. There's nothing owing on your part.'

We sat in silence for a while, looking at the flames. A wind had come up and every now and again it made a hollow sound in the chimney.

'Remember that week fishing on the Delatite?' Drew asked. 'I reckon that was the best holiday of my adult life.'

'You've never said that before,' I said. 'We caught about three fish.'

'Didn't matter a bugger. It was great. It's all the kids seem to remember of their entire childhoods. Apart from the times I'm supposed to have been awful.'

I never thought about that trip. I'd curtained it off. It was the last holiday with Isabel.

'It was good,' I said. 'Like being a kid again.'

'Can't get enough of that.' Drew shifted in his chair. 'Listen, Jack, Danny was probably knocked for some drug scam. This other bloke, from what you say, was a candidate for doing something unpleasant. If there are feral cops involved, the next thing is that *you* have an accident.'

I nodded. I knew he was right. It was too late to do the right thing by Danny McKillop. The guilt that had taken me to Perth was pointless. With a sense of relief, I held out my wine glass.

'We'll just finish this drop in here,' said Drew, 'and then I want to show you a little 1978 shiraz off vines that were ninety years old then. Client gave me a case.'

I ended up sleeping in the spare room.

*

I put in the next day at Taub's, cutting a taper on and hand-morticing the legs of the boardroom table. It was soothing work for someone not feeling all that flash. Charlie didn't make tables any more unless he had to. Having me around meant he didn't have to. 'A table is pretty much a table,' he said. 'When you can't make a complete ruin.'

My cabinetmaking began as a kind of therapy on my way back from self-destruction. I can see that now. At the time it just seemed to happen. I noticed Charlie's workshop while looking at the old tailor's shop that is now my office. I went in on impulse. Sunlight was slanting in through the high windows, the air smelled of wood shavings and linseed oil and Charlie was at his workbench whistling while carving the back of a reproduction George III mahogany chair he was making to fill a gap in what the antique trade calls a long set. In that moment I fell in love with the idea of being a cabinetmaker. No such thought had ever entered my mind before. I knew absolutely nothing about woodwork. I went up to Charlie and said, 'I'll pay you to teach me something about making furniture.'

Charlie had given me his interested look and said, 'Three things let me tell you. Number one, see a doctor. Number two, I'm too old to have an apprentice. Number three, you haven't got enough money.'

After I moved into my office, I began to hang around Taub's, making myself useful where I could. Charlie seemed to like the company. And he couldn't stop himself showing me how to do things.

Just before 4 p.m., the phone rang. It was switched

through from my office. It was Mrs Bishop, Ronnie's mother.

'Mr Irish,' she said, 'I'm sorry to bother you but I'm so dreadfully worried about Ronnie. I've been going over everything in my mind and I remembered him making a phone call. Well, I went to the phone, it's in the passage, and looked at the little pad I keep there and there's two numbers written down. By Ronnie.'

I said, 'Good work, Mrs Bishop. Numbers mean anything to you?'

'No. I don't know them. I was going to ring them, but then I thought I'd ask you first. Should I tell the police? Would they be interested?'

'Let me ring them first,' I said. 'The police often take some time to get around to things.'

I took down the numbers and went around to my office. I had a feeling about the first number. My scratchpad was beside the phone and on it a number was circled.

The first number was Danny McKillop's.

I sat down and dialled the second number. The phone rang two or three times and then a voice said, 'Father Gorman's residence.'

It was another sour day, full of wind and rain. It took a long time to get across the city to the address Father Rafael Gorman had given me. The urban planners wrecked the traffic flow when they turned Swanston Street, once Melbourne's spine, into some kind of half-baked pedestrian mall. Urban planners are people who know best. They should make them all marry social workers.

I sat in the jams and listened to Claude Haynes, the afternoon man on the ABC, interview the Premier. Like most men on the ABC, Claude had started out to be a clergyman but tossed in the frock after going a couple of rounds with God in the seminary. I don't know whether the experience of the religious life left these people sadder but it certainly left them believing they were wiser than anyone else.

'Premier,' Claude said, making it sound like an assumed name, 'the Opposition leader says you and your Planning Minister, Mr Pitman, are turning the State into a paradise for carpetbaggers and quick-buck artists. How do you respond to that?'

'With a smile,' said Dr Marcia Saunders, no trace of amusement in her voice. 'Mr Kerr has no commercial experience and no commercial sense. He wouldn't know a carpetbagger from the chairman of the Reserve Bank.'

Claude said, 'Mr Kerr gave AM a list of what he called "Projects for the Pals" this morning – Yarra Cove, the Footscray Sportsdome, the new privately run remand centre and several others. He says they are all being developed by government pals. Are the developers your pals?'

'Mr Kerr should know about pals,' Dr Saunders replied. 'He's got where he is because of pals. If he'd had to rely on brains or ability, he'd still be teaching geography in primary school.'

With the delighted air of someone who thinks he's trapped Wittgenstein in a logical error, Claude said,

'That doesn't answer my question: Are these developers your pals?'

There was a long silence. Then Marcia said, voice laden with menace, 'Mr Haynes, you shouldn't act as a frontman for these has-beens. If Mr Kerr has any evidence of favouritism, he should produce it. Let me assure the people of this State that this government doesn't do favours. It assesses projects and people purely on merit. It follows all processes and procedures to the letter. The developments you've named are both sound commercial propositions and job creators for this State. The people behind them are highly experienced and astute operators who can be relied upon to do a good job. Are you suggesting anything to the contrary?'

Claude cleared his throat. 'But are some of the developers supporters of your party?'

You could hear Marcia's sigh. It combined disbelief with contempt. 'Are you and Mr Kerr proposing that supporters of a governing party should be excluded from commercial life?' she said. Each word was coated with scorn.

Claude's tone went sugary. 'I think you're shooting the messenger here, Dr Saunders,' he said. 'I'm merely—'

'Don't try to hide behind the messenger argument,' snapped Marcia. 'You media leftovers from the sixties are seldom *merely* doing anything. But you might try to make your agenda a little less obvious.'

It went on like this. Claude kept trying to wrap himself in the rags of his dignity and Marcia kept tearing them off. I enjoyed Claude's discomfort but there was something chilling about Dr Marcia Saunders, PhD in physical education from the University of Kansas and former stockbroker. She wasn't the same person who'd smiled down from the election billboards.

After half an hour of traffic snarl, I'd had enough. I did a savage left turn in the face of traffic into a one-way street. One crime led to another, I had a few altercations and near-misses but I got to Father Gorman's address near Albert Park Lake with all the paint on.

I parked in a no-parking zone. Col Boon could knock a fellow cop and get the pension, he could beat parking tickets on this Celica.

Father Gorman's address was an oddly tapering new building. The tenants weren't short of space: there were eight floors and only six brass plates on the plinth outside. The one for the sixth floor said: Safe Hands Foundation.

The name meant something to me. I remembered as I reached the glass doors: Ronnie Bishop had once worked for the Safe Hands Foundation. Helping homeless children, his mother had said. *Trying to root them* had been the view of his former neighbour in Morton Street.

The tenants were fussy about who came to visit them. A security man with a snub nose, pale eyes and skin the colour of dirty underclothing kept me captive between two sets of glass doors while he wrote down my particulars on a clipboard. A tattoo peeped out from under his wristwatch. He wasn't too flash at writing.

Then he wanted my driver's licence.

'I'm not trying to cash a cheque here, sonny,' I said. 'Just phone the man.'

Tight little smile. 'The body corporate lays down the security procedures.' Flat Queensland voice. Pause. 'Sir.'

'This isn't Pentridge,' I said. 'Didn't they retrain you for this job? Just phone.'

He held my gaze briefly, but I'd got him in one. 'I'll check,' he said.

He made his call, came back, let me in, escorted me to the lift, up to the sixth floor, rang the bell on one of the two doors in the foyer, waited until a handsome dark youth opened the door. Through all this, he said nothing and exuded hatred.

'Come this way,' the youth said. His hair was drawn back tightly in a ponytail and he had the superior and slightly miffed manner of the waiters in most Melbourne restaurants.

I followed him through a large, elegant room and down a passage lined with framed architectural drawings to a teak six-panel door. The youth pushed open the door.

The voice from within was rich, warm and full of authority. 'Thank you, Francis. Do remember to knock next time. Mr Irish, come in. Oh, Francis, bring us a pot of coffee, there's a good boy.'

Father Gorman was coming round from behind a rosewood table with a column and platform base. On it were three or four files, a desk blotter and a fountain pen. He was a large man, probably in his sixties, big shoulders, crisp grey hair with just a hint of a wave brushed back, even features tanned the colour of milk fudge. He was wearing a navy-blue, double-breasted suit over a brilliantly white shirt. His tie had what looked like tiny camels on it.

He held out a hand. It was a surprisingly hard hand for a man of the cloth.

'Pleasure to meet you, Jack,' he said. 'Let's sit down.'

He led the way down the long panelled room to a setting of club armchairs and two sofas around a low military chest. A butler's table with bottles and decanters stood against the inside wall, which was covered with paintings, mostly landscapes. French doors in one exterior wall gave on to a terrace. Deep windows in the other provided a view to the Westgate Bridge and beyond. The beyond was dark with rain.

'Beautiful, isn't it?' he said, gesturing with both hands at the room, the view. 'I thank the Lord for it every day. And I thank Joseph Kwitny, the foundation's benefactor whose generosity allows an instrument of the Lord's will to live and work in such splendour.'

I got the feeling he had said this piece before but he said it very well. I sat down first and he took a chair beside me, close enough to lean out and touch.

'Well,' he said, 'and what part of Ireland do the Irish come from?'

'Not a well-known part,' I said. 'The Jewish quarter of Hamburg. My great-grandfather's name was Isadore Reich. He ran away to sea and jumped ship in Melbourne. When he wrote his name down as I. Reich for his first employer, the man pronounced it as I. Rish. That's what he became. Irish. I'm thinking of changing it back.'

Father Gorman laughed, a sound of deep enjoyment that washed over you, made you want to laugh with him, made you happy that you'd amused him. And while he was laughing, crinkles of pleasure around his eyes, he leaned over and touched my arm.

'Don't you ever do that,' he said. 'You wouldn't be able to tell that wonderful story any more. And you'd be hurting the whole line of dear departed Irishes.' He leaned back and put his hands in his pockets. 'Well now, Jack Irish, what can I tell you about Ronnie Bishop?'

I had told him on the phone that Ronnie was missing. 'Why did he ring you?' I asked.

'Why, he wanted to come around and see me. I hadn't seen him for years. I've known the lad a long time, you know.'

'I gather he once worked for the foundation.'

'Briefly. He wasn't really suited to the work. Not that I say that in any detrimental sense, mind. It's special work, dealing with the young in distress. Not everyone has the gifts needed.'

'And did he come around to see you?'

'Of course. We talked for an hour and then I had to go to a meeting. That was...' He raised his eyes to the ceiling. 'That was last Friday.'

'How was he?'

'Well, Jack, what do you know of the man's situation?' He fixed me with a look of inquiry that said 'Let's trust each other.'

'I gather he's HIV-positive.'

Father Gorman took his hands out of his pockets, sat forward, put his fingertips together. The nails were manicured. He had a slim gold watch on his wrist. Dark hairs fought to get out from under it. He looked out at the view. 'Yes,' he said. 'He told me that and I felt his pain and anger. And his fear.'

He turned his head to look at me, a clear, steady gaze.

'I'm interested in why he came to Melbourne. Did he say anything about that to you?' I asked.

'I assumed he had come to see his family. He said he was staying with his mother.'

There was a sound at the doorway and the youth came in carrying a tray with a tall silver coffee pot. The small cups chattered as he dropped the tray on the table from a height of at least two inches.

'Ah, Francis,' said Father Gorman. 'We may have to send you to waiter school. Perhaps in your home country.' He was smiling broadly, but there was an edge to his tone, a hint of autumn on a warm wind.

The youth gave him a glance of pure malice, tossed his ponytail and left. Father Gorman's eyes followed him. 'Rescued from a life of abuse and poverty,' he said. 'But still uncertain of what the Lord wants for him.'

I thought the Lord probably wanted a good swift kick up the arse for him, but I held my tongue. Father Gorman poured coffee. We both had ours black and sugarless. It was very bad coffee. I went back to Ronnie. 'He was working for the foundation when he testified against a hit-and-run driver,' I said.

Father Gorman took a sip of coffee. 'I recall that well, yes. A tragedy. Lovely young woman.'

'Did Ronnie ever say anything about his testimony?'

'I beg your pardon?'

'Did Ronnie ever talk about what happened that night?'

Father Gorman put his cup down and inspected me. 'I suppose we talked about it at the time. It would have been odd not to. Is there some reason why I should recall such a conversation?'

'Not if you don't. Did Ronnie mention when you saw him that the hit-and-run driver was out of jail and had been in touch with him?'

Father Gorman shot his left cuff to look at his watch. 'Jack, my heavens,' he said. 'I've a speech to deliver. I'm going to have to be dreadfully rude and cut short our talk. No, I can't say that he did mention anything like that. Would the man want to harm him?'

'I don't think so. I think he wanted something else.'

He frowned. 'And what could that be?'

'It's not clear. Have you any idea who Ronnie might turn to if he wanted to hide, Father?'

Father Gorman was already on his feet. 'Hide? That's a strange thing to suggest, isn't it? Why would he want to hide?'

I got up. 'It seems Ronnie was worried about his safety before he disappeared.'

He furrowed his brow, a look of deep concern. 'His safety? I thought you said the man posed no threat to him? My impression was that he was deeply troubled about his health, Jack. He certainly didn't suggest that he wanted to hide. Are you sure about this?'

He was walking me along, holding my arm. I felt like a parishioner in need of comfort. 'Let me see you out. Don't hesitate to give me a call if there's anything else I can do for you. I'm sorry our talk was so short. My work's an endless round of functions and speeches. I try to find an individual message for each group, but it's a battle. You'd know that. Lawyers understand. Every client's a new client, isn't that so? I toyed with the idea of the law, you know, but someone else had other ideas.'

At the front door, something made me ask a final question. 'When did you last speak to Ronnie, Father? I mean, before he rang you about coming to see you?'

Father Gorman stroked his chin. It was shaven to perfection. 'It would have been as much as seven or eight years ago, Jack. I got quite a surprise when I heard his voice, but I placed it straight away. I don't forget voices for some reason. The Lord's compensation for forgetting everything else, I suppose.'

He saw me to the lift. In the lobby downstairs, the ex-screw made a big show of logging me out.

'Well, old sausage,' said Wootton. 'It'd be another matter if this was an inquiry you were pursuing on my behalf.'

I'd tracked Wootton to the street bar of the Windsor Hotel, a Victorian pile near Parliament, after ringing his office on the way back from Father Gorman's. He stopped off there every day on his way home. It was Wootton's sort of place: wood panelling, photographs of cricket teams.

We were sitting at a window looking out on Spring Street. It was just after 5.30 p.m. and the place was filling up with pudgy young men in expensive suits and club ties. Wootton was wearing a dark pinstripe suit with waistcoat, shirt with narrow stripes and a tie with little crests on it. His thinning hair was brushed back on his perfectly round skull and his moustache, dyed jet black, was bristly but trim. He looked like an old-style Collins Street banker and that was the way he wanted to look.

I'd known Wootton in Vietnam. He'd been a sergeant in stores, thankless work in the service of country. In lieu of thanks, he'd taken money from about twenty bars and brothels for supplying them with everything from Fosters beer to Vegemite. Wootton would have gone home very rich if two military policemen hadn't seized his stash of US dollars two days before he was due to fly out. He never faced trial. The MPs thought the loss would be enough of a lesson to him. He never said another word about his money. And nor did they.

'Cyril, I think I've got more than enough credit in my account to cover this little favour. But if it's too much trouble—'

'Steady on, Jack,' said Wootton. 'No need to get shirty.' He took a sip of his whisky and water and rolled it around in his mouth, lips pursed. When he'd swallowed, he sighed and said, 'I'll have to go and do this from a bloody public phone, you know. Give me the number and the dates.'

I sipped my beer and read the *Herald Sun* Wootton had left behind while I waited. The lead story was another police shooting. A policewoman had shot dead a man who came at her with a knife when she attended a domestic dispute in Reservoir. The new Police Minister, Garth Bruce, was quoted as saying: 'As a former policeman, I know the demands and dangers of the job. I am not, of course, passing any opinion on what took place in this incident. The coroner will decide that. But I'm determined that the police force will move away from the culture of the gun that's become entrenched over the last ten years or so.' There was a photograph of the Minister: a big serious man with short hair and rimless glasses.

Wootton was away about fifteen minutes. He came in brushing rain off his suit. 'Can you believe it?' he said. 'Supposed to be a bloody five-star hotel. Had to go outside in the rain to find a phone that worked.'

A black Mercedes pulled up outside and two Japanese men in soaked golf outfits got out of the back. They stood close together in the drizzle, cap peaks almost touching, watching the driver unload two massive golf bags and wheelchair-size chrome golf buggies from the boot.

'Sons of Nippon,' said Wootton, flicking moisture off his moustache. 'Don't know if I'd go swanning around Tokyo if I'd worked thousands of Japs to death in World War II.'

'Those two look a bit young to have worked anyone to death in World War II,' I said.

'Don't be facetious. I need something to eat.' He went over to the counter. A barmaid served him immediately. They knew the man here. He came back opening a bag of salt and vinegar chips. 'Want some?'

I shook my head. He crammed a handful in under the moustache. Pieces stuck to it. 'Well,' he said, 'it'll take about ten minutes for the reverse directory.'

Until Wootton went back to his phone, we continued our argument about how much I'd added to my fee for getting a gun pointed at me by Eddie Dollery.

When he came back, Wootton took an old envelope out of his inside jacket pocket and handed it over. On the back were about a dozen telephone numbers, all the calls to different numbers made on Mrs Bishop's telephone in the three days Ronnie was there. Against each one, in Wootton's neat hand, was a name and address.

'Well,' he said, 'I hope I've contributed to you finding your catamite.'

'Sodomite,' I said. 'He presumably had catamites. I

only asked you to do it for me because I'm sworn to uphold the law.'

Wootton stuffed some more chips in his mouth. Through them, he said, 'Hah bloody hah. Joined the Boy Scouts, have we? Dib, Dib, Dib. Dob, Dob, Dob.'

'That's the Cubs, Cyril,' I said. 'But how would you know?'

I went home and tried Linda Hillier at Pacific Rim News. She was in Sydney, a man said. Back tomorrow. I poured a glass of white wine from an opened bottle in the fridge and studied the phone calls from Mrs Bishop's number. The calls to Danny McKillop and Father Gorman jumped out at me. That left nine calls. I rang Mrs Bishop. We went through the other calls from the beginning of the list. She had made all the calls except the last one. It was to a P. Gilbert, Long Gully Road, Daylesford. Made at 4.07 p.m. on the day Ronnie vanished.

'That must be Paul Gilbert,' she said thoughtfully. 'I haven't thought of him in years. Dr Paul Gilbert, he was. He went to school with Ronnie. Lovely boy, very clever. He had a surgery in St Georges Road.'

'The address is in Daylesford,' I said.

'Well, he's not a doctor anymore,' Mrs Bishop said. 'There was some trouble over drugs. It was in the papers. He started uni at the same time as Ronnie. I used to see Paul's mum sometimes. She was so proud of her boy before it happened.'

I rang the number twice before I went to bed. No answer. I fell asleep thinking about Linda Hillier. She probably had a good laugh at being come on to by the likes of me. Why had Gavin Legge called her a starfucker and a groupie? What star? What group? I hoped she wasn't avoiding me.

The bare limbs of Wombat Hill's English trees still smoked mist as I drove into Daylesford just after 9 a.m. The commuters were all gone and the small town's locals were easing themselves into the day. I parked in the main street and asked at the butcher's for directions to Long Gully Road. Butchers are the most friendly shopkeepers. It must have something to do with working with dead animals.

'Jeez,' said the butcher, 'Long Gully Road. Be out there in the forest, I reckon.' He shouted, 'Les! Where's Long Gully Road?'

A tall youth with red hair came in wiping his hands on butcher's paper. 'G'day,' he said. 'Where's a pen? Have to draw youse a map. It's out to buggery in the badlands.'

I'd tried P. Gilbert's number twice more that morning. No answer. I was eating my microwaved porridge when I decided to take a drive out to Daylesford. I didn't give much thought then to the pointlessness of driving for an hour to a house where no-one was answering the telephone. On the way I did, and almost turned back.

Twenty minutes after leaving the butcher's I was lost. The bush around Daylesford was veined with twisting, rutted roads going nowhere. Les's map wasn't much use after the first wrong turn. I was about to do a U-turn and try to retrace my route when I saw a man in overalls putting in a fence strainer post. Back in the trees a timber shack leant against a woodpile. He must have heard my approach but he didn't look up until I was out of the Celica.

'G'day,' I said. 'Looking for Long Gully Road.'

He looked at me for a while, big beard, eyes slit, jaws chewing cud. 'Back to the T-junction. Left. Third road on the left.'

I found the turnoff. The sign said NO THROUGH ROAD. Just off the ground, a square wooden board with an arrow had Koolanja Healing Centre, Spa, Massage in peeling white paint on a green background. There were old bullet holes in it. I drove about a kilometre through the scrubby regrowth forest before a duplicate of the first sign pointed down a narrow track.

The buildings were behind a fence in a big clearing at the end of the road: a long, low weatherboard with a verandah along the front, a square cinderblock building with narrow windows and, behind them and to the left, a steel-frame shed without walls. The gate was closed and on it a sign saying CLOSED hung at an angle.

A car was parked in front of the cinderblock building: a BMW, not new. I suddenly realised that I'd never asked what sort of car Ronnie was driving. In the shed, I could see two other vehicles, a four-wheel-drive and an old Holden.

I parked outside the gate and let myself in. No dogs.

Dogs appear quickly or not at all. Ahead of me a driveway ran for about thirty metres, ending in a gravelled area in front of the buildings. On either side of the drive, a formal garden had been attempted and long ago given up on. Only the winter rain was keeping the surviving plants going.

I walked down the drive. It had been planted with poplars but they'd never got beyond infancy. Near the house, I could hear the sound of piano music, something classical. The front door was open. The music was coming from inside. I knocked loudly and said, 'Anybody home?' Nothing happened. I tried again. Only the music. Then it stopped and a voice said, 'One of Chopin's loveliest. And now for a complete contrast in composing style...'

The front door led into a long sitting room, furnished with stripped pine country-look pieces. The room was cold and unkempt, as if people had been dossing in it. In a stone fireplace, ashes were a foot deep. There were newspapers everywhere and all the surfaces held empty beer and soft drink cans and dirty plates.

I said my 'Anybody home?' again and went through into a big kitchen. The radio was on a shelf above the workbench, which was covered with the remains of meals long past.

I didn't look at the rest of the house. I went out the way I had come and walked over to the cinderblock building. Nothing happened when I knocked and called out.

I opened the door. A wave of warmth hit me. The air was moist and smelled of chlorine. Chlorine and something else. It was dark inside, the venetian blinds at the slit windows closed. I found a light switch. Two fluorescent tubes flickered, then lit up a sort of reception area, with canvas director's chairs and a glass coffee table holding stacked magazines.

I called out again. Nothing. I crossed the room to a half-open door. Beyond was darkness. I groped around and found another light switch just inside the door. I was looking down a corridor with two doors on either side and one at the end, all closed. The smell was stronger here. The air was also steamier.

My shoes made no sound on the grey felt-like carpet as I walked down the passage. I opened the first door on my left.

It was empty except for a pine upright chair and a large, deep coffin-like object against the end wall. There were pegs on the wall to hold clothes. The smell in here was salty. I guessed the giant coffin was a flotation tank, a bath filled with salt water for experiencing weightlessness.

The hatch on top was closed. Without thinking, I walked across and slid it back. It was empty. I felt foolish.

The room on the right held another tank. I didn't look inside. The next door down on the right opened to reveal a room set up for massage: table, shelves with small bottles. There were posters of Nordic scenes on the walls. Pine forests, snow, frozen lakes.

I didn't enter the room. As I turned to the door across the way, my eye caught a ghost of steam coming out from under the door at the end of the passage.

I went down the passage and put my hand on the

door handle. Then something made me knock. No reply. I waited, knocked again.

Then I turned the handle and pushed the door open.

The smell came out on a great cloud of steam, the smell of stock made with chlorinated water, a pungent, medicinal smell that filled my sinuses and made my eyes water.

I retreated down the passage to the entrance and watched the steam billow out of the room. Just turn around and go home, my inner voice said. Just walk out of this building, down the drive and find your way back to the man putting in the pole. Stop and tell him thanks for giving you shitty directions, you couldn't find Long Gully Road, so bugger it you were giving up. Go back to Daylesford and buy some bullboar sausages from the butcher. Tell Les you couldn't follow his map and it wasn't important. Drive home and have a shower. Forget about Danny and Ronnie and anybody else whose name ended in a diminutive.

But I didn't listen to my inner voice. When the steam thinned, I went back down the corridor.

I'd left the door only half-open.

I pushed it fully open.

The room was still dense with steam but I could see that it was like a large bathroom, tiled floor to ceiling. In the corner to my right, I could dimly make out a large spa bath, above the ground.

I took a step inside the room.

A man was in a sitting position on the floor in the corner to my right. He was wearing a loose pink garment. His left arm was at his side. His right was on his lap with a revolver in his hand. Something long-barrelled.

At first I thought he was wearing something on his head, a kind of big mask. Then I realised his head was twice its normal size, a bloated, suppurating mess.

I felt vomit rise in my throat, but I took another step into the room.

There was something in the spa bath. I couldn't see what. Steam was rising from the surface. The water was much hotter than any bath should be.

I wiped my eyes. Something insubstantial was bobbing gently on the hot bubbles. It was clothing, I thought.

I took another step. And as I did, trapped bubbles turned the clothing around and I saw the skull of a body cooked down to its bones.

The whole spa bath was stock made from a human being. I was going to be sick. I held off until I got outside and then the cold air took the smell out of my nostrils and the urge went away. I stood out in the weak sunlight for a while, thinking. Finally, I took a deep breath and went looking for something to wipe off fingerprints.

You should report crimes to the police. I didn't want to be the one to report this crime. Instead, I drove back to the man putting in the pole. He was tamping with a big metal post. This time I didn't get out of the car. I wound down the window. He looked up.

'You said turn right at the T-junction, didn't you?'

He looked at me with contempt. 'Left,' he said.

I shook my head. 'Well, fuck that for a joke, I've wasted enough time on this bloody call. I've got better things to do than fuck around in this wilderness.'

I took off with the wheels spinning. About two kilometres down the road, I found a signpost to Daylesford. This time Les was in the front of the butcher's shop. Going into a place filled with meat now was an act of sheer will.

'Thanks for the map,' I said, 'but I got lost and I had a flat.'

Les looked mortified. 'Map was okay,' he said.

'Not your fault. I reckon I missed the second turning and took the third.'

Les thought about this, eyes roofward. Then he nodded. 'That'd be right. Then you'd turn into Kittelty's Lane and then you'd be stuffed.'

'Stuffed,' I agreed. 'Anyway, I don't think I want to sell a copier to anyone lives out there. I'd rather do service calls to King Island.'

I bought some bullboar sausages and set off for the city. In Bacchus Marsh, I went to the post office and found the number for the Daylesford RSPCA. A woman came on. There were some animals in shocking condition at the health place in Long Gully Road, I told her. 'You'd better send someone today or they'll be dead.'

'Long Gully Road,' she repeated. 'What's the health place?'

'You'll see the sign,' I said. 'Look in the cinderblock building.'

I was reasonably sure they didn't record calls to the RSPCA. Almost everywhere else seemed to.

On the way back, I thought about Vietnam. In my time there I'd seen a fair number of dead and dying people. It puts another layer of skin on you. I should have been in shock at finding the bodies. Instead, I was feeling mildly elated. My instinct to pursue the trail of Ronnie had been right. Unless this matter was even more complicated than it appeared, one of the bodies was almost certainly his. The other man could be his old pal ex-doctor Paul Gilbert. I thought about the revolver in the man's hand. Had he shot himself? Had he shot the person in the spa first? I tried to remember the colour of the water in the spa. I hadn't registered it as any particular colour. Would it have been dark if the person had been shot in the bath? But the person might have been shot dead earlier and put in the bath.

But even if I had found Ronnie, that didn't advance things much. All I knew now was that the man accused of running down Anne Jeppeson ten years before had died violently, followed shortly by his accuser. I knew that Danny had believed he was innocent of the crime and that his wife said he had been told this by a woman conveying a message from her dying husband. I also knew that Danny McKillop had left messages for Ronnie Bishop. Then Ronnie had come to Melbourne and telephoned Danny.

The only obvious thing about all this was that it went back to Anne Jeppeson's death. That was what linked the dead men. Another obvious thing was that this was a good time to take a holiday in Queensland. I could simply run away from all this. I had run away from the private school my grandfather sent me to. I had run away from my mother's expectations and joined the army. I had run away from my wife's death and from my partner and from my duty to a client. Why not run away? Why change a lifetime's response now?

It's never too late to change. When I got to my office, I rang a man called Mike Drake in the Attorney-General's department. I'd been at law school with him and he had almost gone into partnership with Drew and me.

He sounded tired. 'You want me to ask the NCA if they know someone called Tony Baker? Are you aware that you don't ask the NCA questions? They ask you questions.'

He rang back inside fifteen minutes. The National Crimes Authority denied all knowledge of Tony Baker. 'That might be true,' he said. 'Or it might not.'

'Covers the possibilities,' I said. 'Thanks, mate.' It struck me that a description of Tony Baker might have helped the NCA identify him: five foot six, two hundred pounds, appearance of a .45 slug wearing a leather jacket.

I rang Linda Hillier.

'I've been ringing you,' she said. 'What happened to the answering machine?'

'Forgot to put it on.'

'Listen, that stuff we were talking about. I've been scratching round a bit. Can you meet me in Smith Street?'

Gerry Schuster was fat, and that's putting it politely. She was on a backless ergonomic kneeling contraption in an alcove created out of two computer workstations. I assumed that was what she was on. No part of what supported her was visible beneath a garishly coloured tent big enough to house four small Bedouin.

Linda said, 'Gerry, this is Jack Irish. He's got an interest in this stuff too.'

From beneath a greasy fringe that touched her eyebrows, Gerry gave me the look chefs reserve for three-day-old fish. 'Meechou,' she said. You couldn't have posted a five cent coin through her lips when she spoke.

We were in a large room on the third floor of an old building off Smith Street, Collingwood, not too far from Taub's Cabinetmaking. On the door, a plastic sign said: UrbanData. The room was divided into three by low hessian-covered partitions. Gerry had the biggest one. Gerry had the biggest everything, as far as I could see. There were five women working at computers. In a corner, a bearded man of indeterminate age, about two weight divisions below Gerry, was staring at a monitor showing a bar graph in at least ten colours.

'UrbanData collect and sell data on anything to do with the city,' Linda had said on the way. 'Cat deaths, bicycle accidents, condom sales, anything. They can make the data talk, too.'

Gerry Schuster shifted, wobbled and said, 'I've got inner-city Melbourne property transfers 1976 to 1980 loaded. What you want to know?'

Her fingers lay on the keyboard like tired sausages, each one wearing a ring.

'Transfers in Yarrabank,' said Linda.

Gerry tapped a few keys. An outline map of greater Melbourne appeared, overlaid by a numbered grid. 'Zone 14,' she said and tapped in the number.

The outline disappeared, replaced by a map of an area of the city, also overlaid by a numbered grid.

Topaz-ring sausage touched the screen. 'This is the sub-zone here,' she said. 'Twelve.'

She tapped in 12.

Up came a gridded map showing Yarrabank, the river and part of the area on the opposite bank.

'It's this area here,' Linda said, pointing at the screen.

'Twelve stroke six,' Gerry said. She hit 12/6.

Now there was a detailed map of part of Yarrabank. At its centre was the Hoagland estate.

'Let's look at the picture.' Gerry pulled down a menu from the top of the screen. On it she blipped a command called Aerial. We waited for a second and then the map turned into an aerial photograph of the part of Yarrabank we'd been looking at.

'This is smart,' I said.

Gerry gave me a look of contempt. The sausages

flashed through another set of keystrokes and the aerial photograph changed into a jigsaw puzzle of different-coloured pieces.

'Property boundaries in 14/12/6,' she said. 'Each piece is a separate title.'

She pulled down a menu and blipped a command called Breakdown. A box appeared with about ten options. She chose Number. The figure 27 appeared.

'Number of titles in the sub-sub-zone,' said Gerry.

'Let's say I want to find the owner of that bit,' Linda said. She pointed to a small triangular piece on the bank of the river.

Gerry put the pointer on it and double-clicked it. From a menu called Data, she clicked the Titleholders command. The screen went blank and then a list of names, addresses, dates and numbers appeared.

The most recent was Tilsit Holdings. The date of transfer was 14 February 1984.

'If you've got a name, you can do a search,' Gerry said, looking at Linda.

She pulled down a menu called Search, clicked Name and a box appeared.

She typed in Tilsit Holdings. A list of about eight properties appeared. She typed a command, went back to the jigsaw map and blipped a command called Site. Eight pieces of the mosaic went red. They were dotted along the river frontage in front of the Hoagland estate.

'All owned by Tilsit,' said Gerry.

Linda took a notebook out of her bag, flipped it open and ran a finger down the page. 'Can you try Muscanda Developments?' she said and spelt it.

I looked at her.

'Later,' she said.

The sausages were a blur. About half a dozen pieces of the puzzle in front of and beside Hoagland turned red. Some were tiny, two were quite large.

'Bingo,' Linda said.

I looked at her. Her eyes were shining.

'I've got more names,' she said. 'Can we get the maps and the data printed out?'

'What do you think?' Gerry said. 'This is a business.'

The rest of it took about fifteen minutes. Then we took the folder of printouts around to Meaker's and ordered long blacks. We sat opposite each other, my back against the wall. Linda was wearing a white turtleneck and a leather bomber jacket. Very fetching.

'What's going on?' I asked.

She drank some coffee. 'Well, I was thinking about Anne Jeppeson after our dinner and I mentioned it the next day to a guy at work who was a State political reporter on the *Herald* in those days. Before the drink got to him. He said he remembered there was a huge fight in Cabinet about selling the Hoagland site. The Planning Minister was Kevin Pixley. Remember him?'

I nodded.

'Lance Pitman was the Housing Minister who closed Hoagland. He wanted to sell the site without calling for tenders. Pixley wouldn't have a bar of it and he had a lot of support in Cabinet. Then Harker, the Premier, reshuffled the Cabinet and suddenly Pixley was Transport Minister and Lance Pitman was Planning. And then Pitman approved the sale of the site.'

'Who would have wanted to buy it ten years ago?'

'That's what I asked myself. And why didn't Pitman want to go to tender? The site was bought by a company called Hexiod Holdings, a shelf company with an accountant called Norman Jovanovich and two other people as directors. Hexiod held on to the property until three months ago, when it was sold to Charis Corporation, the Yarra Cove developers. It was sold the day after Pitman and company got back into government.'

'What about the waterfront land, the properties we've been looking at?'

She put out her slim hand and touched my arm. 'Jack, there's something like seventy properties involved. If I read this UrbanData stuff right, at least seven companies started buying or taking options on the riverbank sites about eighteen months before the government announced it was closing Hoagland. At some point, I don't know when yet, another outfit, called Niemen PL, emerged as owner of all the properties. Six years ago, Niemen consolidated all the waterfront properties into one and applied for rezoning of the area as residential.'

Linda paused while what appeared to be members of a female bike gang came in, talking at the top of their voices. Across the street, a white Holden with tinted windows was parked outside a furniture shop. A tall, balding man in a grey windcheater came walking along from the city side and got in the passenger door.

'Anyway,' said Linda, 'the government knocked them back. They went to the Planning Appeals Board and won. Then the Planning Minister overruled the board.'

'Why was that?'

The driver of the white Holden was getting out of the car. He crossed the road to our side and disappeared from view.

'Said rezoning wasn't in keeping with the government's long-term plans for the area.'

I saw a match flare behind the Holden's tinted driver's side window. The man who had got in the passenger side was now in the driver's seat. He opened the window a couple of inches to flick out his match.

Linda looked at her watch and drained her coffee. 'I've got to go,' she said. 'The last act in this saga is that six weeks ago Niemen sold the consolidated waterfront land to Charis.'

'So Charis now owns the whole site?'

'That's right. There's a road between the waterfront properties and the Hoagland land. The government sold the road to Charis a few days after the waterfront deal. And soon after that Charis announced the Yarra Cove development.'

'Tell us thinkers slowed by age and drink what all this means,' I said.

Linda gave me her slow smile. 'I think it means that closing Hoagland was part of a plan to put together a thirty-acre waterfront site. That's a developer's wet dream. The only reason Yarra Cove didn't get started a long time ago is that the Harker government got thrown out at the '84 election. That meant a ten-year wait till Pitman and company got back in.'

I thought about this for a while. 'And if Hoagland hadn't been closed in '84?'

She leaned across the table. 'Then someone was

stuck with a whole lot of falling-down old warehouses and polluted factory sites backed by the toughest Housing Commission flats in the city.'

The driver of the Holden was lighting up again. I said, 'Are we both concluding that Anne Jeppeson's death suited some people?'

'I've got to find out more about the companies involved. But the answer is Yes. I think we should talk to Kevin Pixley.'

'What became of him?'

'Retired. Lives in Brighton. The bloke at work is an old drinking mate of his. I'll see if he can get Pixley to talk to us.'

I said, 'Can we have dinner? I've got to tell you something about Ronnie.'

She gave me an interested look. 'Ring me before eight-thirty. I'm working till then.'

I took my time finishing the coffee. Then I took a stroll down Brunswick Street, marvelling at the dress sense of the young, crossed over to the other side at Johnson Street, walked back to my car.

The white Holden was gone.

I went back to my office and rang the last number Cam had left. He didn't seem to leave the same number twice running. A woman with a French accent invited me to leave a message. My eye fell on the mobile phone in its little plastic case next to the Mac. I'd bought it in a fit of technological anxiety and used it about four times. I left the number with the French lady and walked over to Charlie's.

'So,' he said. 'Had the breakfast. Ready for the day's work.' He was preparing a length of wood for steam-bending, using a block plane to chamfer the edges that would be in tension. This was to stop the wood fibres breaking loose. In the corner, the low potbelly stove was fired up, and Charlie's ancient steam kettle was starting to vibrate.

'I've been out since dawn,' I said. 'Looking for people.'

He shook his head sadly. 'A man with a profession. What does he do? He goes to the races and he looks for people who should stay missing.'

The mobile phone went off in my pocket, a nasty, insistent electronic noise. It was Cam. 'The big man wants to have breakfast tomorrow,' he said. 'You on?'

I said yes.

'Pick you up quarter to eight.'

I felt Charlie's eyes on me as I closed the flap and put the phone in my pocket.

'So,' he said. 'Mr Big Business Man. Mr Executive. So busy he can't go to the telephone anymore, has to take it with him. Next it's no time even to go for a shit. Take a little shithouse around with you, do it in the motor car.'

'You need to keep up with things in my line of work,' I said.

'Yes,' he said, disbelief in his tone. 'When you going to finish that table, Mr Walking Telephone?'

'Friday. Well, Sunday.'

'Got a big job yesterday,' he said. 'Man wants me to make him a library in Toorak. Panelled. Carved. Don't know if I'm up to it anymore.'

'No,' I said, 'you're not up to it. Play bowls instead. Give the work to somebody who can do it.'

'I just might,' Charlie said. 'Or maybe I'll get an apprentice, hey? Smart girl. Strong. Not afraid of work. Reliable even.'

'Good idea,' I said, heading for my bits of table. 'Anyone would want to spend five years making mortice and tenon joints and finding out about the finer points of lawn bowls.'

Charlie finished his planing and took the boards over to the steam box. It was a length of glazed sewerage pipe, eight feet long, sixteen inches in diameter, plugged at both ends. The steam went in at one end and escaped through a hole at the other. He gave it an appreciative smack with a huge hand. 'You want to know something?' he said. 'You can give a schmuck a walking telephone. But what you got then is a schmuck with a walking telephone.'

'Gee, you can learn a lot around here,' I said, 'just by listening.'

The workshop was warm from the steam box and the rest of the afternoon slipped by. At quarter to six, we called it a day and went around to the Prince. What Charlie called the Fitzroy Youth Club was in position at the bar.

'Jack, my boy,' said Wilbur Ong. 'Did I tell you I tipped eight out of eight three weeks in a row now? In me granddaughter's tipping pool, round this place she works. Hundreds in it. I give her me tips Thursday nights when she comes for tea. Me daughter's girl.'

Norm O'Neill's huge nose came around slowly, like the forward cannon on the USS *Missouri* swivelling to speak to Vietnam. 'You can only get eight out of eight, Wilbur,' he said slowly and with menace, 'if you tip against the Lions.'

Wilbur gave him a pitying look. 'Norm,' he said, 'if you was forty years younger I'd take you outside for jumpin to that conclusion. 'Course I don't tip against the Lions. It's the girl. She takes all me other tips and changes that one. She reckons tippin against the Lions is the only sure thing left in the footie.'

'I don't think you brought your daughter up right,' Eric Tanner said.

Stan came out from behind the bar and switched on the television set on the wall in the corner. It was news time. When the set was first put in, Stan tried to keep it on all the time but the Youth Club kept switching it off. Now it went on for the news and football.

The news opened with a helicopter view of Dr Paul Gilbert's health centre with at least ten vehicles parked outside the front gate.

'Two men have been found shot dead at an isolated property bordering on the Wombat State Forest outside Daylesford,' the woman newsreader said. 'One of the bodies was in a hot spa bath. Police said the men might have been dead for as long as a week.'

The helicopter went in for a closer look. I could see two men in plain clothes standing outside the house. They looked up at the helicopter and the one on the left's lips said, 'Fuck off.'

'Police said the bodies had been identified. Their names are expected to be released later this evening. The property is owned by Dr Paul Gilbert, a Melbourne general practitioner who was permanently barred from practice in 1987 after being found guilty of a variety of drug offences. He served two and a half years of a six-year sentence. Dr Gilbert lived on the property. He has not been seen in Daylesford for more than a week.'

The news went on to other things. I finished my beer and drove home. The streets seemed to be full of white Holdens. Had a white Holden followed me to Daylesford? My neck hair prickled.

When I got home, I rang Linda Hillier. She wasn't at her desk, said a man. He took a message. I was looking sadly into the near-empty fridge when the phone rang.

'We need to talk,' Linda Hillier said.

'Endlessly,' I answered. Then I went for it. 'Can you come around here? No. *Will* you come around here?'

'What's the address?'

I walked around the corner to Papa's Original Greek Taverna and bought some bread, olives, dolmades and an unidentified fish stuffed with thyme and basil from Mrs Papa. Menu price less fifteen per cent, that was our deal.

I was just out of the shower when the bell rang. I pulled on underpants, denims and a shirt.

'Well, hello,' she said. There was rain on her hair.

'You're wet,' I said.

'So are you. At least I've got shoes on.'

She had changed since this morning. She was wearing a trenchcoat over grey flannels, a cream shirt and a tweed jacket. I caught her scent as I took the coat and jacket. It was, in a word, throaty.

'This is nice,' she said, looking around.

We stood awkwardly for a moment, something

163

trembling in the air between us. I looked around at the books in piles on every surface, the CDs and tapes everywhere, the unhung pictures, seeing the place for the first time in years.

'It's sort of gentlemen's club mates with undergraduate student digs,' she said.

I cleared my throat. 'Come into the kitchen and I'll give you a drink. What would you like?' The kitchen was respectable. I'd cleaned it recently.

'Whisky and water if you've got it.'

She had a good inspection of the contents of the open shelves while I got the drinks, watching her out of the corner of my eye and telling her about my visit to Father Gorman. I poured myself a glass of Coldstream Hills pinot noir from a bottle I'd started on the day before.

'Cheers,' I said.

'Cheers. I've met Gorman a couple of times. He's a walker for high-society hags. Something slimy about him.'

'A walker?'

'Takes them to the theatre, to parties. When their husbands are too busy fucking the secretary.'

'You're very knowledgeable,' I said. 'I've got a fish. If you're hungry.'

'A fish,' she said thoughtfully. Our eyes were locked. I couldn't look away. I didn't want to look away.

'It doesn't have to be fish.'

She bit her lower lip. 'What else have you got?'

I wanted very much to bite her lower lip. 'There's some steak,' I said. 'Sirloin. Frozen.'

We had somehow got closer. I couldn't remember moving. She put out her left hand and touched the hollow in my throat with one finger.

'Sirloin,' she said. She put her glass down on the counter and slowly folded her arms under her breasts. It was somehow a hugely erotic gesture. 'Anything else?'

'Dolmades?'

We looked at each other in silence. I wanted to move my erection to a more comfortable position but I was paralysed. She looked down at it.

'Have you got a condom?' she said.

I swallowed some wine with difficulty. 'I suppose you'll think I'm predatory if I say yes?'

She nodded. 'Possibly.'

I put my glass on the counter. She put a fingertip against my lips. I kissed it. As her mouth came nearer I could smell the malt whisky. I put my hands on her buttocks and pulled her close. I could feel the elastic of her panties under my thumbs.

Our lips came together. Her right hand moved between us and cupped me. I thought I'd swoon.

'I'm going to swoon.'

'Perhaps,' she said, 'you should lie down.'

I took her hand and led her into the bedroom. We undressed with the urgency of people shedding burning clothes.

'Bugger buttons,' she said thickly, pulling her shirt over her head. She shrugged out of her bra and, for a moment, stood there naked to the waist, big breasts over prominent ribs. Then she stripped off her grey flannels, pantyhose and white bikini pants. She was built for movement: long bones and long muscles that showed under the skin.

The sheets were like ice. But only for seconds.

Around midnight, we ate sirloin steak sandwiches and drank the rest of the Coldstream Hills. It was too late for fish.

'Did you live here with your wife?' Linda said in a neutral tone.

'Yes. But we didn't sleep in that bedroom. That was the spare room. I couldn't bear to go into the bedroom for a long time.'

She said, 'You knew what I was thinking. Do all the girls ask that?'

'One hundred per cent of them.'

She looked at the ceiling, nodding.

'One girl, one question. That's a hundred per cent, isn't it?'

She smiled. 'I knew this would happen,' she said. 'When I saw you coming down the newsroom with that twerp Legge.'

We were on the sofa, backs against the arms, legs entwined, chewing. Linda was wearing a sort of kimono thing my daughter had left behind. She was about a foot taller than Claire, all of it leg. I was in my old towelling dressing gown.

'I know what went through your mind,' I said. 'Here comes six foot two of solid erotic pleasure.'

'No,' she said. 'I thought, here comes exactly the kind of rumpled, predatory, middle-aged sleazebag I always end up fucking.'

'I thought you said you wouldn't think I was predatory.'

'I said I possibly would. Anyway, that was tonight,' she said. 'You didn't have to be predatory tonight. All you had to do was lie back.'

'I liked the lying back bit,' I said. 'You're born to the saddle.'

'All it takes is a good pommel,' she said and rubbed her instep down my right calf. 'What's that funny shaped scar on your stomach?'

'I was hoping you'd ask. A man shot me.'

'Why?'

'Trespass,' I said.

'Trespass where?'

'In Vietnam. How come you've got such strong legs?'

She put her head back and looked down her nose at me, eyes narrowed. 'Is that a flattering question? Don't answer. Think. Think about the proximity of my heel to your groin.'

I said, 'Higher. A little higher. Gently.'

She moved her foot up my leg. 'I was an athlete,' she said. 'From about ten to eighteen. Then I went to uni. One joint, one paper cup of cheap wine, one night in the sack. Ex-athlete.'

'Ex-track athlete,' I said. 'There are other places to display athleticism.'

Linda put her plate on the floor and slid down the sofa. The kimono rode up above her pubic hair. She lifted one long, strong leg and rested it on my shoulder. 'That is so,' she said. 'What do you know about the leather sofa half mile?'

167

'It'll leave a wet spot,' I said.

'Wet spot? It'll float the sofa into the fucking kitchen.'

Later I told her about my trip to Paul Gilbert's health spa.

'Jesus Christ, Jack,' she said. 'How the fuck can you be so calm? You should have gone to the cops.'

'No,' I said. 'Too messy.' But I was starting to have doubts about my decision.

Harry met Cam and me at the front door. He was wearing a hacking jacket in soft grey checks, grey flannels, a pale yellow brushed-cotton shirt, and a silk tie in shades of grey and lavender. We went through into the breakfast room. Rain misted the french doors on to the terrace but concealed lighting made the square room's lemon walls glow and the whole house was warm enough for shirtsleeves.

We helped ourselves to muesli or porridge from the buffet. Harry and I had oatmeal porridge soaked with raisins overnight. Cam had a teaspoon of muesli. Then Mrs Aldridge brought in poached eggs, grilled ham, pencil-thin beef sausages, and grilled tomatoes. Harry once told us she had cooked for an English trainer. He said the man didn't give him a ride for two years after he stole Mrs Aldridge by offering her five pounds a week more than she was getting. 'Ate like a prince after that,' he said. 'Didn't eat often but when I did, by Jesus.'

In the study after the first sip of Mrs Aldridge's coffee, dark and viscous as mapping ink, Harry said,

'Jack, this Dakota Dreamin. We're thinkin of goin for a ride.'

'From what we saw?' I said.

Harry scratched inside an ear. 'Tony Ericson won't run the bugger in a proper trial. Don't blame him. Too risky, history like that.' He sniffed his cup. 'He's happy to see him take it easy on his first outin, though. But we know, there's only a couple of nags runnin around in the mud now could show him a bum.'

I said, 'If form's a guide, this thing may never run like that again, never mind improve.'

'Chance of that.' Harry sipped his coffee. 'Still, Ericson reckons he'll take a race or two. Cam here likes him.'

I looked at Cam. He'd gone off with the boy, Tom, and the horse after the gallop.

'The boy reckons he's taken the horse around that 2400 in just on two-thirty,' said Cam. 'Didn't tell his dad. Tony would have paddled his arse.'

I'd come to realise that Cam's judgment was vital to Harry's operations. Harry watched jockeys. Cam looked at horses. 'Fella's got the Eye,' Harry said to me after my second photography mission. 'Not one in a thousand around horses got it. Can't learn it. Mystery.'

Harry held up the silver coffee pot inquiringly. 'Two-thirty on that sheep paddock is hot stuff. Add a few seconds, it's still smokin.' He poured for Cam. 'Still. Spring would've been best. But we can't hold this thing together that long.'

'Who's inside so far?' Cam said.

'Ericson says it's just Rex Tie,' Harry said. 'Might

well be true. Told Rex, he says one word, in his sleep even, he'll train polar bears in Siberia for a livin.' He swivelled his chair, looked out into the dripping garden for a few seconds, completed the circuit. 'I reckon we've got a better than usual chance to keep this thing tight. Not your whole stable and the connections in the know here. Just a few yokels.' He looked thoughtful. 'Fair few things to think about concernin this horse, though. Number one is: do we want to go first up?'

We sat in silence for a while. I wasn't sure that I had a sensible opinion about when to mount a betting coup.

'First,' Cam said. He stretched his legs. You could see he was thinking about a cigarette.

'What's the reasonin?' Harry said.

Cam smiled his thin smile. 'There's two points,' he said. 'One, like Jack says, there might not be a second up. Two, the first time this horse turned out twice in a reasonable time, he bled. The second time he came off lame. I say put on the money and pray.'

Harry was doodling with his Mont Blanc on the blotter. 'What do you reckon, Jack?' he asked without looking up.

'How much is involved here?' For once I wanted to know.

Harry shook his head. 'Not yet. Money clouds the judgment. We want the horse to win for us. Question is, do we want to try for first up?'

I said, 'If we don't, the whole world gets a look at him. If he finishes in one piece and he backs up again inside a reasonable time, someone's going to be looking for the party. We'd be, wouldn't we?'

Harry pushed his coffee cup and saucer away, opened the brassbound cedar cigar box on the desk and took out the first of his three Havanas of the day.

Cam was out of the gate as Harry's fingers touched the porcelain cup. He was blowing Gitane smoke out of his nose before Harry had the cigar band off.

'Not an easy one,' Harry said. Eyeing the cigar suspiciously, he rolled it between the thumb and fingers of his left hand. Then he picked up a silver spike and violated the rounded end. After several exploratory sucks, he lit the cigar with a kitchen match, leaned back and waved the small baton at me. 'Sure you won't, Jack? Makes it all worthwhile.'

I shook my head sadly. You can get over love affairs but you never get over Havanas.

'Horse's goin racin with us or without us,' Harry said. 'Thing is, if it's not with us, Ericson and Rex Tie'll go looking for the stake money. They might as well go on the wireless with the news.'

We sat in silence again. The smoke from Harry's Havana drifted up towards the lofty ceiling, meeting and mingling with that from Cam's Gitane. Outside, a gust of wind plucked at the last few leaves on the elm.

Harry made a clicking noise. 'Okay,' he said. 'First up it is.' He opened a drawer and took out a yellow legal pad. 'This is a big one, Jack. We have to spread the risk around, that's the way we do it. Done a few quick sums here. I'm assumin we'll start in the fifties, see the price shrink like a prick in a cold shower when we get movin. If you're in, it's twenty-five grand apiece from you fellas.'

He looked at Cam, at me. 'What's your thinkin?'

171

Cam blew a perfect smoke ring. 'I'm in,' he said. 'Jack?'

Twenty-five thousand dollars. I was broke as usual. Most of the Ballarat payout had been distributed among my creditors. What would Charlie Taub say? I knew what he'd say. He'd say: *Horse business. Never met a man it didn't ruin.* In any event, the creature would probably break down soon after leaving the barrier and be shot behind a screen.

'How long have I got to raise it?' I asked.

Harry took a draw, studied the cigar, reluctantly tipped off an inch of ash. 'Your credit's good. Day before'll do.' He looked at me. 'I'd offer you a loan, Jack,' he said, little smile. 'Only my late dad always said never lend a gambler money. You're sidin with the devil if you do.'

'A wise father,' I said, 'is worth more than a clever child.' We went into the cinema and watched films of all Dakota Dreaming's races. Only the first one gave me any hope.

Kevin Pixley, former MP for Peterslee and Minister for Urban Development, lived in one of a row of mansions with the bay at the end of their gardens. Peterslee this wasn't. Peterslee was little brick veneers with concrete yards cringing in the flightpath from Tullamarine.

Linda had set up the appointment with Pixley. Then she'd been summoned to see the boss at the headquarters in Sydney. 'It's just bullshit,' she said. 'Randy little Pom with a wife in Singapore. The creep's been trying to get into my pants since he arrived.'

I said, 'Inexplicable. Why would he want to do that?'

'I'll deal with you when I get back tonight. I told Pixley you're helping with legal aspects of a story I'm doing on city planning. Try to keep it as general as you can to start with, okay? No cross-examination. Ask him what he thinks of the Planning Appeals Board, how attractive is Melbourne to developers, that sort of thing. Work him around to 1984. See if the bile surfaces.'

'Can I wear a hat with a little Press card in the band?'

'Only if that's all you wear. They say his second wife liked a bit of rough trade. New one's probably the same.'

I had to announce myself into a microphone behind a grille next to a door set in a two-metre wall. The door clicked open immediately. Beyond was a short brick path flanked by cumquat trees clipped into perfect balls. It led to a two-storey mock-Georgian structure painted to look like a down-at-heel Roman palazzo.

The front door opened when I was a couple of metres away. It was a woman in her late thirties, dark, pretty in a nervous way. She was dressed for dry sailing: boat shoes, white duck trousers, striped top, little kerchief at the throat.

'Good morning,' she said. She had a professional smile, like an air hostess or a car hire receptionist. 'I'm Jackie Pixley. Come in. Kevin's just having a drink before lunch. He's not supposed to. He's had a bypass, you know.'

It was 11.30 a.m.

We went through a hallway into a huge sitting room with french doors leading out to a paved terrace. An immaculate formal garden led the eye to the view of the bay. It was its usual grey, sullen winter self.

There were two sets of leather chairs grouped around massive polished granite pedestals with glass tops. We went around the setting on the left and through a door into another large room. This one was panelled floor to ceiling in dark wood. A snooker table with legs like tree trunks dominated the room. Against the far wall was a bar that could seat about twenty. Behind it, mirrored shelves held at least a hundred bottles and dozens of gleaming glasses. The top shelf appeared to have every malt whisky made.

Seated behind the bar was Kevin Pixley. I remembered his press photographs of a decade before: built like an old-time stevedore, strong square face, dark hair brushed straight back, oddly delicate nose and mouth. The man behind the bar was a shrunken and blurred version of the one in those pictures. He was tanned like his wife but the colouring looked unhealthy on him. In spite of the warmth of the room, he was wearing a bulky cream sweater. He leant over the counter and put out a hand.

'Jack Irish,' he said. 'Spit of your old man. He was one of the hardest bastards ever to pull on a Fitzroy guernsey.'

We shook hands. I used to get a lot of this kind of thing when I was younger. It always embarrassed me.

'Sit,' he said. 'What'll it be?' There was a tic at the corner of his left eye.

I said beer and he slid along to a proper pub beer tap. His stool was on wheels. I caught sight of the back of a wheelchair sticking out from the corner of the bar.

'Something for you, madam?' Pixley asked. I realised his wife was still standing in the doorway.

'Not just yet, thanks,' she said. 'We'll be lunching at twelve-thirty, Kevin. I'm going shopping. Goodbye, Mr Irish.'

'Pretty economically done, eh,' said Pixley, putting down a beer with a head like spun candy. 'I've got my instructions, you've got your marching orders.' He took a swallow of the colourless liquid in his own glass. There was just a hint of a tremble in his hand as he raised it. 'Now,' he said, 'why are you snooping around for Ms Linda Hillier? Didn't I used to see your name in the papers defending criminal slime?'

'This is just a little job Linda thinks a lawyer might be useful for. I'm not quite sure why. Did she tell you what it's about?'

'Something about planning. Sounded like a cock and bull story to me.'

He finished his drink and turned to the serving counter.

He took down a bottle of Gilbey's gin and poured half a glass. Then he added a dash of tonic and stirred the mixture with a big finger.

'Cheers,' he said. 'I'm not supposed to drink. Fuck 'em. What else is there?' He took a sip and licked his lips. 'She thought a lawyer might be useful, hey? Be the first time. Cabinet was full of bloody suburban lawyers. Think they're the bloody chosen race.'

'We're looking at decisions like the one to close the Hoagland estate,' I said. 'It leaked out in May 1984. We're interested in what happened in Cabinet.'

Pixley put his glass on the bar, put his elbows on the counter and looked me in the eyes.

'This is about Yarrabank, right? What's the shithole going to be called now?'

'Yarra Cove,' I said.

'Yarra fucking Cove. That what it's about?'

'Yes.'

'What are you lot trying to do?'

'It's just a general piece of planning.'

He gave me a smile of pure disbelief. 'Planning shit, Jack,' he said. 'I've been dealing with the fucking media for forty years. Ms Hillier thought she'd have a better chance of getting me to tip a bucket if she sent you.' He leant forward until his face was a handspan from mine. 'I've got it, haven't I?'

I sat back on my stool. There wasn't going to be a general discussion about planning. 'Well, I suppose there's a public service element in shafting the shaft-worthy.'

Pixley laughed, a throat-clearing sound. 'I can think of a couple of dozen shaftworthies,' he said. 'So ask me a question.'

I took out my notebook. 'Who made the decision to close Hoagland?'

He shook his head in mock admiration. 'You've got good timing, Jack. I was looking at '84 in my diaries the day before yesterday. The answer is Lance Pitman. He convinced the Premier that shutting the hellhole was a good idea. Stop all the publicity about rapes and fires and general mayhem in the place. Thought he had it all stitched up, usual breezy fait a-fucking-ccompli style. Then he got to Cabinet and some people weren't happy.'

'But the Premier overruled them?'

'No. Harker didn't try too hard to get his way. There wasn't a decision taken then. Pitman looked like he'd been bitten in a blow job. He couldn't believe Harker wouldn't push it through.'

Pixley paused to drink. 'Stage two. After the meeting, someone leaked it that Cabinet had *approved* closing the place. Next afternoon, we had the usual rent-a-lefty crowd outside Parliament screaming "Save Hoagland". Bloody unions making threats. And some cop jockey rides his horse over a twat in a wheelchair.'

'So at that point the Premier could simply have said it wasn't going to happen? Hadn't been approved by Cabinet.'

'And that's what he was going to say, mate. That's what I advised him to do. I heard him tell Pitman that was what he was going to do. He was nervous as hell about the protests. Never expected a reaction like that. Walking up and down in his office saying, "That fucking little bitch". We had an election coming up, all the bleeding hearts in the party on the phone to him saying we had to soften our image after the way we chainsawed the bloody power workers. Last thing anyone wanted was all the clergy and the social welfare industry getting on heat. Next thing you find bloody independents coming up in the marginals like pricks at a pyjama party. What Harker was scared of was that the party would lose the election and blame it on him closing bloody Hoagland. He wasn't going to close it in a fit.'

'But he did?'

'Well, everything changed in a flash when the Jeppeson woman got hit by that prick.'

'What happened in Cabinet?'

'The woman was running the whole protest single-handed. We didn't know that. Once she was gone, it just fizzled out. Meantime, Pitman's people are putting it around that the Premier's authority is on the line, battle for control of Cabinet, leadership challenge brewing, all that sort of shit.'

'So what happened?'

'Harker jumped on all the people who'd opposed closing Hoagland. We had a Cabinet meeting and now everybody's crapping on about we can't have mob rule, need a show of support for the Premier, in the public interest to close the dungheap anyway, that sort of shit.'

'So Lance Pitman won.'

'That's right. Touch and go for the bastard, though. That Jeppeson woman came within a rat's foreskin of getting the closure stopped.' Pixley started coughing and only stopped when he took a mouthful of gin and tonic. 'Jesus, if it's not one thing it's another,' he said weakly. 'Can't even take a piss any more without splashing my boots.'

'And when the estate was sold, there was a bit of a barney over that, wasn't there?'

Pixley studied me for a while. 'You could say that. In spades.'

I said, 'Pitman wanted to sell it without calling for tenders.'

'That's right. Stank like last week's roadkill.'

'Why's that?'

'Well, people who knew Pitman didn't swallow all the bullshit about we'll never get an offer this high again if we put it out to tender until doomsday.'

'What did they know about Pitman?'

He studied me some more, the tic going in his eye. Then he knocked back his drink and busied himself fixing another one. He poured me a beer in a clean glass without asking.

When he handed it to me, he said, 'Let me tell you something about my life, Jack. I joined the party with my dad when he came back from the war. I was seventeen. I just missed the war. I wanted to go, lie about my age, be a hero, fight the bloody Japs. Mum wouldn't hear of it. And I couldn't bring myself to go without her blessing.'

He took a sip and studied his glass. 'Four blokes in my class went. Just the one came back. You couldn't recognise him. Just bones. A skeleton. Bobby Morrisey was his name, little fellow. Never well again in his life. Fucking Japs. There were lots of blokes like that around where we lived. Think the local MP would do anything for them? Not on your bloody life. Too busy fighting factional wars to give a bugger about the voters. Well, I ended up taking that seat from the bastard. No-one thought it was possible. There wasn't even a branch of the party there when I joined. When I got into Parliament I did what I could for Bobby Morrisey and the others. Felt I owed it to them. Something personal, like they'd gone instead of me. Nonsense that, but there you are.'

I nodded. I didn't see where this was going and time was running out before Mrs Pixley closed the proceedings.

Pixley did some more coughing. 'What I need is a fucking smoke,' he said. 'Don't have one on you? No. Bloody woman searches the house like the Gestapo. Bugger that. Thing is, Jack, I found it wasn't an unusual thing to do, look after people. Sure, there were a lot of toffee-nosed dickheads on our side. But they weren't in there to feather their own bloody nests, not in those years. That's why I couldn't understand people like Lance Pitman when they came in, when I realised what the cunts wanted out of politics.'

He looked away for a while, down the bar. Then he

jerked his head around and said, 'Nice house this, eh Jack? Cost a bit more than my super, you'll say to yourself. That bastard Pitman put it around that it came out of graft. He's still putting it around, every chance he gets. Well, I'll tell you where it came out of. It came out of me mum's will, that's where. And she got it from Uncle Les when he died in Queensland. I'm not saying the old bastard was straight. I'm not saying he got it by the sweat of his brow. There's a lot of stories about him. But it came to me out of the cleanest hands on earth.'

Pixley lapsed back into coughing. His eyes were streaming. The big bar clock said 12.15. I'd have to come back. I gestured and made to stand up. He waved me down.

'Sit. I'm not done. Pitman. I'm talking about Pitman. You want to know about him? That's why you're here, isn't it?'

I nodded.

'This is all off the record, right? That bloody newspaper even suggests I'm a source, you'll find out I've still got friends, understand me?'

I nodded again.

'Yes, well, Lance Pitman. Mr Lucky, we used to call him. No bigger disgrace to the party ever walked. It means nothing to him, dogshit. He was a fucking little real estate agent out there in Allenby when he saw the whole place was changing. All the basketweavers and potmakers and bloody unemployed architects making houses out of mudcakes were moving back to Carlton and the place was filling up with young people with kids, big mortgages. Next thing he's joined the party, he's branch secretary, he's signed on hundreds of these beancounters and computer salesmen. Before you look the cunt's in Parliament. He'd have joined the Nazi Party if he thought it would carry Lance Pitman to glory.'

Behind me, Jackie Pixley said, 'Lunch is served, Kevin. You'll have to excuse us, Mr Irish.' Her voice was as cold as the wind on Station Pier.

Pixley's eyes narrowed. 'Leave us alone, woman,' he said. 'It'll be closing time for me soon e-bloody-nough. And get me my diary for 1980.'

I heard her turn on her heel on the polished boards. It made a squeak. We sat in silence. Inside a minute she was back, slamming a leatherbound book down on the bar and leaving. Squeak.

'Nice girl,' Pixley said. 'Met her on the plane to Europe after Ellen shot through. My second wife, that was. She couldn't stand being alone. Took to fucking plumbers, electricians, any bloke in overalls with a tool. Now Jackie can't bear that I can't go out much. And the bloody people around here don't want to know us. Christ knows what that'll lead to.'

'I can come back,' I said.

'Bugger that. I'm warmed up. How's your drink? I'll give you another one.'

When he'd poured the drinks, he said, 'Anyway, the bastard went around brown-nosing every living thing in the caucus. We get into office in '76 and Pitman's in Cabinet. Minister for Police. That's a laugh. He should've been the first one arrested. But they liked him there, the cops. He made a lot of cop friends. They know a shonk when they see one. He howled like a dingo when Harker moved him to Housing.'

I didn't have time for a complete history of the Harker government. 'About Yarrabank,' I said.

He ignored the hint. 'What the bastard really wanted was Planning,' he said. 'He'd have put on lipstick and a party frock and sucked off the whole caucus for Planning. But not even Harker was stupid enough to give it to him. Not then, anyway. Later on, they were like bumboys.'

I said, 'Why did he want it so badly?'

Pixley looked at me sadly. 'Come on, Jack. Where've you been? Cause that's where the big graft is. That's where the big boys play.'

'And that was your portfolio.'

'From '80 till '84. Then Harker dumped me for Lucky Lance over the Hoagland sale. Just before the voters dumped the bloody lot of us. I never took a quid, not a bottle of Scotch, in the job. And it was lying around. Made some fucking horrible decisions, mind you. Some places in the city I can't hardly bear to go. Still. Bloody honest cockups. Pure ignorance and led by the nose by certain people in the department. Some of them pals of Lance Pitman. The bastard came to see me in '80. I'll find it here.'

He picked up the diary with 1980 in gold on its cover and riffled through the gilt-edged pages. 'Got it. Listen:

' "Pitman came to see me this morning. Slimy as ever. Said he understands that I'm much more suited to the job than he could ever be. Knows all about Ellen. Said it's a tragedy the way women don't understand the demands of high office, etc etc. Beat around the bush till I asked him what he wanted. Nothing, he says. Just wanted to say he's there if I need anything. Then he asked would I like some company. He's got a young woman friend, lost her husband, understands grief and so on. Told him no thanks. He hung around a bit more, then asked me how I was going on the Baygate project. I said it was going through due process. He said he thought it would be bad for the party's image with business if it got knocked back. Also, the developers were likely to be generous donors at election time. I didn't show any interest. Then he asked me if I'd heard there was a chance ColdRoads could put their new packing plant in my electorate. I said I thought it was going to Orbison. That wasn't settled yet, he said. Raelene came in and said my appointment had arrived. At the door, Pitman turned around and said, as if he'd just remembered it, that, by the way, did I know that the major shareholders in Baygate were also on the board of ColdRoads. I don't have any doubt about his meaning, but I don't want to go to Harker with something the bastard will say was just an innocent remark."'

He looked up at me. 'You know what happened?'

I shook my head.

'Baygate got built. I couldn't bring myself to throw it out just because Pitman wanted it built. I should have. That was a good enough reason. But I wanted it to be a fair planning decision. And the department was divided about it. So I ended up going along with the senior man, a bloke called Malcolm Bleek, who reckoned it was a good thing. And come the election, some of the directors of the company, in their individual capacities mark you, came over with big contributions to the party.'

'Could be just sound business practice,' I said.

'Bullshit. But listen to this. Peterslee was always a marginal seat. Held it because people trusted me, bugger my party. But it only took about three hundred pricks to cross over and I'm gone. And in this business you don't come back. Ten days before the election, ColdRoads Australia announces it's putting its new plant in my electorate. Jobs in construction, a whole lot of new permanent jobs. Like a marginal MP's wet dream, eh?'

I said, 'You're saying Pitman believed you'd delivered the goods.'

'I don't think he was sure. But he came in to see me again after the election. Before he could open his mouth, I said to him, "You slimy little shit, if you ever mention the name of a project to me again, that project is dead in the water. I don't care what it is, can be the landing strip for the second coming, it is fucking stone dead." He never said a word, just turned and walked.'

Pixley stared into his glass. 'Like I said, Jack, your timing's good. Three months ago, I'd have told you to fuck off. I took the view that I couldn't get Pitman without hurting the party. And I couldn't do that. Party's been my whole life. Been everything to me. Cost me two marriages, kids who don't want to know me, but that was my choice.'

He finished his drink. 'One for the road,' he said and set to work again.

I drained my beer and waited for him in silence. When he'd put the glass in front of me, he said, 'Mortality, that's what changed my mind. I was lying in the Epworth waiting for the knife and I thought about dying and fucking Lance Pitman coming to my funeral. I thought, fuck me, if I come out of this and a chance comes up, I'll shaft the fucker. It'll hurt the party, but in the long run not shafting him will hurt it more.'

'Is there likely to be any kind of evidence against him?'

'You and Ms Hillier are going to have to find that out. Let me tell you the rest of the story.'

Pixley seemed to have gone down a gear. His eyelids were drooping. He shook himself alert. 'About a year after Baygate, the same senior man in my department talked me into chucking out a planning decision against a company called Hexiod Holdings. Big shopping mall in Apsley. Millions involved. I also had the local MP camping in my office and a man called Massey, Dix Massey. Know of him?'

'Owns racehorses.'

'And other things. He's Charis Corp's chief cocksucker and standover man. Well, a couple of months later the same man in my department, Bleek, comes to see me. He's sweating blood. He says there are things he wants to tell me but he wants indemnity first.'

Pixley drank deeply. 'I said, "Tell me what it's about, I'll think about the indemnity." He won't. The bastard wants forgiveness before confession. We went on like this for a while, I told him to go away and think about it, come back tomorrow. He comes back the next day, says he had a brainstorm, he was talking rubbish on medication. Stress. Overwork. He's taking sick leave. Please forget about the matter. Never came back. Early retirement. Never set foot in the building again. He's dead now. Killed himself about six months later.'

'You're saying this was connected with Pitman?'

Pixley shrugged. 'You can make your own connections. You know the name of the company that had the foresight to buy Hoagland?'

'Yes. Hexiod Holdings.'

He nodded. 'That's the company. Sold it to Charis Corporation the other day, I see.'

'Can I get this straight?' I asked. 'You're saying that Pitman closed down Hoagland so that Hexiod could buy the site and turn it over to Charis?'

'Draw your own fucking conclusions.' He leaned forward. 'What do you reckon's the company that ended up building Baygate?'

'Charis?'

'Fast learner. That's right. Came from nothing to be one of the biggest developers in the state in about ten years. Bloody miraculous. And now Pitman's in the Planning chair again, old Joe Kwitny's two boys can get seriously rich. Charles and bloody Andrew really can't miss now. Next thing the Kwitnys are going to want their pederast pal Father fucking Gorman in Parliament.'

Father Gorman's fulsome tribute to Joseph Kwitny came back to me. 'Close to the Father, are they?' I asked.

'Old Joe's the biggest donor to that shonky foundation of his. And I think Dix Massey's one of the directors or whatever they call them.'

Pixley had another coughing fit. When it stopped, he

pushed his glass away. He looked utterly worn out. 'I've said enough, Jack. Time for some lettuce and my nap.'

I stood up. 'Just one last thing,' I said. 'The death of Anne Jeppeson.'

'Spot of luck for Mr Lucky Pitman, eh? Or do people make their own luck? See yourself out, Jack. Come again.'

I said thanks again. On the way out, I saw Jackie Pixley looking out at the bay. I said goodbye and she said something without turning.

We were sitting in front of a fire in the house Anne Jeppeson grew up in, drinking tea out of bone china cups with little roses on them. The room was comfortable: good furniture scuffed by life. Outside, it was raining on the big garden, the usual thin Melbourne drizzle that dampened the heart more than anything else.

'I'm sorry to ask you to talk about something so painful,' I said. I meant it. There's a special kind of dread you don't know about until you have children.

Mrs Jeppeson shook her head. 'Nothing can make it any worse than it is,' she said. She was in her sixties, a thin and pretty woman with short hair and a faraway look. She was dressed for outdoor work: trousers, shirt, sleeveless jacket and short boots. 'Sometimes I'm glad to talk to someone about it. My husband can't bring himself to. But Anne's death lies there all the time.'

'Did you see much of her?'

'Not as much as we wanted to. She was always busy and she had her own friends. But she came for most Sunday lunches, well, perhaps every second Sunday here and at the sea. We have a place at Portsea. She was there with us for a few days that summer. Our son and his family were here too. They were living in Hong Kong then. He's in banking, like his father.'

She looked out of the window. Some bedraggled sparrows were pecking the terrace. 'Do you find the winters depressing?'

'Yes. Except for the football.'

'Anne liked football. Richmond. The Tigers. No-one else in the family has any interest in it. My husband pretends to be interested when we're with people who are. I don't know why. It's a male thing, I suppose. I spend as much time outside as possible in winter. I try to ignore the weather.'

'Does that help?'

'I'm not sure. I'd have to stop to find out. Why is Anne's death of interest now?'

'There's a possibility that the person convicted of knocking her down didn't do it.'

She didn't react. 'More tea? I think I'll have some.'

'Thank you. It's very good.'

She poured. 'Have another biscuit. They're homemade. Not by me. I bought them at the church fete. I can't bring myself to go to church any more so I go to all the fundraising efforts and buy things that never get eaten.'

I took another biscuit. 'Perhaps you can tell me something about the days before...'

'Her death. We hadn't seen her for a fortnight. She phoned on the Sunday to say she couldn't come to lunch. That Housing Commission business was on the go, so we saw her on television all the time. My husband was secretly quite proud of her, I think.

Although you'd never have known it from the fights they had over those squats in people's houses she used to organise.'

'So you never had the chance to talk about the Hoagland protests?'

'Just a few words on the phone. Well, more than a few words, I suppose. It was very difficult to limit Anne to a few words. She was always so passionate about everything, even when she was little. When she was thirteen or fourteen she knew everything about every oppressed group in the world. It drove her father up the wall. He even complained to the school about one of the teachers putting ideas into the girls' heads. They couldn't agree on anything political. If she wasn't arguing with her father, she was fighting with her brother. She enjoyed baiting him. He's very like his father. Conservative, I suppose. He used to call her Annie the Anarchist. It's funny how different children grow up to be, isn't it? Do you have children, Mr Irish?'

'Just the one.'

'I wish we'd had ten, spaced over twenty years. A stupid idea, isn't it?'

'No.'

She smiled. 'Of course it is. You're very diplomatic.'

The time had come. I said, 'Do you know of any reason why someone would want to murder Anne?'

She put her cup and saucer down and looked at me steadily. She had the inner stillness of someone who has found meaninglessness in everything. 'Are you saying that Anne's death might have been murder?'

'There's a possibility she was murdered.'

She looked away. 'I don't know what to think about

that. Who would do something like that? No-one ever suggested...'

'It's just a possibility,' I said. 'Both the man who went to jail and the witness have been shot dead in the last ten days.'

'Are the police investigating?'

'Not Anne's death, no.'

'So it's *your* idea that Anne might have been murdered?'

'My first concern was my ex-client's death but other things have turned up. Anne's death may be the key to what's happened since.'

She gave me a doubtful look. 'I don't know what I can do to help you, Mr Irish. Don't you think it's a police matter?'

'Not just yet. Is there anyone Anne might have confided in? I mean, if she had any fears for her safety, been threatened, anything like that?'

'I suppose the people in that group of hers. Right to a Roof? We never knew any of them.' She thought for a while. 'About her safety, I can remember her saying, it must have been at our wedding anniversary party, I can remember her saying she could go anywhere in safety because the Special Branch were always lurking somewhere.'

'At the squats she organised?'

'I think she meant generally. She was on about mining companies cheating Aboriginals, but I'm afraid I wasn't paying much attention. She usually had something she felt strongly about. Her father used to say she was only scored for percussion.'

There didn't seem to be anything left to ask. I

thanked her for seeing me. The passage leading to the front door was wide enough for us to walk side by side. One side was hung with Australian paintings from the thirties and forties: outdoor scenes, sunlit interiors. I recognised a Gruner and a Tidmarsh. The other wall was covered with framed family photographs.

At the front door, I looked to my right and saw a photograph of four solemn-faced girls in school uniform, two blonde, two dark-haired. They looked about sixteen. Under the picture, it said, 'Coniston Ladies' College Debating Team, 1976'.

I looked at the names. Anne Jeppeson was on the top right, blonde, with a snub nose and rebelliously tousled hair. The girl next to her was one of the brunettes.

Her name was Sarah Pixley.

'She loved debating at school,' said Mrs Jeppeson. 'My husband never went to hear her.'

I pointed at Sarah Pixley. 'Was she friendly with Anne Jeppeson?'

Mrs Jeppeson touched the photograph. 'Sarah Pixley. They were great friends at school. Two of a kind in many ways. Her father's the politician. Sarah hated him. She took her mother's name when she left school. Life can be cruel to parents, can't it?'

'It can, Mrs Jeppeson,' I said. 'It can.'

I drove away down streets where the naked branches of elms and oaks were woven overhead like basketwork and you could glimpse the pert backsides of BMWs and Saabs in brick-paved driveways. It took a while before I found a place that looked as if it might make a hamburger. I was starving.

The hamburger was of the old school: pressed flat as a powder compact, burnt mince topped with burnt onion and cold-storage tomato. It was made by a new-school Aussie, a Vietnamese with rings in one earlobe and a beanie in the Richmond colours. It wasn't a bad hamburger. A slice of sun came out and fell on my lap as I sat in the car, eating and watching a deal taking place across the street in a small park. Two boys in Melbourne Grammar blazers were scoring something off a tall youth with a ponytail wearing an oversized leather jacket. Answers to that day's maths homework, probably.

When I'd finished, I had a sudden urge to see what was happening to the Hoagland estate. I set off down Malvern Road in the direction of St Kilda Road. At Albert Park, I got on to Kings Way and went up King Street through the drab end of the business district. As I waited to turn into Dudley Street at the Flagstaff Gardens lights, a dero in a mauve polyester suit with a filthy Fitzroy FC scarf wound around his neck knocked on the passenger window. I leaned across and wound it down.

'Help a bloke can't get a job?' he asked. He had a long, narrow face, with deepset eyes and a big nose. He looked like a country boy lost in the city for forty years.

I found a five-dollar note and gave it to him. 'Go the Roys.'

'You're a prince among men,' the man said. 'Go Roys, make a noise.'

The future Yarra Cove was much larger than it had appeared on Gerry Schuster's computer screen. I parked near a wooden observation platform next to one of the three site gates. A burly man in a dark-blue uniform with a red shoulder patch that said AdvanceGuard was talking to the driver of a ute in the gateway.

There must have been twenty earthmoving vehicles, giant yellow insects, attacking the glum expanse of grey mud. At least as many trucks moved around the area on temporary roads, stretches of coarse aggregate sinking into the clay.

Not a trace remained of anything that had been there before. I stood at the rail, ten metres up, and after a while the ripping and pushing of the machines began to make some sense. They were gouging massive trenches, the width of streets, running from the waterfront. All of them led to an oval-shaped area, bigger than a football field, marked out with yellow nylon cord threaded through the eyes of metre-high steel needles stuck in the ground. The site huts, a small village of them, were in the middle of the oval. Eventually, the oval would be a yacht basin, with the trenches becoming canals leading from the riverfront. The Hoagland flats must have stood where a small digger was unearthing pipes in one ploughed-up patch.

For a while, caught up in the sheer scale of the operation, I watched the machines roaring and grinding, scooping and reversing, dumping, wheeling, their grey breaths pumping out and being snatched by the sharp-toothed little wind off the river. The whole scene was one of power: man and machine changing a landscape by sheer force.

This was what it was all about.

Sheer force.

Anne Jeppeson thought she was taking on the power of Heartless Bureaucracy. What hit her was the sheer force of Money.

She died so that someone could make a fortune out of rich people's desire to park their boats outside their front doors.

It came to me with absolute certainty that my little inquiry into the lives and deaths of Danny McKillop and Anne Jeppeson was of no consequence whatsoever. Nothing would change what had happened, no-one would be called to account for it. Anne, Danny, Ronnie Bishop, the doctor, me – we were all just minor nuisances.

I felt like shouting Fuck into the wind but there was someone else on the platform, a thin man with a week's grey stubble and wispy hair sticking out from under a beanie. He was drinking a can of Vic Bitter. Looking at me, he drained the can and threw it over his shoulder. 'Used to live here,' he shouted over the noise. 'Fucking shithole. Should've flattened it years ago.' He took another can out of his anorak and popped it.

The daylight was almost gone when I parked outside my office. I had the key in the lock when I sensed someone behind me.

'Mr Irish.' It was a friendly voice. I turned. Two men, solid-looking, in dark suits. The one who had spoken held up an open badge wallet. 'Detective-Sergeant James,' he said. 'The Commissioner of Police would like a word, if it's convenient.'

'It's not,' I said. 'Tell him to make an appointment.'

'If it's not convenient, I have instructions to arrest you,' he said, voice still friendly.

'On what charge?'

'Several charges. One is conspiring to pervert the course of justice.'

'In what matter?'

'Murders. Two of them.'

A gap appeared in my social calendar. I rode in the back of their grey Ford. No-one said anything. When it was clear that we weren't going to police headquarters, I asked where we were going.

'Collins Street,' said the spokesman.

At the Hyatt on Collins, the driver showed the attendant a card and we drove into the underground carpark. We parked in a reserved bay next to the lift.

'Let's go,' said the spokesman.

The three of us went up to the twelfth floor. When the lift door opened, Detective-Sergeant James's partner went out first.

'After you,' said James. 'Number seven.'

I followed his partner down the hushed pink and grey corridor. As he passed a door, he indicated it with his thumb and kept walking. I knocked at number seven. The partner had turned around about ten metres down the corridor and was looking at me. James, near the lifts, was studying a print on the wall.

The door was opened by a man in shirtsleeves and red braces. His tie was loose and he had a drink in his hand. 'Come in, Mr Irish,' he said.

It was the Minister for Police, Garth Bruce.

*

The suite was pale grey and pink like the corridor. We went through a small hallway into a large sitting room furnished with French period reproductions. A bottle of Johnnie Walker Black Label, an ice bucket, a water carafe and cut-glass whisky glasses stood on a table against the wall. A briefcase was open on a small writing desk between opulently curtained windows.

'Thanks for coming,' Bruce said. 'Sorry about the escort. Let me give you a drink. Whisky, anything.'

I said no thanks, curtly.

He was at the side table with his glass. He put it down and turned, a big man, bigger in life than on television. He'd boxed. There was scar tissue around his eyes. It hadn't shown up on television. That would take skilful make-up. 'Jack,' he said, 'this is friendly. Let's have a quiet drink together. It's very much in your interests. Okay? What'll you have?'

I asked for whisky and water. He made two drinks and brought mine over. We sat down a metre apart. He took a big drink.

'That's better,' he said, sighing. 'Jesus, what a day. Politics. Win one, lose ten.' He took a cigarette out of a packet and offered the packet to me. I shook my head.

Bruce lit up with a lighter, blew out a long, thin stream of smoke and tapped the cigarette in the direction of an ashtray. Ash drifted to the carpet. He sat back, shoulders loose, and said, 'Jack, I'm told you've been asking around about a lot of old business, things that happened nine, ten years ago. That right?'

'Who tells you?'

He had another big drink. His eyes never left me.

There was an appealing sadness about them. 'Let me tell you a story,' he said. 'I haven't got a lot of time. I don't want to dance around with you. When I got this job, I appointed a new Commissioner and a new deputy. The first thing I said to them, I said: "The fucking joke's over." '

He leaned forward. 'I was a cop for nearly twenty years, Jack. I know the system, I know what goes on. Everything. These new blokes knew that I knew what I was talking about. Cops've been bullshitting politicians for years. They can't do that to me. I'm not going to sit in a high chair and be fed shit with a spoon. That's why the Premier wanted me in this job.'

He drew on his cigarette and studied me. The silence and the open gaze were disconcerting. He hadn't been a cop for twenty years for nothing.

'Anyway,' he said, 'the point is, when this Danny McKillop got knocked behind the Trafalgar, I called in the file. I've had it with all this Dirty Harry shit. They see it on television. Twenty years, I fired three shots, all in response to cunts firing at me.'

He sat back, stubbed out his cigarette, put his hands in his pockets. 'I read the wife's statement, reckoned there were some questions about what made McKillop so scared. Told the Commissioner that. He came back with all the background, the Jeppeson trial stuff, and the missing person's report on this Bishop.'

Bruce got up, took out another cigarette, flamed it with the lighter, went to the windows. 'Can't sit for long,' he said. 'Back's buggered. Anyway, Jack, what the Commissioner tells me is that the blokes he's had going over this business find your tracks all over the place. You're giving Vin McKillop money, you're in Perth, you're everywhere.'

He turned his head towards me. 'What's really worrying, Jack,' he said quietly, 'is that you were out there in the bush at Daylesford and it looks liked you wiped clean a whole lot of places. Places that could have had the prints of whoever topped Bishop and the druggie quack.'

He looked out into the night again. 'Now that is very, very serious,' he said. 'You know how serious, Jack.'

I had seen this coming but I still didn't know how to handle it. Bruce turned. There was a sheen on his face and on his scalp showing through the short, thinning hair.

'I never found the doctor's place,' I said. 'Got lost.'

He gave me a slow cop smile. 'That's a porky, Jack. If you were going to tell porkies, you should've changed the tyres on that motor Col Boon loaned you. Your tracks are all over the place.'

He came back to his chair and sat down carefully. 'That was a really stupid thing to do. The Commissioner wants to charge you. But he came to me first. That's why you're sitting here, not in metropolitan remand.'

We sat in silence for a while. The little carriage clock on the mantelpiece chimed the half hour, a silver splinter of sound.

Bruce picked up his glass, looked at it, rolled it like a thimble between his big, hairy hands. 'I knew that prick killed your wife,' he said, not looking at me. 'Wayne Milovich. Knew him for years. He was always a dangerous animal. Only had to look at his eyes.'

I didn't know what to say. There was silence again. Bruce rolled his glass.

'Crim tried to shoot my daughter,' he said. 'She was in the kitchen, looking in the fridge. Went through her hair, through the cupboard, through the wall. Couldn't pin it on him. Bloke called Freely. We knew it was him. His whole fucking family, about fifty of them, said he was watching TV at the time. Couldn't shake them. And by Jesus we shook some of them.'

'I never heard about that,' I said.

'No. We kept it quiet. You don't want to give the other animals ideas.'

He got up, collected my glass and made the drinks. While his back was turned, he said, voice just a little rough, 'She was sixteen, lovely girl. Not the same again. Ever. Lost to me. To all of us. In and out of the funny farms. Cut her wrists, swallowed anything she could find. They found her on the beach just before Christmas. Her birthday was Boxing Day. Twenty-first that year. My fault, I suppose. My wife thought so, anyway. Never forgave me.'

I looked at the big back, the way he was holding himself. 'You can't take the blame for what mad people do,' I said. 'You couldn't know.' My voice seemed too loud.

'You could say I did know,' Bruce said flatly. 'He told me he was going to do it. Outside court. He said, "Watch your family, Bruce, something could happen to them." I told him, "You wouldn't have the guts, you chickenshit little bastard." I laughed at him. He was a runt, five foot fuckall. You'd never credit that he would do it.'

He brought my drink over. I got up to take it. We stood together awkwardly, not knowing where to look, some kind of bond of loss between us. I knew now why I wasn't in metropolitan remand.

'Cheers,' Bruce said.

'Cheers.'

We drank.

'Never said anything to you? Milovich.'

'Just the normal abuse. I wouldn't have paid any attention if he had. I wouldn't have done anything.'

'Would you have told your wife?'

I shook my head.

Bruce nodded. He drank again, wiped his mouth and said, 'You see Danny McKillop after he got out?'

'No.'

'So what, you heard about the shooting, started poking around?'

'No. I was away for a couple of days. When I came back there were messages on my answering machine from him. I didn't even remember who he was. He was waiting for me at the Trafalgar that night. Only I didn't play the tape till the next day.'

'What did he say?'

'Said he was in trouble. He was scared.'

'You talk to the wife?'

'Yes.'

'She tell you about the phone call, about Danny getting the idea he didn't kill the Jeppeson woman?'

I nodded.

'You reckoned there might be something in it, did you?'

I nodded again.

Bruce shook his head. 'And Vin McKillop? He help you along with the theory?'

I shrugged.

Bruce gave me the look. 'Jack,' he said, 'don't come the lawyer with me. If I don't help you, you're going to have to practise in Somalia, somewhere like that.'

I didn't ponder the matter. 'Vin says someone saw Danny miles away from his car and dead drunk about twenty minutes before Anne Jeppeson was killed. And there was a cop with Danny earlier. Someone called Scullin. Vin says Danny was Scullin's dog.'

Bruce sighed and shook his head. He went over to his briefcase and took out a manila folder. He waved it at me. 'I can't show you this,' he said, 'but I'll tell you what it says. Sit down.'

I sat down.

'Danny wasn't a dog. Vin was a dog. Vin was Scullin's dog in those parts. And Vin thought that being an informer gave him some kind of immunity. The next thing Scullin hears is Vin is dealing speed on a fair scale and he's claiming he's got police protection. Scullin didn't like that. He put him away. Four years. Vin's been trying to get even ever since. He's obsessed with Scullin.'

I said, 'So?'

Bruce tapped the folder. 'It's Vin fed Danny all that stuff about being innocent, about Scullin being around that night. It's all bullshit. There's no question that Danny was the driver. Vin's idea was that Danny might go nuts and nail Scullin for him.'

I thought about this for a while. Bruce sat down again, gingerly, and lit a cigarette.

'There's something else,' he said.

I waited.

'The gun Danny had on him at the Trafalgar.'

'The gun the cop says he had on him. Yes.'

'It's the gun that knocked Ronnie Bishop and his druggie doctor mate out at Daylesford.'

This took a bit of absorbing too.

'You know what that means, Jack?' Bruce was holding the folder against his chin.

I had an idea. 'Tell me.'

'Danny was going to kill you that night. You and Scullin and Ronnie Bishop were the trifecta. Good thing you didn't listen to your messages. Danny wanted to knock you, mate. He reckoned you helped fit him up.'

My mouth was dry. I finished my drink, got up and opened a bottle of soda. The realisation that you've been a blind prick is not an easy one to come to terms with.

'What about the doctor?' I asked. 'Where's he come into this?'

'Wrong place, wrong time. That's what it looks like. You can tell me something else. This Hillier woman. She's scratching around the Yarra Cove history. What's that all about?'

I said, 'There's not a lot you don't know, is there?'

'I'll be open with you. The Yarra Cove history is a sensitive subject for the Premier. For the whole fucking party. What's Hillier looking for?'

'I don't think I can tell you that.'

Bruce got up, big hands holding his back, and walked over to the desk. He began to pack up his briefcase. 'You can go,' he said. 'Those blokes brought you will take you up the road and charge you. Good luck.'

I didn't feel like going anywhere. I didn't want to be charged. I didn't want to tell my pathetically naive story in court. I didn't want never to be able to call myself a lawyer again.

'She thinks closing the Hoagland estate was part of a plan to put together the Yarra Cove site. It looks like Lance Pitman closed down Hoagland so that some mates could buy it. They'd started stitching up the properties around it long before.'

Bruce stood his briefcase upright. 'She work this out all by herself?'

I said, 'I talked to Kevin Pixley. He as good as shafts Pitman.'

Bruce took his hands off the briefcase and looked at them. 'Jack,' he said quietly, 'do you know who the biggest crook ever to hold ministerial office in this State is?'

'Be an open field, wouldn't it?'

'No. There's a clear winner. Kevin fucking Pixley. You are sitting here and telling me that you and this journo woman are taking the word of a man who was in the pocket of every shonky developer in the State. Did you go to his big house? Did he tell you about the place at Portsea? Tell you about that little six-bathroom shack in Port Douglas? Didn't happen to mention his old uncle who left him the money, did he? Or his brother, good old Wal Pixley, the one who always seemed to know where to buy property? The one with the instinct for buying cheap just before the rezoning sent prices through the roof?'

I drank some more soda water.

'Let me tell you about Hoagland,' Bruce said. 'I know all about bloody Hoagland. Closing it was decided on about eighteen months before it came to Cabinet. Only three people knew. The Premier, Pitman and Pixley. Putting together a big waterfront site was Pixley's idea. He told his mates, small fry, little property crooks he'd helped out, and they started to buy up the land around the site. But things went sour. They say he wanted a huge payoff for his tip. One last payday before the South of France. His mates didn't want to come over with a massive sum of money before they could sell the properties. So Pixley turned nasty. Said, I'll fucking show you. And when it came to Cabinet, all of a sudden Pixley doesn't want a bar of closing Hoagland. He organises a little Cabinet revolt. They say he got his daughter to tip off the Jeppeson woman. And he leaked it that Cabinet had approved the bloody thing.'

I said, 'All or nothing? That doesn't sound smart.'

'It was smart,' Bruce said. 'The story is his mates said okay, okay, we'll come over with the money. Just stop opposing it. Unorganise your little Cabinet revolt. And he did. End of opposition in Cabinet. Then of all the fucking luck, Danny McKillop gets off his face and decides to go for a drive. End of opposition outside Cabinet.'

'What about when it came to selling the site? Pixley opposed that too. How does that fit?'

'Well, there's two schools of thought. One says it was just a replay of the first scam. The bastard wanted another bite at the cherry. More money from his mates. Blackmail. The other school says it was just a big sham. He knew he was going to be rolled out of Planning. He'd corrupted the whole bloody department. Him and his offsider Bleek, the department head. The Premier'd had enough, thank God. So Pixley thought, here's a way to go out with dignity. Rolled on a matter of principle.'

There was a knock at the door. Bruce went out and closed the door behind him. I drank more soda water and thought about Pixley.

Bruce came back in, leaving the door open. He said, 'I'm pressed, Jack, I've got to be somewhere. If your friend Ms Hillier goes on with her inquiries, she's going to find out what a crook Pixley was and how a couple of his mates, small-timers, made a few quid out of Yarrabank. None of it's got anything to do with the Yarra Cove developers. Charis is clean. The site was offered to them and they bought it. But the Pixley part's not a bad story, the fucking *Age* will love it, the ABC's little turds will come in their pants. Their panties.'

He looked at me for a while.

'Jack, I want a favour from you,' he said. 'You've made a cunt of yourself over Danny McKillop, right?'

He waited.

I nodded.

Bruce looked away. 'I think you've had enough pain with this Milovich. I'm going to lean on the Commissioner. I'm going to get them to wipe you out of this like you wiped your Daylesford prints. I'll get the files cleaned up. No charges. No trace of you.'

I felt a surge of gratitude, a great sense of relief.

'What I want from you is that you get Ms Hillier to

back off the Yarrabank story. If it was up to me, I'd give her a hand with it. Pixley deserves his name written in shit on every building in town. But the Premier takes the view that it will sink the government. Taint everything we've ever done, everything we do in future. We'll just limp through our term. And then the voters will dump us. All because of Kevin Pixley.'

Bruce came over and stood in front of me. 'What do you say, Jack? It's not a big ask.'

I stood up. 'I'll talk to her,' I said. 'And thanks.' I put out my right hand. He took it in both of his.

'I'll give you a number for me,' he said. 'Got a pen?'

I got out my notebook and wrote down the number.

'If anything comes up,' he said, 'ring it and say…what shall we say? Say John English wants to talk to the Minister.'

At the door, we shook hands again. 'You're doing the right thing, Jack,' he said. 'This is the only way to do it.'

The two men drove me back to my office, silence all the way.

We were eating ravioli and drinking red wine in front of the fire when I asked, 'What did Legge mean about the return of the starfucker?'

Linda looked at me thoughtfully while chewing. A large piece of glossy hair had fallen over one eye. She was wearing an old pair of my pyjamas. It came back to me that there is a brief stage in relationships when women like to wear your clothes.

'In what context was this remark made?' she said.

'The day I met you. Talking about you coming back to Melbourne. Later on, he called you an ex-groupie and you said something nice about his wife.'

'You give good ravioli,' she said. 'The *Age* is full of people like Legge. Done all their growing up there, can't work anywhere else. What do you do around here, generally speaking, after ravioli?'

'Oh, around here we just horse around, generally speaking.'

'Horse around? Can you show me how that's done? I'm a city girl.' She slid off her chair into a sitting position on the carpet. The pyjama pants tucked up into her groin. 'Is there any special equipment needed?'

'Generally speaking, we make do with the bare minimum. Improvise.'

'Is that so?' she said, unbuttoning her top button with her left hand.

Later on, I fetched another log from the pile under the fire escape. The lights were off and the firelight made the room look both mysterious and comforting. We sat side by side on the couch, silent for a while, companionable.

'Starfucking,' I reminded her.

Linda said, 'I went off with a singer in a rock band. I walked out on my husband of three years and my job. It seemed like a good idea at the time.'

'Good band?'

'Not bad. Power and Imagination, it was called. They looked like artists and poets are supposed to, sort of pale and dreamy and wasted. They got that way on a strict diet of smack, speed and Bushmills.'

She swung her legs over mine and leaned back. 'Eric was just chipping in the beginning. "Everything's under control" was his favourite expression. We had a great time. Played all over Europe, did a tour with Fruit Palace, went to a party with Mick Jagger, met Andy Warhol. What a prick.'

'Were you in love?' I said.

'Madly. I was just a kid. Only I didn't know it. I was twenty-three, never really been out of Melbourne, married to a doctor I met at uni. Then one day this utterly strange and exciting creature came into my life. He had a kind of erotic presence, it was overpowering. And he lived in a world that had nothing to do with shopping and dishes and catching trams and alarm clocks and meals at certain times and lunch with your husband's parents every Sunday. He put his hand on me and I was gone.'

I found the red wine and poured some into our glasses.

'So that's starfucking,' Linda said. 'And it all ends in tears, believe me.'

'Everything's got a price.'

She leaned over and kissed me half on the mouth. 'Mine's cheap. Plate of ravioli is the going rate. You've got a bit of an erotic presence yourself, if I may say so. Of the wounded rogue bull-elephant variety.'

'Many a cow has told me that,' I said. 'I want to tell you something.' I'd been putting this off all night.

'So soon? There's another woman already?'

'I got escorted to see the Police Minister this evening. The cops know I was at the doctor's place. They know I wiped my prints.'

Her eyes were wide. 'How did they find out?'

'Somebody must have remembered the Celica's rego. Bloke I asked for directions, I suppose. They seem to have traced it to the guy who lent it to me. And matched its tyre prints with some I left at the scene. He says they matched them, anyway.'

'What now?' There was concern in her voice.

'There's more.' I told her everything Bruce had told me.

'That's quite a session you had,' she said when I'd finished. 'You believe him?'

'Mainly. It makes more sense than the version I half convinced myself was true.'

'So Danny McKillop ends up getting lumbered with

everything. Revenge killer. How come he didn't start with this Scullin?'

I shrugged. 'Could be any number of reasons. No-one will ever know.'

Linda lay back and looked at the ceiling. 'What did Pixley tell you?'

'Lots. He hates Pitman. He says Pitman tried to get him to do things for big donors to the party and shut down Hoagland so that he could sell the site to mates. He says Cabinet didn't approve the sale the first time Pitman raised it. But someone leaked that it had been approved.'

Linda pushed back her hair. 'Pixley says this outright?'

'More or less.'

'Paydirt,' she said. She had the shine in her eyes I'd seen when the fat woman played the computer at UrbanData.

'Not quite. He won't go on the record. I also talked to Anne Jeppeson's mother. Pixley's daughter, Sarah, was in Anne's class at school. They were close friends.'

'Jesus. That's stretching coincidence a bit. Wait a minute. The Cabinet leak about Hoagland...'

'Bruce says Pixley told his daughter, who told Anne. Pixley also suggested that Bleek, the senior officer in the Planning department, was got to by Pitman. He's dead too. Bruce says Bleek was corrupted by Pixley.'

'Did Pixley mention companies?'

'Hexiod and Charis. He says they're the same thing.'

'This is heavy stuff,' Linda said. 'Pass the wine.'

I poured some more of the red. 'You won't be able to drive after this,' I said hopefully.

Linda looked at the fire through her glass. 'Dear me,' she said, 'I'll just have to stay over and fuck your face off. Listen, I think Bruce is trying to bullshit you. I've searched all the Yarrabank titles. What it looks like is that about eighteen months before Pitman decided to shut Hoagland eight companies began buying up the area.'

'*Eight* companies?'

'That's right. Eight companies with names like Edelweiss Nominees Number 12 and Collarstud Holdings and Rabbitrun. And they in turn are owned by companies registered in places like the Cayman Islands and Vanuatu and Jersey.'

'Dummies.'

'Your normal shelf numbers. I've talked to five of the sellers. At least three real estate firms were involved. The owners were made reasonable offers. There was no hurry for possession, the agents said. They could stay on, no rent, if they wanted to. They would get sixty days' notice to move. And there was a secrecy bonus if the buyer was satisfied that no word of the deal had leaked out for thirty days after the sale.'

'Was it paid?'

'Yes. More than a year before Pitman went to Cabinet with his proposal the whole area around Hoagland was stitched up by the eight companies. Well, all except one bit, a sheetmetal works. That changed hands about six months after the others. The land anyway. The factory burnt down.'

'Someone who wouldn't sell?'

'Could be. I'd have to talk to the owner.'

'What's all this add up to?'

'I'd say somebody had the idea for Yarra Cove and quietly bought up the properties through the nominee companies. The companies warehoused them, waiting for Hoagland to be closed and sold to Hexiod Holdings. But before anything could happen, the government lost the election. The nominee companies then one by one sold their waterfront properties to a company called Niemen PL and Niemen consolidated them into one property, a semicircle around Hoagland. Niemen applied for a rezoning for the consolidated property as residential. But the new government blocked them. So nothing happened for nine years. Then Pitman's mob came back into power and the next day Hexiod sold the Hoagland site to Charis Corporation. Soon after that, Niemen sold the waterfront strip to Charis. Hey presto, the jigsaw's complete. All is in readiness for a six hundred million dollar development.'

I felt tiredness creeping over me. 'So Charis might only have come into the picture at the end?'

Linda put her glass on the floor. 'I'd guess that all parties were in on the deal from the beginning. Hexiod wouldn't have bought Hoagland if it wasn't sure it could buy the rest of the land. The people behind the nominee companies wouldn't have bought up the whole area unless they were part of a deal with Hexiod and Charis.'

'And nobody,' I said, 'would have done anything unless they knew that Hoagland was going to be closed down.'

'And sold to Hexiod.'

'But you're just guessing,' I said. 'It's possible that Pixley was the one who tipped off the first buyers and that Charis is just the innocent last link in the chain.'

'I doubt that.'

'But nothing you know says that the whole thing was more than a little scam involving some small-time friends of Kevin Pixley's.'

'I don't know what you'd call a big scam,' said Linda.

'Leaving Hoagland aside,' I said, 'there's still no real evidence that Anne Jeppeson was murdered. Or that Danny was framed. In fact, I now think it's extremely unlikely that Danny was framed.'

She hugged herself. 'Because Bruce says so? Five minutes with the Minister and you come out in reverse.'

'What he says makes more sense of the evidence than my conclusions. And no-one's going to prove any different. Even if Pitman was somehow involved, you won't nail him. You'd have to demonstrate a connection between him and one of the other parties. A tangible link. A beneficial link.'

Linda took my right hand and put it inside her pyjama top, under her right breast. 'I love it when you sound lawyerly,' she said. 'Cup that. And demonstrate a connection.'

I wanted to cup it. And its twin. And to show a tangible link. But I felt a dread stealing over me and I took my hand away. 'Linda,' I said, 'I think we've got to close the book on this thing. I've given my word to Bruce.'

She leaned back. 'Your word? Your word what?'

I found it hard to say it. 'I've told him that neither of us will take this any further. That includes the Hoagland sale.'

Linda stood up. 'I don't understand. Why? Why would you do that?'

How do you tell people about your fear that you might lose one of the few things that has given your life any meaning? 'Bruce offered me a trade,' I said.

'A trade?'

'Back off or be charged with a whole raft of offences over my Daylesford excursion.'

Linda shook her head in disbelief. 'Bruce didn't offer me a trade. You can't speak for me. This whole thing doesn't belong to you. You can't suddenly take your ball and go home. This is a huge story. It could bring down a Cabinet Minister. Maybe the whole government. You can't just switch it off because you've got cosy with the Police Minister.'

'Listen to me,' I said. 'I'm not cosy with him. I'm scared. I'm under the gun. They'll charge me. I'll get convicted. Even if I don't go to jail, I'll get struck off the roll. I'll never be able to practise again.'

She looked at me for what seemed to be a long time. Then she turned and went into the bedroom. I waited, stomach tense, not knowing what to do, knowing I was losing her. When she came out, she was dressed. She went over to where her jacket was hanging over a chair.

I said, 'Can we calm this down? I'm—'

She cut me off, voice even. 'Jack, as far as I can see four people have died over Hoagland. It's likely that there's been a spectacular piece of corruption. I was under the impression you cared about that. Now you're telling me that the nice Police Minister has explained the whole thing to your satisfaction. And to help convince you, he's threatened you with legal action. So to hell with justice, you've agreed to shut up. And you've agreed to shut me up. Well, I'm not yours to shut up. I don't know what made you think I might be.'

I tried to get angry. 'Hold on. A minute ago you were talking about a huge story. Now you're campaigning for justice. Which one do you want to sacrifice me for? Justice or the huge story?'

There was something approaching contempt in her eyes. I knew about contempt in people's eyes. In my life even outback barmen had looked at me with contempt in their eyes.

Linda took her jacket and walked to the door. When she got there, she turned and said, 'If your new chum the Minister drops you in it because you can't control me, my view is you should've asked me first. That's about my pride. About your pride, I'd have thought you wouldn't have given a fuck about getting struck off the roll if you could find out the truth about what happened to Danny McKillop. And if you think the Minister's going to supply you with the truth, you have been living on some other planet for the last forty years. Goodbye.'

I rang twice before I gave up. She had the answering machine on. Halfway through my second message I felt pathetic and broke off. What was there to say anyhow? I lay down on the sofa and tried to sort out my thoughts.

It hadn't occurred to me that Linda wouldn't go along with what I'd done. I'd kept nagging at the thing because I felt I'd let Danny McKillop down. Twice. I didn't think that anymore. I believed Bruce: Danny had probably intended to confront me over my part in his jailing; he might well have intended to kill me. And if Danny wasn't framed for killing Anne Jeppeson, then she wasn't murdered. That left the matter of finding out the truth about Hoagland. But I wasn't going to give up my attachment to the law in pursuit of the truth about Hoagland. There wasn't going to be any truth about it. No-one was going to go on trial for what would probably be regarded as a smart piece of property dealing. So it wasn't a choice between getting justice for Danny or facing serious criminal charges. It was a choice between achieving nothing and getting struck off.

When I finally went to bed, I slept badly, the dream coming back for the first time in years, and, after it woke me, the unbidden and random memories of childhood. The dreams began when I was about nine, when we went to live in the grand house in Toorak with my grandfather, my mother's father, after my father's death. My screams would wake my mother in her huge room miles down the corridor. I could never explain the dream or why it was so frightening. It is about surfaces and textures: smooth, cold surfaces like great sheets of iced marble that suddenly become hot and buckle and twist; steel bars that become dense forests of hot, slippery entrails; pale surfaces that feel solid before they turn to blood-red ooze, sucking you down like quicksand. The dream comes with no warning, as if a trapdoor opens and I fall from the safe and known world into a world that is nothing but terrifying sensation in which I am utterly alone.

The childhood memories started after Isabel's death. They rise up in the margin between wakefulness and sleep and they lie on the mind like prints floating in fixer. All of them seem to date from the years before my father's death. In one, I see the back of the house of my childhood friend Chris Freeborn. Chris's little sister is outside the back door, stirring something in a zinc tub. Through the open back door I can see down a passage all the way to the street. There are people on the pavement outside, moving in and out of the frame of the front door. From inside the house, I can hear someone sobbing and saying something I cannot catch over and over again. In another, my mother is standing behind a high fence, her hands above shoulder-height, fingers hooked in the diamond mesh. She is wearing a dress with large spots on it and her hair is pulled back. The expression on her face is one of anxiety: her chin is lifted, her mouth is open slightly as if she is breathing shallowly through it. There are other women on either side of her, but she is not with them. I am looking at her from the other side of the fence and as I get closer I see that her left eye is full of blood.

These two memories and at least a dozen others fill me with unease, but they have no meaning. I have no other memories of Chris Freeborn's house. Indeed, I cannot bring to mind Chris Freeborn's face. Nor do I know anything about the fence behind which my mother stands. Or, in another memory, who the men are in the car full of cigarette smoke. Or, in another, why my mother and I are shivering in a doorway in the dark, hiding from the headlights of cars. There is no-one I can ask about them. My mother is dead, my sister was born after my father's death, the Freeborn family is scattered to the winds.

At 5.40 a.m., exhausted, I declared the night at an end, got up and made a pot of tea. While it was drawing, I found a novel called *Over Ice* I had been meaning to finish. I read until 8 a.m., when I wrenched myself away from the excitement of a pension in postwar Vienna to clean the flat. Some of the flat. One room. Partly. At 8.30, I drove down Brunswick Street to Meaker's. The street was almost empty, just me and a few party animals in leather and dark glasses moving towards the caffeine with the care of blind people in a strange place.

I almost missed the item on page five of the *Age*. 'Former Minister found dead,' the headline said. The story said Kevin Pixley had been found dead in the bathroom of his Brighton home. A heart attack was suspected. Mrs Pixley was in London.

What appetite I'd mustered was gone. In the night, I'd turned over the idea of going back to Pixley and putting Bruce's accusations to him. In the end, I'd concluded that it would be pointless. Kevin Pixley wasn't going to fall in a heap and confess anything to me.

And what did it matter? Guilt over Danny had started me off. Now I had little doubt that Danny had driven the car that killed Anne Jeppeson. I had nothing to feel guilty about.

I drank a short black and went around to Taub's. The wood and oil smell of the workshop had the power to cheer me at even the lowest times. Down at my end of the workshop, Charlie had laid out on trestles the wood for my boardroom tabletop: three perfect walnut boards, fifteen feet long, eighteen inches wide and one-and-a-half inches thick. They came from what Charlie called The Bank, the timber stacked in the rafters. The first time Charlie had given me a job using timber from The Bank, I'd asked: 'What's this?'

'Piece wood,' Charlie said. '*Swietenia mahagoni.* Cuban mahogany. One hundred years old.'

'I don't think I'm quite ready for this,' I said.

Charlie had taken the cheroot out of his mouth and given my statement some thought. 'Jack,' he said, 'till you make something nice out of it, it's just a piece wood.'

I studied the rough walnut boards with reverence. This was one of the classic furniture timbers. Very few makers ever had the chance to work with wood of this quality and size. I turned one of the boards over. Chalked on the other side was the date Charlie had laid the resawn boards down: 10/3/46. This wood's moisture content was so low that not even the ducted central heating in some Collins Street tower was going to cause it to move. Did an emerging mining company deserve a table made from unobtainable timber air-dried for at least fifty years? Wouldn't some lesser, wetter timber do? The miners wouldn't notice. I'd once asked Charlie the same question about a bureau he was making for a hotel owner with drug connections. 'This *arschloch* I'm not making it for,' he said. 'He's just the first owner. I'm making it for all the owners.'

I set aside my feeling of awe, put on my overalls and went to work. I gave the boards a preliminary pass over the pride of Charlie's life, a near-new high-speed 24-inch surface planer bought from a bankrupt furniture factory. I took off a tissue-paper-thin layer, exposing the figure in the wood. I went outside and stood in the drizzle for a few moments so that I could come back in and smell the fragrance of the walnut filling the workshop. After that, I gave the edges two passes each over the long-bed jointer to prepare them for edge-jointing. Then I set the planer and put the boards through again. They came out almost polished. I dipped a finger in a pot of Charlie's own oil, cold-pressed linseed oil prepared on the workshop stove without chemicals. It was like putting a finger in honey. I drew a squiggle on one of the boards and rubbed the oil in. The wood came to life: smooth, fine-textured, glowing.

I had the three boards on the trestles, admiring the fit of my edge joints, when Drew said from the door, 'I never saw you look at a client that way.'

I looked at my watch. Three hours had slipped by. 'I never had a client wanted to be planed, jointed and oiled,' I said.

We picked up Norm O'Neill and Eric Tanner at the Prince. Wilbur Ong was going to the game with his grandson, Derek Ong, society dentist.

'They can't give this bunch a sheilas a beltin, might as well merge with Brighton Bowls Club,' Norm O'Neill said.

'I heard Vanotti's got a groin problem,' said Eric Tanner. 'There's a number of the fellas got things missing in their groins,' Norm said gloomily.

Things were more cheerful on the way back from the Western Oval. Things were riotous on the way back from the Western Oval. We'd beaten St Kilda 84–79. St Kilda was one of the league's most improved sides and we'd come from behind to win. It was coming from four goals down – that was what mattered. That was the sweetness. Fitzroy had played its usual game: players dropping chest-marks and handballing at each other's knees. But then, in the final quarter, Ansell and McCracken kicked two each. Then Grimmer kicked one. We were in front. And we stayed there, fighting off the Saints for ten agonising minutes. At the final siren, in the rain, we embraced one another and drank toasts from Drew's little silver flask of malt whisky. Around us the Fitzroy supporters croaked out the club song with the joy that comes only to those who have kept the faith through the darkest nights.

At the Prince, the atmosphere was like VE Day. Even Stan was smiling. Even Stan's wife cracked a joke. We had a few toasts, a few songs, relived a few great games. Then Drew and I took his car home and got a taxi to Vlado's in Richmond. The warm room was full of Japanese tourists exclaiming at their handbag-sized steaks. We had almost finished ours and a bottle of '88 Bailey's shiraz when Drew said, 'Hear anything more from that bloke who tried to heavy you?'

I told him about finding the two bodies.

He looked at the roof, looked at me. 'Fucking oath, Jack. Have you gone completely out of your brain?'

'Listen,' I said, 'there's more.' I told him about Linda's digging into Hoagland and my discussion with the Minister.

When I'd finished, he cut the last of his rump in two. 'Jack,' he said, 'you won't mind my saying you're a stupid prick, will you?'

'Not really.'

He put a piece of steak in his mouth and chewed thoughtfully, looking around the room. 'Mate, you don't seem to have got a grip on something,' he said.

'What particular thing is that?' I asked.

'You've gatecrashed a party at the big end of town. With McKillop, I thought you were getting mixed up with some drug business and someone was giving you a chance to pull your head in. Now you tell me you've been trying to tie up the Jeppeson death and McKillop's conviction and death and Bishop's and the doctor's, the whole bloody mess, with Yarra Cove.'

He looked around again. 'This is dangerous stuff. We shouldn't even talk about it in public places.'

'Come on, Drew,' I said. 'This is Melbourne.'

Drew drank some wine. He leaned forward. 'Jack, I think you're out of touch. You're still stuck in the days when the Melbourne Club ran this town. All those pompous arseholes who owned factories and insurance companies and played the market. All went to Melbourne Grammar or similar and basically silly buggers who didn't like Jews or Ities or other kinds of wogs. Otherwise reasonably harmless twerps. Their day's gone, Jack. They woke up one day and found the real money was in property development. Residential sub-divisions. Hotels. Shopping centres. Office blocks. And most of the people making the money didn't give a shit about joining the club.'

He dropped his voice. 'I'm talking about people like Joe Kwitny, mate. Came out here with two pounds and holes in his socks. Got a job as a brickie, didn't know a brick from a banjo. Some old bloke in Preston gave him a crash course for ten bob. Next thing Joe's the gun brickie, the union's telling him to slow down or a wall's going to fall on him. So bugger the union, Joe borrows a few quid, goes off concreting over backyards, putting up brick-veneer houses. That was the beginning. The next thing people like Joe were employing hundreds, doing million-dollar deals, putting up buildings overnight, building whole fucking suburbs out there on the fringes. And on the way they found out how to make sure government gave them the decisions they wanted, how to get the unions on side.'

Drew paused and looked at me for a while, the way teachers look at less-than-quick pupils. 'These people don't think bribery is a crime, Jack,' he said. 'It's just an alternative way to get things done. Blackmail? Well, some people won't co-operate. Rough stuff, murder maybe? Well, accidents happen. Some of the smarter ones even take the long view. They've gone into politics, stacking party branches, getting the right people into Parliament.'

Drew paused, spoke slowly. 'I'm talking about Joe Kwitny, Jack. Charis fucking Corporation.'

He sat back. I didn't know quite what to say. Drew didn't normally deliver lectures. We ate in silence for a while. Then he said, 'Well, that's the lecture. That's the way the world is now, and mate, you have been wandering around in it like some yokel from Terang in town for the day. You think you're doing something good, not so? You see it in terms of right and wrong, justice, that kind of thing. Well, pardon me, you know and I know that the system is not about fairness. It's not about good and bad. It's not about right and wrong. It's about power, Jack. I know that. You should know that.'

'At least I knew when to back off.'

Drew shook his head. 'I don't know if you've backed off in time. One thing's for sure. Bruce is no white knight. He's going to rebury this smelly stuff you've been digging up. You just have to make sure he doesn't put you in the hole too.'

'I could get myself some insurance.'

He cocked his head. 'Don't follow you?'

'Say it gets into the papers.'

Drew didn't reply until he had aligned his cutlery, wiped his mouth with his napkin, folded it, put it under his side plate, signalled the waiter and ordered two brandies.

'Mate,' he said, 'don't let the thought cross your mind. If they can hang this stuff on anybody, it'll be on small fry and people already dead. And you'll keep. These people have got long memories. They'll come back for you.'

At home, I could smell Linda's perfume on the pillows. For a moment, I lay there, drowning in a sense of loss. Then I got up and changed the sheets and pillowcases. I slept better. The first night is always the worst.

Phillip Epstein, art dealer, didn't ask to see the provenance, although I had it.

'You'd expect, what?' he said.

'I need twenty-five thousand as soon as possible,' I said. 'They should cover that.'

He patted my arm. 'Sisley,' he said. 'I think that's a reasonable expectation. Where on earth did you get them?'

'From my wife. Her grandfather once owned the whole notebook.'

He frowned. 'You've got more?'

'No,' I replied. 'They're the only material thing I've got left that's worth anything.'

'I'll be happy to advance the twenty-five thousand. We'd want to take our time selling.'

'It would help,' I said, 'if it was in cash.'

He smiled. 'Let's go in the back and have a drink. We're not talking used notes in small denominations, are we?'

'Large denominations would be better.'

Hardhills was as we'd left it: cold, damp, three utes and a dog outside the pub. On the way, Harry said, 'Fill you in, Jack, next Saturday's the day. Caulfield, race four. Two thousand four hundred. Bit short for the bloke's breeding but it'll do. Next point. We're puttin a girl on him.'

'I thought it was going to be Mick Sayre,' I said.

Harry popped a Smartie. 'Turns out Mickey's a bit of a worry,' he said. 'Cam here was talkin to a clocker, fella who knows a few things. Says Mickey put a whole Greek syndicate on a plunge up in Sydney. On the day the stable got such a fright when they saw the odds go to buggery, they told Mick, bugger this, we're not goin on at four to one, we'll do it another day. Trouble was, Mickey's more frightened of the Greeks than the stable. Wins three lengths clear. Next start, two to one favourite. Greeks love Mick but he doesn't ride for that stable any more.'

'Who's the girl?'

Harry turned and gave me a wink. 'You might've seen her. Nicest little bum on the turf.'

'That's her qualification?'

Harry smiled. 'Nancy Farmer. Rides for her dad. Harold. Two city wins. Mostly she rides the cattle out in the bush. Cam's happy. Wanted a girl from the start.'

'Why's that?'

Cam was driving the big BMW. He took it around a speeding semi with a smooth change-down and a burst of power before he gave me a glance. 'There's two reasons,' he said. 'One, women can keep their mouths shut. They don't get on the phone, go down the pub, do all their mates a favour. Reason two, a little girl's been looking after this bloke fulltime for a year. They're in love. Her and her brother's all that's ridden him. You don't want to put some cocky bastard on him, hard hands, knows it all, thinks he can thrash him home.'

'I'm convinced,' I said. 'What about her bum?'

'Bum?' Cam said. 'Since when do jockeys have bums?'

We parked in the same place as before. Cam got out to have a smoke. Harry put his seat back.

'She'll be along in a minute,' he said.

'The jockey?'

'Staying at Ericson's till the race. I want her to get to know this Dakota Dreamin.'

An old Land Rover pulled up next to us. A woman in her early twenties got out, moleskins, checked shirt, short hair, windburnt face: lean as string. Cam went over. They shook hands, said a few words.

Cam came back and got in, drove off. She followed us around and over the low hills and parked next to us at Ericson's. She was out quickly, waiting, hands in flap pockets.

It was just as cold as the time before. Cam said,

'This is Mr Strang and Mr Irish, Mr Strang's lawyer.'
We shook hands. She was good-looking, big mouth,
no make-up, a hint of wariness in the eyes.

'You're on time. That's good,' said Harry.

Tony Ericson came up the gravel path from the
stables. More handshakes.

'Use your kitchen table, Tony?' Harry said. 'Bit of
talkin to do.'

Ericson led us inside the house and down a passage
to a big, warm kitchen with an old Aga stove. We sat
down at the table. Harry was at the top. Nancy
Farmer was opposite me. She put her elbows on the
table and laced her fingers. She had big wrists and
strong hands like Harry's.

'Nancy,' said Harry. 'Mr Delray told you he wanted
you to ride a bit of track on this Dakota Dreamin
before Saturday.'

She said, 'That's right.'

Harry said, 'This horse is goin to win.'

She kept looking at him, no expression.

'It's goin to win,' Harry said, 'because it's the best
horse in the race. There's nothin else happenin.'

Nancy nodded. A little tension went out of her
shoulders. 'Why me?' she asked.

'Like your style, good hands, got a bit extra out of
that Home Boy in the spring.'

'Didn't get me any more races in town,' she said.

Harry smiled. 'This'll be the makin of you. Tony,
tell Nancy about this bloke.'

Tony Ericson didn't do much public speaking but he
got through it. At the end, he said, 'He goes down the
beach every day. Me girl rides him in the water, on the

sand. Four days he does a bit of track, not too much. Not the way the others do it, but he's rock-hard now. Just right.'

Nancy said, 'You trialled him at the distance?'

Tony shook his head. 'No. He's bred for the two miles but he'll run a strong race at anything over two thou.'

She looked around the table. 'I'll do my best.'

Harry said, 'You'll understand if I say you can't make any phone calls without Mr Ericson's with you? You got a mobile with you?'

She shook her head. 'Is this big?' she asked.

Harry nodded. 'Big enough.'

The tip of her tongue came out and moistened her lower lip. 'I don't have any calls to make,' she said.

'Good,' said Harry. 'There's a thousand for the week's work here. You want to talk about the race fee?'

Nancy looked at him, unsmiling. 'It's laid down.' She paused. 'Excuse me, are you *the* Harry Strang...?'

'Things go right,' Harry said slowly, 'Mr Ericson here is a generous owner.' He patted the table with both hands. 'Well, business over. Let's have a look at the bloke.'

At Dakota's stable, a small girl in overalls was waiting, stroking the horse's nose. She had short red hair and freckles.

'This is me girl Denny,' Ericson said. 'Slim's sort of her horse.'

Nancy shook hands with Denny. 'Pleased to meet you, boss,' she said. 'Now that's what I call grooming. You want to bring him out?'

The girl blushed with pleasure.

Dakota came out calmly, gleaming like a horse in a painting. Denny handled him as if he were a big labrador. He was saddled and bridled inside a minute. We walked behind Nancy, Denny and the horse to the track. Dakota had his head down, his neck extended. He looked as if he were deep in thought, a horse at peace with himself and his surroundings.

'Walks like a stayer,' Harry said. 'You can always tell.'

At the track, Nancy adjusted the stirrups, swung up effortlessly.

'Have a little muck about, get the feel of him,' said Tony Ericson.

We watched for fifteen minutes while she took him up and down the track, trot, canter, short gallop, bit of walking around. When she came back to us, she said, 'Nice horse, likes to run,' rubbing his jaw. She got off and gave the reins to Denny.

'Walk with me,' Harry said. They hung back. When I looked around, they had their heads together, Harry talking with his hands. At the top of the gravel path, they caught up.

'Friday, I'll be back, talk some tactics, look at some movies,' Harry said.

On the way home, Harry said to Cam, 'Girl can ride. Strong, too. You got a feelin?'

Cam flicked a glance at him. 'You know what Oscar Wilde said? Only one thing makes more of a fool of a man than a woman. And that's a horse.'

Harry said, reflectively, 'That so? Didn't know old Oscar rode horses. Knew he rode everythin else.'

The sun came out as we drove over the Westgate Bridge. Off to the left, far off in the distance, I could see the observation platform at Yarra Cove. They had put three flags on it now. Big flags.

I got in another two hours' work at Taub's. The three tabletop boards had to be joined with hide glue. Charlie wouldn't use anything else for this kind of work. Some cabinetmakers use epoxy resin glues. The joints were claimed to be stronger than the woods they joined. When I mentioned this to Charlie, he said, with feigned incomprehension, 'Stronger than the wood? You want joints stronger than wood, welding is the trade.'

I measured out a quantity of hide glue, golden granules, dissolved them in water, added some more granules and heated up the liquid in the glue pot. While it was warming, I put the boards on the gluing stand and dry-clamped them. The fit was good. I unclamped them and, when the glue was hot, I carefully painted it on two interior edges with a hog-bristle brush. Then I put hardwood strips down the outside to protect the outer edges and one-inch dowels outside them to spread the clamp pressure. I tightened the eight bar clamps, the outside pair first, then alternately on each side. At each end and at three intervals along the surface, I used three-by-three hardwood cauls and C-clamps to make sure that the pressure of the bar clamps wasn't distorting the assembly.

It had to be absolutely flat. There were no second chances.

Then I tinkered with the clamps for a good fifteen minutes, trying to ensure that I had enough pressure but didn't force out glue and starve the joints. 'Trust your hands,' Charlie used to say in the early days. 'If you're straining, it's too tight.' I didn't quite understand this: Charlie could tighten the nuts on the Sydney Harbour Bridge with his bare hands without taking any strain.

When I'd cleaned up, I went home. Reluctantly.

Sunday night. I cleaned the kitchen and the bathroom, fed the dishwasher, tried to read the *Sunday Age*, opened a bottle of wine, drank half a glass, stared at the contents of the fridge. Made a cheese and gherkin sandwich. Women come into your life and all the hard-earned self-sufficiency deserts you. Suddenly you're half a person again.

The phone rang. Long-distance beeps.

'Jack Irish?' Ronnie Bishop's friend Charles Lee in Perth.

I said I was sorry about Ronnie's death. I didn't have the heart to tell him I wasn't interested in Ronnie anymore.

'Jack,' he said. 'I should tell the police this now that Ronnie's dead. Remember I told you about the answering machine tape? How it was missing?'

'I remember.'

'Well, I found it. About half an hour ago. Under the drinks cupboard next to the phone. It must have slid under there when the burglar tipped out the phone table drawer. It's got the messages from Melbourne for Ronnie.'

'Have you listened to them again?'

'Yes. They're from different people. The first one left a name and phone number. Danny McKillop. Do you want the number?'

I said, 'No. I've got that number. What about the other one?'

'There's just a message. No name. It's a man.'

'What's the message.'

'I've written it down. He said, "Ronald, listen to me carefully. It's absolutely vital that you bring the evidence. You were stupid to take it and now you've been doubly stupid. I'll have to extricate you." Then he says something that sounds like "sculling's the one in trouble". And then he says, "Ring me when you get here."'

'Can you play that to me over the phone?' I said.

Charles hesitated. 'I can try. I'll put it on the stereo tape deck and hold the phone near the speakers. Hang on.'

I could hear him moving about the room. There were a few false tape starts, then he came back on and said, 'Here goes.'

There was an electronic whine, a pause, a throat-clearing. Then the rich voice of Father Rafael Gorman said, 'Ronald, listen to...'

When the message finished, Charles said, 'Did you get that?'

I said, 'Loud and clear.'

'Do you know who it is?'

237

'I think so. Well done, Charles.'

'I should tell the police, shouldn't I, Jack? It could be very important.'

I made a decision without a second's conscious thought. 'Charles,' I said, 'this is important but I want you to wait until I call you before you tell the police. It won't be more than forty-eight hours, I promise. Will you do that?'

He didn't hesitate. 'Yes. Yes, I will. Jack, there's something else.'

'Yes?'

I waited.

'This is probably quite meaningless.'

I waited.

'I certainly wasn't going to tell those men, but there *was* something the day Ronnie left for Melbourne.'

'What was that?' I said encouragingly.

'Well, I drove him into the city that morning. I had the day off. He said he had to get something out of his safe deposit box at the bank. I dropped him outside and waited, double parked. He was only about five minutes. Then we drove back to his place. His suitcase was already packed and he opened the zip compartment and he took something out of his jacket pocket and put it in.'

'Any idea what?'

'No. Something flat, that's all.'

'And you think that's what he'd got out of his safe deposit?'

'Yes. Well, I can't be sure. I felt bad about not telling you before.'

'I'm glad you have now. It could be useful. Keep it

to yourself. Thanks, Charles. Ring me if you think of anything else. I'll get back to you as soon as I can.' Then a thought occurred to me. 'Maybe you can help with something else. Someone I don't know knows I was in Perth asking about Ronnie. Have you told anyone about me?'

Again, he didn't hesitate. 'No. It'll be that architect bitch next door. When you were in your car I looked around and I could see her shape against the venetian blind upstairs. She thinks you can't see her, but there's light behind her. I've seen her there before. Once when my friend from work came to keep me company while I was tidying up Ronnie's garden she had a good look. And then she came out and took the dog up the street and back. It was because she couldn't see his licence plate from the window, I'm sure.'

'Who would she tell?'

'Those men, I suppose. The ones I told you about.'

I said, 'Thanks again, Charles. I'll be in touch.'

In the kitchen, I poured a glass of wine. There was a little tingle in my body. I found a piece of paper for doodling and sat at the kitchen table.

Father Gorman had said, *Scullin's the one in trouble*. Trouble over what? Danny McKillop's attempt to get his case reopened? Not if Bruce was to be believed. Why then had Ronnie come to Melbourne if not in response to Danny's phone call? How would Scullin be involved? What was the evidence his old employer wanted him to bring? Evidence of what? Had Gorman steered Ronnie out to the doctor's establishment in the bush so that he could be murdered? Did this have any connection with Danny?

The phone rang again. Blinking, I looked at my watch: 11.15. It was Linda. Just when I'd stopped missing her for three minutes at a time.

'You alone?' she said.

'No,' I replied. 'I had three girls home delivered from Dial-a-Doll.'

'I've been burgled. The place is a shambles.'

I sat upright. 'What's gone?'

'My laptop. All my disks. Whole filing cabinet emptied. Not the television or the VCR or the stereo.' There was a pause. 'It's a bit scary.'

'Don't touch anything. Grab some clothes and come over here. We'll get the cops in tomorrow.'

'No,' she said. 'I'm okay. I've already rung the cops. If I don't stay here tonight I'll never come back.'

'I'll come over.'

'No. It's fine. I just wanted to tell you. Hear your voice, really. There's something else.'

'What?'

'Everything I've put into the computer system at work is gone. Wiped.'

'Accident?'

'I don't think so.'

'Don't you have some kind of security?'

'Yes. There's more.'

I waited.

'That creep in Sydney I told you about? The regional director?'

'Yes.'

'He's told my boss here that I'm to drop any story about Yarra Cove or anything to do with Charis Corporation.'

Suddenly the room felt cold. 'What did you say?'

'I said I'd think about it.'

'Sure you don't want to come over here?'

'Yes. I'll call you in the morning.'

'Call me any time. How did they get in?'

'Don't know. The front door was still locked.'

'Have you got a chain?'

'Yes. And two bolts.'

'Lock up tight after the cops leave. And don't let the cops in without showing you their ID. Get them to push it under the door or through the letterbox. Okay?'

'Right, O Masterful One.'

'I think you're back to normal.'

'Getting there. Talk to you tomorrow.'

'Early. Before you go to work. Goodnight.'

There was a moment's silence. Neither of us wanted to be the first to hang up.

'Well,' she said. 'Missed you.'

'Me too,' I said. 'Life's been lacking something.'

I put the bars on the front and back doors and looked down the lane for a while before I went to bed. I tried to sleep but I kept thinking about Drew's description of the rise of the Kwitny empire. He was right. I had been a bit like a yokel from Terang. For a whole decade, I hadn't paid any attention to anything except cabinetmaking and plodding around looking for people who didn't want to be found.

Linda rang at 7.30 a.m. I was up, just out of the shower.

'Let's have breakfast,' she said. 'I haven't got much time.'

We met at Meaker's at eight and ordered orange juice and muesli.

'I'm not sure what to do,' she said. She looked thinner somehow. 'I'm not as brave as I thought I was.'

'It comes to us all.'

'It's not just the burglary,' she said. 'I was being followed yesterday. I tracked down the man whose sheetmetal works across the road from Hoagland burnt down. He didn't want to know me. Then he rang yesterday and said he'd thought about it and he'd talk to me. I went out to his house, out in Swanreach. Lives all alone in this brick-veneer palace. He says he didn't want to sell at first because it suited him to be in Yarrabank. Then he sniffed that the whole place was being bought up, so he held out, thought he'd get twice what they were offering.'

She was silent while our breakfast was served. We both drank some juice.

'He says two men came to see him at home. Just arrived at the front door. They offered him ten per

242

cent more than the agent's offer. When he said no, one man said there wouldn't be any more offers. No threats. After that, a whole series of weird things began to happen. The two family dogs died, poisoned. About ten kilos of broken glass was put in the swimming pool. Undertakers got calls to go to the house. One night, five different pizza deliveries were made. Then his wife's car went in for a service and when she drove it again the brakes failed. She broke her arm and some ribs.'

'Did he go to the cops?'

'Early on. They said there was nothing they could do. Hire a security firm.'

'Did he tell them about the pressure to sell his factory?'

'He says yes. He went to his local MP, too.'

I said, 'Swanreach? Don't tell me.'

She nodded. 'His MP's Lance Pitman.'

'Eat your muesli,' I said, not feeling like mine. We sat there, eating and looking at each other.

'And then?' I asked when we'd almost finished.

'He says business began to fall off even before the men came to see him. He depended on five or six major customers. Two went, and then after the visit his biggest customer, more than half his business, went elsewhere.'

'Reasons?'

'They gave him a story he didn't believe. He says they couldn't look him in the eye.' She paused and ate a spoonful. 'And then one Friday night the place burnt down. Blew up, actually. Full of gas cylinders.'

'Cause?'

'Made to look like negligence, he says. Insurance wouldn't pay. He thinks one of his workers set it up.'

'So he sold?'

'Yes. He was ruined. He says he could have sold the business for half a million before it all started. After the fire, it was worth nothing. No customers. No premises. The agents came around and offered half of the original offer and he took it.'

'Why did he change his mind about talking to you?' I asked.

Linda was studying the street. 'He says it's been boiling inside him all these years. He's convinced the whole business killed his wife. And his divorced daughter, who lived with him with her kids, she said he'd gone neurotic and went to live somewhere else.'

'Tell me about being followed.'

She smiled, a thin smile. 'Talking about neurotic,' she said. 'All day Saturday I had this feeling someone was watching me. Then yesterday, after I left Swanreach, I stopped for gas and a car, ordinary cream Holden or something with two men in it, pulled up at the air hose. I realised I'd seen it parked way down the road from the house I'd been at.'

She took a deep breath. 'Anyway, I went in to pay and I buggered about, bought a drink, looked at the magazines, studied the engine additives, fanbelts, whatever. The guy at the air hose pumped three tyres and then he stuck on the fourth one, at the back. His head kept bobbing up. Finally, he hung up the hose and they drove off. I went outside quickly and they were pulling up by the side of the road about a hundred metres down. In front of a parked car. I went by them – I didn't have any choice – and they zipped out, forced their way into the traffic and sat about five cars behind me. I pulled in at a liquor place in Alphington and when I came out, they were at the kerb about two hundred metres back. So I changed direction, went back past them.'

'You realised that would tell them for sure they'd been spotted?'

Linda shrugged. 'I hate to say it, but I was completely spooked. I was hoping I was wrong. I hoped they'd go away.'

'But they didn't?'

'They did a U-turn right in the face of traffic. I drove on for a bit, did an illegal U-turn at some lights, saw them on my right, and then I didn't see them again.'

'Where'd you go?'

'Home first. Put the interview notes on the laptop. Then to work. That's when I got the message from this arsehole in Sydney. Via this spineless arsehole in Melbourne. And discovered my computer wipeout.' She smiled another wan smile. 'First I'm followed, then at work I get two quick kidney punches. Go home for the knockout blow. Every square inch of the place searched. I kid you not. My old photo albums, Christ. They took the top off the lavatory cistern. Left it in the bath.'

I thought about Eddie Dollery and the money in the dishwasher. Was that only two weeks ago? Our coffees came. I was trying to think of something to say that wouldn't reveal the jellyback in me when Linda said, voice low, 'Oh, and about your friend Ronnie Bishop.'

'What?'

'I talked to someone I know from when I was on the compassion beat at the *Age*. She's a welfarey, a youth worker, knew Ronnie Bishop from way back. She says she wanted to give a party when she heard he was found dead.'

I waited.

'She says she thinks he got a whole lot of street kids into porn movies. She says she's heard that Father Gorman runs the Safe Hands Foundation as a kind of brothel for sleaze-bags looking for under-age sex. Ronnie was a recruiting agent on the street.'

I remembered something Mrs Bishop had said: *Ronnie loved films. He saved up to buy a movie camera. He was always filming things.*

Linda lowered her voice even further. 'Here's the really interesting bit. My contact says that around the time of the Hoagland business, she was working in a youth refuge, lots of street kids with drug habits. One of them, a girl about fourteen, saw a man on TV one night and said, "That's the bloke who fucked me and my friend."'

'Ronnie?'

She shook her head. 'No. Lance Pitman MP, then Housing Minister.'

I closed my eyes and said, 'Jesus. Did they go to the cops?'

'No. No point. The girl wouldn't talk to the cops. But she fingered Ronnie Bishop as the one who set it up.'

I looked out the window. Ronnie and Father Gorman and Lance Pitman and Scullin the cop. Under-age sex and porn movies. And the Kwitny family, patrons of the

Safe Hands Foundation and owners of Charis Corporation. 'What did they do about it?' I asked.

'This woman and another youth worker went to see Father Gorman. He gave them a lot of charm, said he'd look into it. They didn't hear anything more. Ronnie wasn't seen on the streets again.'

'And they left it at that?'

'They're both good Catholics. He's a priest.'

I said, 'What are you going to do now?'

She gave me her unblinking look. 'What the burglars didn't know is that I'd backed up everything at work and on the laptop on disk. And the disk is in my bag. I'm going to try to link Charis Corporation to the companies that bought up Yarrabank. That's the link I need. But if I can't tie them together, I'll write the story of the buy-up and see if the *Age* will run it.' She blinked. 'I'm sorry, Jack, I have to.'

I sighed and put my hand on hers. 'Don't be sorry,' I said. 'Let me tell you about my phone call from Perth.'

There was a piece of cardboard torn off a beer carton slipped under my office door. On it was written: *I rembered somthing else about what you was asking about. See me at my house.* It was signed: *B. Curran, 15 Morton Street, Clifton Hill.*

It didn't mean anything for a moment, and then I remembered I'd left my card with the man who'd lived next door to Ronnie Bishop in Clifton Hill.

A car hooted outside. It was Cam. We had a meeting organised with Cyril Wootton and his chief commissioner at the pub in Taylor's Lakes. Cam favoured places in the suburban wastelands for meetings like this.

It started to sprinkle with rain as we hit the freeway in Kensington.

We were in the fast lane, doing ten over the limit. On the right-hand bend coming up to the Coburg exit, Cam shifted into the middle lane, giving a furniture truck no more than a second's warning.

Five hundred metres further, he went back into the fast, no warning. A hooter blared at us.

'Having fun?' I asked.

'Two pricks on a bike been with us since Carlton,' Cam said, voice normal. 'Just wanted to see what they'd do.'

'What'd they do?'

'Dropped way back. Put your hand under the seat, will you, mate. There's a little case.'

I found what looked like a small aluminium brief-case under the seat. It was heavy.

'It's loaded. Keep it out of sight,' Cam said.

I unsnapped the lid of the case. Inside, nestled in hard foam, were a long-barrelled revolver, cleaning equipment and about thirty rounds of ammunition.

'Ruger Redhawk,' Cam said.

'That's nice. What the fuck's going on?'

Cam had his eyes on the rear-view mirror. 'Dunno. Could be just two pricks out for a ride. Could be someone thinks we've got the cash for the Commissioner on board.'

'Who knows we're meeting him?'

'It's a her. Just Wootton.'

The Essendon exit was coming up. Cam waited

until it was almost too late and then swung off sharply on to it without signalling. 'I'm going first left, round the sports fields,' Cam said. 'Hold your tummy.'

I looked back. Three hundred metres behind us, four cars in between, a motorcycle with two figures in black wearing fullface helmets on it was coming off the freeway.

'Bloke on the back's got a little bag,' I said.

'His playlunch maybe,' Cam said. 'When last you shoot anything?'

I felt fear for the first time. It had seemed a bit of a joke up to then. 'In the Mallee about ten years ago,' I said. 'Shot a few rabbits.'

'Take that thing out of the box.'

I took the Ruger out and looked back again. The motorcycle was accelerating past the cars, closing the gap between us quickly.

The engine screamed and the tyres squealed as Cam changed down and took the left, but the car held its line. 'Nice bus this,' Cam said. 'But it hasn't got the legs for this kind of thing.'

The bike leant over at forty-five degrees as it came around the corner behind us, perhaps two hundred metres away.

We were on a street with houses on our right and sports fields behind a high wire fence on the left. We had to turn right at the corner coming up or go into a parking lot for the sports complex.

'I think we've got to show these boys the iron,' Cam said. 'Can't outrun them. I'm going to broadside in this parking lot. Get out quick, I'm coming out the same door.'

My eyes flicked to the speedo. We were doing a hundred when we went into the parking area. There were three cars in it, all near the gate at the left.

I looked back again. The bikers were close now, perhaps a hundred metres. The sun had come out and their leathers gleamed like otter skins.

Cam swung left towards the cars, slowed, then swung right. As the car came around, he hit the brake.

We went into a broadside skid across the tarmac, the right-hand wheels lifting. We came to a stop side on to a fence a few metres away.

'Out we go,' said Cam calmly.

I opened my door and half fell out. Cam was right behind me in a crawl.

'Keep down,' he said. 'Give me the gun.'

We crouched behind the front of the car. I could feel the heat from the engine on my face. Cam pulled back the Ruger's hammer.

The bike came into the parking lot almost without slowing and went right. As it turned half side-on to us, I got a view of the passenger.

His bag was slung around his neck by the strap now and he was holding something black and blunt.

'Fucking Christ,' said Cam.

It was a sub-machine gun.

The rider slowed and swung left. He was going to make a run parallel to us.

We both ducked. They must have been about twenty metres from us when the passenger opened up, flat, coughing sounds, not loud. Most of the first burst was high, over the top of the car. But the last rounds hit the front windscreen with sharp tapping noises. A large, jagged hole appeared on the passenger side and the rest turned to mosaic.

A second later, the next burst of hard coughing. They went low. Some hit the car, some hit the tarmac underneath, ricocheted and pinged off the chassis.

The bike was past, accelerating into a turn for another run.

'Fuck this for a joke,' Cam said. He straightened up, Ruger in both hands, and leant his long forearms on the bonnet.

I put my head up. The bikers were side-on, just starting the turn towards us. The passenger saw Cam and raised the fat barrel of his weapon.

Cam fired.

He missed.

He fired again.

The bullet hit the back of the gunman's helmet. His left arm went up as the impact lifted him off the bike and spun him on to the tarmac.

The rider, unbalanced, veered sharply towards us, gained control and swung savagely away.

'One down,' Cam said softly, steadying himself for a shot at the rider.

The passenger got to his knees, left hand to his helmet, sub-machine gun still in the other. He was small, no bigger than a fourteen-year-old. He shook his head like a dog, then turned to look at us.

Cam was aiming at the rider.

The small man brought the sub-machine gun up.

'Down!' I shouted, grabbing Cam's coat and pulling him onto me.

The weapon coughed again, bullets whining just over the bonnet where Cam had been.

'Little fucker,' Cam said.

The bike's engine roared.

Cam put his head up. 'Party's over,' he said.

I stood up. They were going out of the parking area exit, sun glinting on their helmets, engine screaming in second gear.

We listened to the sound of the bike going up the road, turning left, getting fainter. Then it was still, just the hum from the freeway and the jungle sounds of small children playing far away. It had taken no more than forty seconds from the time the bikers came into the parking area. Now only the smell of cordite hanging in the cold air spoke of violence and near-death.

I looked around, expecting to see people everywhere. There was no-one. The silenced sub-machine gun had probably gone unheard, Cam's shots taken for a car backfiring.

Cam finished putting his Ruger back into its case and took a packet of Gitanes out of his top pocket. 'You smoking?'

'Just this once,' I said. I cupped my hands around the lighter flame. They weren't shaking. Not yet. The first draw almost made me sit down.

'Well, you can rule out money,' said Cam. 'That ain't the way they go about taking it off people.'

Something was gradually dawning on my adrenalin-soaked brain. 'Where did you say you first saw them?'

'Top of Elgin Street. They couldn't have been behind me long. I'd have seen them on the freeway.'

I took another draw. Another reel. 'Mate,' I said, 'I don't think this is connected with the horses. Something else. Little job I've been doing.'

Cam blew smoke out of his nose, looked around. 'Don't take any big jobs,' he said. 'You want to get the cops over here?'

'No,' I said. 'I'll have to take care of it myself.'

I didn't need to think about it. There wasn't anything the cops could do for you if people wanted to kill you. Not unless there was something you could do for the cops, and then you ended up living in a caravan park in Deniliquin on the witness protection program.

We inspected the car. Apart from the windscreen, there were about half a dozen bullet holes.

Cam took out his mobile. 'It'll probably go,' he said, 'but I don't want to explain these holes to the jacks. I'll get a mate to bring some wheels around, take this away. Wonder where that prick got an Ingram?'

I said, 'Is that what it was?'

'Not your normal scumbag piece of iron.'

Cam got through to someone. 'Henry,' he said. 'I want you to think about how much you owe me...'

Fifteen minutes later, a Ford Granada came into the parking lot, followed by a tow truck. The tow truck driver, a huge man with a beard, stuck masking tape over all the bullet holes. He'd done this sort of thing before. We were on the freeway in the Ford in five minutes.

After a while, Cam gave me a quick look. He was steering with his fingertips, cigarette drooping from his mouth. 'Knew their business,' he said, 'we'd both be looking at the lid.'

'I'm glad they don't know their business,' I said. I put my hands out and looked at them. I was shaking. 'I'm just starting to react.'

Cam said, 'Want somewhere else to stay?'

I was thinking about phone calls. Calls from Charles and Linda last night. All my calls in the past weeks. I really was a yokel.

'I'll need room for two,' I said.

'Two, twenty,' Cam said. 'You can use my current's place. She's gone to Italy.'

'I wish I was in Italy,' I said. 'Italy, Bosnia, anywhere.'

Cam opened the window and flicked his cigarette out. 'Things go right Saturday,' he said, 'we can all go to Italy. First class.'

Wootton was waiting in the parking lot of the pub, a hideous pre-cast concrete affair with flagpoles all over the front. He was in his XK Jaguar, reading a magazine. He put it away when he saw us coming. I went around to his side. The window was down.

'Can you get someone to debug my place?' I said.

He frowned. 'Really, Jack, are you sure you're important enough for people to want...' My expression stopped him. 'When do you want it done?'

'Now,' I said.

'Now?'

'Now. The person can pick up a key from the ground-floor flat. Number one. Say Jack sends his fondest regards and the bloke will hand over the key.'

Wootton took out his mobile phone and got out of the car. 'What's the address?' he asked. He punched in a number and spoke to someone in cryptic terms, giving the address and the introduction. 'It's urgent,' he said.

The commissioner was waiting for us in the lounge, a pinkish chamber, full of angular chrome and plastic furniture. I didn't know there were people who'd place your bets for a commission who didn't look like Eddie Dollery or like market gardeners in town for the day.

Wootton did the introductions. He introduced me as Ray and Cam as Barry. The Commissioner was called Cynthia. She was in her late thirties or early forties, grey suit, tall and slim, an intelligent face of sharp planes relieved by a lower lip as plump as an oyster. Her shoulder-length dark hair slipped silkily around her head.

She was business-like. Harry would approve.

'How big?' she said.

'As possible,' Cam replied.

'They're gun-shy these days,' she said. 'You'll have to spread it around.'

Cam nodded. 'This is the drill,' he said. 'You wait for the second call. We expect the price to drift. Then we want as many fair-sized hits as we can get without collapsing the price. Then send in the troops, like they've heard the late mail. Take it all the way to the floor.'

She smiled a cautious smile, cocked her head. 'Some organising here. Small army. There's not that many reliables around.'

I thought I caught a hint of working-class Tasmania in her voice, perhaps one of those bone-hard timber towns, full of red-faced men with pale eyes and bad breath, the girls with one pretty summer before the babies and the cigs and the mid-morning start on the wine cask. Cynthia would have got out early, escaped to the mainland.

'We're told you can do it. But if you can't...' said Cam.

She crossed her legs. In my trained observer way, I registered that they were exceptionally long legs. Part of me couldn't believe that I was sitting in this garish place looking at legs and listening to talk about backing horses when people had recently been trying to kill me.

'I can do it,' she said. 'What happens interstate?'

'You get first go,' Cam said. 'We'll take what we can get elsewhere.'

'The TAB?'

'Don't worry about it,' he said.

'When do I know?'

Cam lit a Gitane and blew smoke out sideways. 'Cyril will tell you where to be,' he said. 'You've got to be ready to push the button, go straight off.'

'Not even the race number?'

Cam shook his head. 'No.'

'Makes it hard if it's going to be the eighth.'

'Life's hard,' Cam said. 'Cyril says we don't have to worry about collecting. Is that right? We hate worrying.'

Cynthia gestured with her hands, palms upward. 'You don't have to worry,' she said. 'I'm not going anywhere. I've got three teenagers to look after.'

'I know that,' said Cam. 'Think about them. We'll need a full accounting. Every bit of paper. Anything else I can tell you?'

She shook her head and stood up. 'Nice to do business with you,' she said.

'We hope so,' Cam said. 'We hope so.'

We were waiting at the St George's Road lights when the ambulance came through and did a screeching right turn.

'Just live for speed,' said Cam.

I saw the smoke before we turned into my street, a dark plume against the cigarette-smoke sky. When we turned, we saw the street was blocked by three police cars. People were everywhere. Further down, a fire engine was paralleled to the pavement. Its ladders were up and firemen on them were spraying water into a huge hole in the building's roof.

It was my building.

The huge hole was in my roof.

My home was burning.

Cam pulled up and looked at me. 'Your place, right?' he said.

I could only nod.

'Better wait,' he said, opening his door.

I slumped against the door pillar. I could recognise at least a dozen people standing around. Neighbours. The man from the corner shop.

Cam was back inside five minutes. He didn't say anything, did a slow U-turn. We were heading down Brunswick Street when he spoke.

'Cop reckons the bloke turned the key and the whole place went up. He might live. Door could have saved him.'

'It was supposed to be me,' I said. Cam didn't need telling. I needed to say it. I wasn't feeling scared. All I could think about was the flat. It contained everything I valued. My books. My music. The paintings and prints Isabel had bought, always as presents for me. The leather sofa and armchairs we'd bought together at the Old Colonists' Club auction. It was my home, the only place that had ever meant anything to me since leaving my first home at the age of ten. It was my history, my link with Isabel. If Cam could have taken me directly to the person responsible for destroying it, I would have committed murder.

After a while, Cam said, 'Where to?'

My first thought was my office. Then it sunk in. I couldn't go near my office or Taub's. People were trying to kill me. They'd been prepared to kill Cam this morning. They would kill Charlie if he got in their way. They probably intended to kill Linda.

Now I felt fear, a knot in my stomach.

'I've got to make a call,' I said. 'Talk to someone.'

Cam turned into Gertrude Street and parked next to the Housing Commission flats. Three men in overcoats, all bearded, were sitting on a scuffed knoll, passing around the silver bladder of a wine cask.

I took the mobile and got out. In my wallet, I found the number Garth Bruce had given me. I'd transferred it to the back of a business card. About to press the first button, I hesitated. How could I trust Bruce? Linda didn't. Drew didn't. Then I remembered the awkward way we'd stood together, two men struggling to come to terms with their grief, and his words: *I think you've had enough pain with this Milovich.*

I punched the number. It was answered on the second ring. A woman. I said John English wanted to speak to the Minister.

'Please hold on,' she said.

I leaned against the car. The sun had come out, making the day seem colder. One of the bearded men on the knoll was trying to strangle the last drop of wine out of the bladder.

'Yes.' It was Bruce.

'Someone's trying to kill me,' I said. 'Twice today.'

He said nothing for a moment. I could hear him breathing.

'God,' he said. 'You all right?'

I said yes.

Another pause. 'Where are you?'

'In the street.'

'Jack,' he said, 'this is getting out of hand.' His speech was measured. 'I think I've underestimated Pixley's old mates. We'll have to put you somewhere safe till we can shake some sense into them. The Hillier woman too. Can you get in touch with her?'

'Yes. She's being followed.'

'That so? Be the same people. Okay, listen, we've got to do this carefully. Yarra Bend. There's a park up there, near the golf course. Know it?'

'Yes.'

'Get hold of Hillier and get up there, park as far away from those public toilets as possible. What are you driving? What's the rego?'

I walked around the back of the car and read out the number. 'Ford Granada,' I said. 'Blue.'

'Right. Let's make it in an hour's time. The two blokes from last time will pick you up, get you somewhere safe.' He paused. 'Now this is important. Don't talk to anyone except Hillier. And don't say a word about this arrangement to her on the phone. She's probably tapped.'

'Right,' I said. 'An hour from now.' The lead ball of fear in my stomach was dissolving.

'Good,' he said. 'You'll be fine. Just take it easy. We can fix this up in a day or so. I'll see you tonight.'

I rang Linda's number. She answered straight away.

'I want you to make sure you're alone and get a cab to the place where we ate. The first time, remember?'

'Yes,' she said. 'What's wrong?'

'Something very serious. I'll tell you when I see you. Get the cab to park as close to the place as possible. Wait in the cab until you see me.'

'Jack, what's going on?' she said.

'Half an hour from now. Okay?'

'Yes. Okay.'

'See you then. Love.'

'Yes,' she said. 'Love.'

I got back into the Granada. Cam was reading the paper, smoking a Gitane.

'I'll get off your back in an hour's time,' I said. 'I won't take up that offer of yours. Need to disappear for a day or so.

Cam gave me a long look. 'I'll miss the excitement,' he said.

I was looking in my wallet to see how much money I had. There was a piece of cardboard in the note section. I took it out: *I rembered somthing else about what you was asking about. See me at my house. B. Curran, 15 Morton Street, Clifton Hill.*

Clifton Hill was as safe a place as any to pass the half-hour until it was time to pick up Linda.

'Can we take a little drive around to Clifton Hill?' I said.

The man was wearing the same outfit as before: dirty blue nylon anorak, black tracksuit pants. There was every chance that it hadn't come off since our previous meeting.

'Wondered when you'd come,' he said.

'You remembered something else about Ronnie Bishop,' I said.

He looked at me, said nothing.

I took out my wallet and offered him a twenty.

He took it. 'Had to walk round to your place,' he said. 'Bloody long way. Had to take a cab back. Me legs is bad.'

I found a ten and gave it to him.

'Wait,' he said. He shuffled down the dark passage and came back a minute later, folded newspaper in his hand. ''Member I said cops come around next door couple times?'

I nodded.

He coughed and spat past my right shoulder. 'One's a cunt called Scullin.'

'You told me that.'

He sniffed. 'Didn't know who the other was. Do now.'

'Yes? Who?'

He unfolded the paper. It was the *Herald Sun*. He looked at the front page. 'This bastard,' he said.

He turned the newspaper to face me. There was a large colour photograph of a man sitting in front of microphones. He was flanked by two high-ranking policemen in uniform.

'Which cop?' I said, studying the policemen.

'Not the cops. The cunt in the middle. The fucking Minister. That's him.'

I was about to put the phone down when the woman answered.

'I need to get in touch with Vin McKillop,' I said.

She started coughing, a loose, emphysemic sound. I

waited. When she stopped, I said again, 'Vin McKillop, I need—'

'Vin's dead,' she said. 'Overdose.'

I didn't ask her any questions.

I went into the sitting room. Linda was standing in front of the huge fireplace in the centre of Cam's absent girlfriend's place off Crombie Lane in the heart of the city. Her apartment occupied the top floor of an old six-storey warehouse. She was an artist. Paintings were everywhere, mostly landscapes at different stages of completion.

'Vin McKillop's dead,' I said. 'Pixley's dead, Vin's dead. It's like a battlefield.'

'Oh, Jesus,' Linda said. 'Oh, Jesus.'

'Garth Bruce visited Ronnie Bishop with Scullin more than once around the time of Anne Jeppeson's death,' I said. 'If Scullin fixed up Danny for killing her, Garth Bruce must be part of the whole thing. He was setting us up.'

Cam was lying on a sofa, long legs over the arm, head propped up by cushions, drinking Cascade out of the bottle.

'So Bruce's got the motor's number,' he said. He'd had no trouble grasping my explanation of what was going on. It didn't seem to surprise him either.

'I suppose that was dumb,' I said, 'but you don't expect the Minister for Police to try to kill you.

'It's just possible he's not involved,' Linda said. She was dressed for business in a suit, cream silk blouse, black stockings and high heels. Overexcited though I was, the sight aroused a frisson of lust.

'I don't think we should operate on that assumption, I said. 'What can we do about the car?' It was now in the girlfriend's garage on the ground floor.

Cam swung his legs to the floor. 'It can stay where it is. I'll get my mate to report it stolen, give me another one.' He stood up and walked off down the long room in the direction of the kitchen.

Linda's eyes followed him. 'What does he do for a living?'

'He's a gambler,' I said. 'He shot a midget firing a sub-machine gun off a motorbike this morning. That's how I'm here.'

She nodded. 'I can believe that,' she said. 'What do we do now?'

'Think. Think about evidence. Evidence is the only thing that can help us now.'

'Did you tell me once,' Linda said, chin on her palms. 'Did you tell me that Danny's wife said there was evidence he didn't do it?'

I thought back to the night, in the family room Danny built. 'Yes. She said a woman phoned Danny. The woman said her husband had died.'

'But she didn't give Danny the evidence?'

'No.'

'I don't suppose it follows that if it's evidence that proves Danny didn't do it, it's evidence of who did,' Linda said.

'It might be.' I was thinking. 'What kind of person would have the evidence? It would have to be a cop, wouldn't it?'

'Could be someone connected with Charis Corp.'

I sighed. 'That's right. This is a dead-end.'

Linda got up and crossed to a huge steel-framed

window. Her high heels went tock on the polished concrete floor. She had to stand on tiptoe to look out. Her calf muscles tensed deliciously. At any other time I would have been seized with an impulse to rush her from the rear.

'Let's say it's a cop. Was a cop,' she said. 'What then?'

'Died some time before Danny was shot. At least a month.'

'How do you know that?'

'I'm assuming the woman got in touch with Danny soon after her husband's death. That's when she rang. About a month before Danny was killed.'

Linda turned around. 'What date was that?'

I told her.

'Where's the phone?' she said.

'Coming up.' Cam was coming back, carrying a cordless phone. 'I'm taking a stroll to pick up some other wheels. I'll come back, see if you need anything.'

Linda took the phone from him. 'Phone book?'

'In the kitchen. On the fridge.' He gave me a wave.

When she came back, Linda took a notebook out of her bag, sat down and punched a number.

'Hello, Police Association? Can I speak to the secretary? Right. Who could I speak to about membership records? Oh, you've got a membership secretary. Denise Walters. I'd like to, yes.'

Linda waited, looking at me. 'Denise, hi,' she said. 'My name's Colleen Farrell. Dr Colleen Farrell. From Monash University Medical School. Denise, I wonder if you can help me. We're doing a study on police mortality in Australia. Do you know about that? No?

It's at the early stages, but we think it'll help the police case for a stress loading on salaries.'

Pause. 'Yes. Abnormally high levels, we think, Denise. We've run into a little problem you might be able to help us with. We don't have any data for Victoria for the last two months.'

Pause. 'Yes, that's right. We got the other data directly from the Commissioner's office but the person there has gone on leave and I'd like to get up to date before *I* go on leave.'

Pause. 'That would be terrific, Denise. I'll wait on.'

We sat in silence looking at each other. Linda reached down, took the hem of her skirt and began to work it up, slowly, one thigh at a time, flexing her thigh muscles and moving her bottom from side to side. I could see the dark at the fork of her legs when she said, 'Still here. Right. No serving members so far this year. Good. What about non-serving?'

Pause. 'Two in January. None in Feb. One in March. One in April. Okay. Now, Denise, I'll need the names to check against our register.'

Pause. 'H. J. Mullins. T. R. Conroy. M. E. F. Davis. P. K. Vane. That's V-A-N-E, is it? Terrific. I see we've got them all except Vane. You wouldn't have any biographical data there, would you, Denise?'

Pause. 'Just service dates. Um. '63 to '88. Special Branch 1978 to '84. Look, Denise, you've been a great help. Thanks very much. Much appreciated.'

Linda put the phone down and pulled her skirt back to respectability. 'I can't bear to see a man salivate,' she said. 'The only possibility is P. K. Vane. He was in the Special Branch when Anne was killed, though.'

'I'd say that lets him out. They spent all their time hanging around anarchist meetings. Six people and a collie dog and two Special Branch. Our bloke would probably be in Drugs, one of Scullin's mates.'

There was a sound in the hallway. I felt my shoulders tense. Cam came in.

'All fixed up,' he said. 'Listen, I'm shooting through. You want me, press auto and 8 on the phone. It'll page me.' He opened his jacket and showed the pager on his belt.

'I'm in your debt, mate,' I said.

Cam said, 'Saturday, that's the day we pay off debts. There's plenty of food here.' He eyed Linda appraisingly. 'Try the cupboards in the big bedroom for clothes. You're not far apart in size. Jack, there's men's clothes in the other bedroom. One of her exes. Biggish fella, I gather. Nice line in shirts. Help yourself.'

I went with him to the front door. He was outside when he said, 'That little case of mine, that's in the kitchen now. Under the sink. I wouldn't open this door to anyone if I were you.'

I detoured to the bathroom on my way back, looking for aspirin. Pumping adrenalin leaves you feeling dull and headachey. I was studying the contents of the medicine cabinet when it came to me out of nowhere.

I can remember her saying she could go anywhere in safety because the Special Branch were always lurking somewhere.

Anne Jeppeson's mother. That was what she had said.

The Law Department at Melbourne University looks the way universities should. It has courtyards and cloisters and ivy.

I loitered downstairs, near where a girl had set fire to herself during the Vietnam War. Nobody paid any attention to me. The whole campus was full of people in ex-army overcoats wearing beanies. I was just older than most of them. By about thirty years.

My man came out ahead of his students, striding briskly, looking the way lecturers usually look after a lecture: happy and smug. His name was Barry Chilvers and he taught constitutional law. He was also a civil liberties activist and knew more about the Special Branch than most people.

'Barry,' I said when he was level with me.

He jerked his head up at me, eyes startled behind the big glasses.

I took the beanie off.

'Jesus Christ, Jack,' he said, exasperated, 'where'd you get that coat? And the beanie, for Christ sakes. It's a Collingwood beanie. How can you wear a Collingwood beanie?'

'Ensures that I'm not recognised,' I said. 'Got a moment?'

We went upstairs to his office. It was the same mess I remembered: books, papers, journals, student essays, styrofoam cups, newspapers, bits of clothing everywhere. Two computers had been added to the chaos.

I cleared away a briefcase and a pile of files from a chair and sat down. 'You were looking very pleased with yourself,' I said.

He scratched his woolly grey head. 'One of the better days at the pearl–swine interface,' he said. 'Some days I come back and headbutt the door. To what do I owe this visit?'

'Do you remember Anne Jeppeson?'

'Sure. Got run down. She was a spunk. Politically loony but a spunk.'

'Would the Special Branch have watched her?'

He put a thumb behind his top teeth, took it out. 'It's hard to say. Who says so?'

'She said something to her mother.'

'There was a lot of paranoia about the Branch. If you believed all the people who said the Branch was watching them, it wouldn't have been a branch, it would have been the whole bloody tree.'

'But it's possible?'

He shrugged. 'More than most, I suppose. She was into a whole lot of stuff the Branch would have had an interest in – Roxby Downs, Aboriginal rights in Tasmania, East Timor. You name it.'

'East Timor? The Special Branch? I thought it was only interested in local stuff?'

Barry shrugged again. 'The Branch, ASIO, ASIS, you can't separate them. They scratched each other's backs. So it's possible, yes.'

I told him what else I needed to know.

He groaned. 'Where some Branch goon was at a certain time in 1984? Jesus H. Christ, Jack, you don't have modest requests, do you? When in '84?'

I told him.

'Not long before Harker got the boot and the new government closed the Branch down.'

'That's right. There'd be records somewhere, wouldn't there?'

Barry shook his head. 'Shredded. On orders from the highest authority. All records to be destroyed.'

'So there's no record of what they were up to?'

He clapped his hands. 'Shredded,' he said. 'But not before being copied.'

'Shredded? And copied?'

'What do you expect?' said Barry. 'I think it was something the cops and the new Opposition found themselves in agreement on. Think about it. The files represent about five billion hours of coppers standing around in the rain dying to have a piss. You shred them and a couple of years later another government gets elected and wants you to start all over again, spying on the same bunch of harmless sods. They say they went through three copiers. Twenty-four hours a day for days.'

'Who's got the copy?'

'What copy? No-one's ever admitted the files were copied.'

I said, 'Barry, I'm talking life and death.'

He did another big head scratch, rolled his chair back till it hit a pile of books. The pile toppled, slithered to become a ziggurat.

'Okay,' he said. 'I can't promise you anything, though. I'll ask a man who might be able to ask another man, who might know someone.'

I stood up. 'I need to know today. It's that bad.'

Barry stood up. His eyes were level with my middle greatcoat button. He looked up at me. 'You serious?'

I nodded.

He nodded back, sadly. 'I'll go after my tutorial. You can't phone him, this bloke. Paranoid. Give me the date and the name, anything that'll help.'

'God loves you, Barry,' I said.

'There is no God and you know it. Ring me at home after five. But I can't promise anything. I don't know if they copied this kind of thing.' He paused. 'I'm only doing this because of your old man's record for Fitzroy, you know. I wouldn't do it for you.'

'I know that,' I said. 'Go Roys, make a noise.'

I found Linda at a laptop computer in a long, narrow room off the kitchen. A bench down one wall held three computers, one with a huge monitor, and two printers. The other wall was covered in corkboard, with dozens of computer-generated colour images stuck up. They seemed to be tryouts of the landscape paintings.

'Cam's woman's a computer freak,' Linda said. She was scrolling text on her screen. 'She's got enough power here to run the tax system.'

'What are you doing?'

'Tell you when I've done it.' She was tapping keys.

I went into the vast sitting room. It was 4.30 p.m. Both the fire in the fireplace and the day outside were dying. I brought in a log from the woodpile in the entrance hall, put it on the steel dogs and scraped all the embers together under it. Then I did an inspection of the premises. Apart from the sitting room, computer room and kitchen, there were two huge bedrooms, two bathrooms, and a studio the size of a pool hall. Next to the steel front door, another steel door opened on to the building's internal staircase.

When I'd done the tour, I sat down in front of the fire, put my hands in my pockets, stared into the flames and tried to work out how we could come out of hiding safely. All I could think of was to have Drew negotiate with the police. Negotiate over what, was the question. The bombing of my flat was certainly proof that I needed protection. Or was it? People had been known to boobytrap their own houses. After all, it wasn't me who was blown up. Maybe I'd set a trap for someone else.

What about the men with the sub-machine gun on the motorcycle? We hadn't reported it. We'd had the car spirited away. By now, the body was probably crushed to the size of a tea chest. Cam's friend who took it away wasn't going to jump up and testify for me.

As for Linda, what exactly was she in hiding from, they would ask? No-one had tried to kill her. She'd been burgled, that's all. Everyday occurrence.

And the Minister? The Minister wouldn't recognise my name.

It was 5.30 p.m. before Linda emerged, carrying a printout.

'Hey, let's get some light here,' she said. 'It's like a set for *Macbeth*.'

I realised with a start that the room was in deep gloom, the firelight playing on the unfinished landscapes around the walls.

Linda found a panel of switches next to the kitchen doorway. 'Fuck. Like a Boeing.' She hit several switches. Concealed lighting came on all over the room.

'That's more like it,' she said. 'Save the firelight for later. I've got something. Remember all the companies in the Yarrabank buy-up turned out to be owned by other off-shore companies?'

'Yes.'

'Well, I've been searching all the finance databases for anything on the offshore companies and one database turned up three of the companies at once. The Jersey companies. They were suspected in 1982 by the Securities Commission in Britain of warehousing shares for an Irish company that was trying to take over a British construction group.'

'I'm lost already,' I said.

'Wait. It becomes clearer. The three companies were all run from Jersey by an accountant. The securities people forced him to disclose where the money had come from to buy the shares in the construction group. It didn't come from the Irish company. It came from the company that owned the Jersey companies. This one was registered in the Cayman Islands. It's called Pericoe Holdings. That's where the story stops. The Securities Commission lost interest in the inquiry.'

She paused.

'But you didn't?' I said.

She nodded. 'I was searching a new South Pacific database at the university in Suva. Just to see what it held. And I turned up a little item from 1981 in a defunct publication called *Pacific Focus*. Just been scanned into the system. They reported that a Cayman-registered company had a shareholding in a company that wanted to set up a bank in the New Groningen Islands. And what was the Cayman company's name?'

'This is a test, isn't it? My answer is: I don't know.'

'Pericoe Holdings.'

'This is it?' I said.

She nodded. 'Pericoe was obliged under local law to disclose its shareholders.' She read from the printout. ' "Shareholders: J. Massey of Carnegie Road, Toorak, Melbourne, Australia; M. Jillings of Miller Street, Kew, Melbourne, Australia; and H. McGinty of Carnham Close, Brighton, Melbourne, Australia." '

'Do we know these people?'

Linda came over and stood in front of me. 'J. Massey is Jocelyn Massey, ex-wife of Dix Massey, Charis Corp's fixer-in-chief. M. Jillings is Maxine Jillings, wife of Keith Jillings, a major shareholder in Charis Corp. H. McGinty is Hayden McGinty, who sucks to get on the social pages and is the wife of Martin McGinty, chief executive of Marbild, a wholly-owned subsidiary of Charis Corporation.'

She flicked the printout in the direction of the coffee table and put her hands on her hips. 'This is the jackpot,' she said. 'This is it. This is the connection between Charis and the buying up of Yarrabank. It's going to take an awful lot of explaining away. And it sure as fuck ain't gonna work to say these Charis Corp girls put their spare housekeeping money into real estate.'

'You're pretty smart for a good-looking person,' I said. 'Do people tell you that?'

'Only when they want to fuck me. What about the Special Branch man?'

'I've got to phone Barry Chilvers.'

A child answered at Barry's number. A girl. Barry had obviously started on a second round of procreation, probably with a graduate student. That was the price of academic life. Inexplicably, first wives stopped being turned on by your mind.

When he came on, he said, 'Chilvers.'

I said, 'It's the man in the Collingwood beanie.'

'That's got to be cryptic enough. Hello, phone-tappers. Mate, your conjecture turns out to be correct. The female person was an object of attention.'

'And the male person?'

'Not attending on her, I'm afraid. He was keeping an eye on an East Timor activist in town for a rally. Does that make life easier?'

'Barry,' I said, 'it may make it possible. What does his log record?'

'Nothing. Uneventful. He said the man spent the evening with known friends in Scott Street, Fitzroy, then went back to his hotel. That's it.'

'The man in the Collingwood beanie thanks you very much.'

Barry said, 'Go Roys, make a noise.'

I went back into the sitting room. Linda was at the bank of windows. She turned.

I said, 'I want you to think very carefully. On the night Anne was killed, P. K. Vane of the Special Branch was keeping track of an East Timor activist visiting Melbourne.'

Linda nodded. 'That'd be Manuel Carvalho,' she said. 'He was here often. I remember now, there was talk of Anne having an affair with him at some stage.'

'Can you remember where Anne was earlier that evening?' I asked.

'With friends. In Fitzroy.'

'Sure it was Fitzroy?'

'Absolutely. Scott Street. I knew the people vaguely.' She lifted her head. I saw the shine in her eyes. 'Wait. You're going to tell me Carvalho was in Scott Street that night, aren't you?'

I gave her a double thumbs-up. I felt like someone who'd tipped a 500-1 shot for the Melbourne Cup. 'That's exactly what I'm going to tell you. I'm betting that Manuel Carvalho went back to Richmond with Anne. And that P. K. Vane, doing his duty, followed them there. And then P. K. saw something. And for some reason he kept quiet about it. He's our man. He's the one. His wife rang Danny. He's the one with the evidence.'

Linda put her head back, closed her eyes, smiled and ran her fingers through her hair.

I slumped on to the sofa, legs outstretched, flooded with elation and relief. There was hope.

Linda walked across the room. When she was standing between my legs, she reached down with both hands and began to pull up her tight black skirt, working it up slowly over her thighs. When her stocking tops and suspenders came into sight, I said, trying to speak normally, 'Since when do you wear a suspender belt?'

She wriggled her skirt up higher. She wasn't wearing panties. My eyes were level with her dense pubic bush. She put her hands on her hips and pushed her pelvis at me.

'I always wear a suspender belt,' she said, 'when I want someone to fuck me senseless on the floor in front of a fire.'

She started unbuttoning her blouse. I reached out

and put my hands around her waist. She stopped unbuttoning and pulled her skirt up over her hips.

'Now you've seen mine, Irish,' she said. 'Take off your pants and show me yours.'

How can you make love when people are trying to kill you? You can. Does perfect love drive out fear? For a while. I reflected on these matters afterwards as I lay naked, sweat beginning to chill, in front of the fire.

Linda came in wearing blue jeans and a denim shirt. 'This girl's got everything,' she said. 'Maybe I should start painting.'

I got up. I have always felt silly naked the minute the other person puts something on. I kissed her and went off to shower.

I was under the spray in the room-sized shower when Linda said from the door, 'Get a move on. I've found the champagne.'

The ex-lover's clothes did fit me. I borrowed a corduroy shirt. I was passing through the kitchen when Linda said from the computer room, 'Your glass's on the fireplace. I'm just trying the name P. K. Vane on the *Age* news database.'

It was Krug, vintage, utterly delicious, the tiniest prickles on the tongue. I felt my whole body relax.

We were going to get out of this. For the first time, I felt that.

Linda came out of the kitchen.

'There is a God,' I said. 'Where's your glass?'

She said, 'Paul Karl Vane didn't die of natural causes. He was shot dead in the driveway of his home in Beaumaris. Shot six times, four shots from close range, three of them in the head.'

Linda went to bed at 10 p.m., subdued. Finding out about Paul Vane had taken the gloss off linking Charis Corp to the Yarrabank buy-up. I sat in front of the fire, drinking a small amount of malt whisky. My bombing was the second item on the 10.30 Channel 9 news. The helicopter looked right down into my sitting room through the hole in the roof. I looked away.

The newsreader, a woman with the teeth of a much larger person, said, 'Police are tonight looking for the owner of the flat, Jack Irish, a Fitzroy lawyer. He is described as in his forties, tall, heavily built, with dark hair. He may be with another man, Cameron Delray, of no fixed address. Delray is in his thirties, tall, slim, dark hair and sallow skin. The men may be accompanied by a dark-haired woman, also tall, wearing a dark outfit. Police say the men were involved in a shooting incident earlier today and are believed to be armed. They should not be approached. Please ring the number that follows if you think you have seen these people.'

Jesus.

I felt the panic rising again. I got up and added some whisky to my glass. Now I had to get hold of Drew or we were going to meet the fate of Danny McKillop in the Trafalgar carpark.

First, my sister. She picked it up instantly. 'My God, Jack,' she said, 'what on—'

I spoke quickly. 'Rosa, listen. I'm okay. I want you to ring Claire and tell her I spoke to you and I'm fine. It's all a misunderstanding. Don't worry about the television. I've got to keep down for a bit but it's going to he okay. I'll ring you.'

'Does that mean our lunch is off?'

'Not necessarily. I'll be in touch. Love.'

I put the phone down. Lunch. I shook my head in wonder. Drew. I was putting out my hand to dial when the phone rang.

I picked it up. 'Yes,' I said, tentatively.

'Jack.' It was Cam. 'Listen, mate,' he said conversationally, 'time to go. There's blokes coming up for you. With guns. Go into the studio. There's a ladder in there, extension ladder, against the left-hand wall. You'll see a square hole in the roof in the left-hand corner, like an inspection hatch. You with me?'

'Yes,' I said. The phone was trembling in my hand.

'Get up there. You can slide the cover open, get on the roof. Pull the ladder up. First thing, go round that lift housing building up there and bolt the steel door to the stairs. Okay?'

'Okay.'

'There's no other way up there. It'll give you a bit of time. Get moving now. They're on their way up.'

The line went dead.

'What is it?' Linda was in the doorway, pillow marks on one side of her face. She'd fallen asleep fully dressed.

I tried to imitate Cam's calm. 'Put your shoes on.

Get the disks. Quickly. We've got to get out of here. Come to the studio.'

The ladder was aluminium, lightweight. I had it up against the wall beneath the hatch in the roof when Linda came in, wide-eyed, carrying a laptop and her bag.

'I'll go first,' I said. 'Get the hatch open.'

It was at least six metres to the roof. The ladder flexed alarmingly, not made for my weight.

I was halfway up when the banging started at the front door.

'Jack Irish,' a voice shouted. 'Police. We know you're home, Jack. Open the door. No-one gets hurt.'

I put one hand up and found a handle on the hatch cover. I tugged it. It didn't move. The hatch cover wouldn't open.

Something hard hit the front door. They were trying to break in.

The ladder was flexing alarmingly. I braced myself and got both hands to the handle.

I tugged. It wouldn't budge.

There was a louder impact from the front door.

I tried again. I moved the handle from side to side, desperately. It shifted.

I tried again. Backwards, forwards. It moved. I'd been forcing it in the wrong direction. I pushed the handle away from me and the hatch slid open. I grabbed the edge of the hole and pulled myself up the last steps and out on to the roof.

By the time I'd turned back to the hole, Linda was half-way up the ladder. When she was near enough, I leant down and took her bag and the laptop. Then I pulled her up.

The ladder came up easily. We stood panting on the concrete roof in the dark, cold night air.

'Close it,' Linda said, pointing at the hatch. As I bent down to slide the door over, there were four sharp sounds from below. Gunshots. They were trying to shoot open the lock on the front door.

I slid the hatch closed and stood up.

What was I supposed to do now?

The roof door to the internal stairs.

I looked around. About ten metres away I could make out a large, square structure. The lift housing.

'Wait here,' I said and ran. The roof was slippery, some kind of moss growing on the concrete. At the corner of the housing, I fell, sliding across the rough surface. I got up, sharp pain in the left knee. The door was a few metres away, open. I got to it, closed it and felt for the bolt.

There wasn't a bolt. The door couldn't be locked.

I opened it slowly, stuck my head in and listened.

Silence. The men weren't at the front door any more. They were in the flat. There was nowhere to hide there. They would very quickly know we had got out.

I closed the door again and looked at it, felt it. Nothing on the surface of the door.

My fingers touched something on the door frame to my left. I felt to the right of the door. The same. Steel brackets.

The door was meant to be barred, not bolted.

Where was the bar? I felt around frantically, seeing better now, eyes getting used to the dark. No bar.

I looked around the roof. Away to my left, there was something moving.

I squinted, trying to see better.

Washing. Someone had hung a line of washing on the roof. Hung the line between what? I limped over. Two lengths of one-inch pipe with welded crossbars held up the washing line.

I went over to one, put both hands around it and pulled with all my force. It came out so easily that I fell over backwards, pipe clutched to my chest. Scrambling to my feet, I wrenched off the washing line and ran for the door, pipe at the port arms.

I was a few metres from the door when someone in the stairwell shouted something. I could only catch the word 'stairs'.

I got to the door. I could hear footsteps thudding metres away.

The door wouldn't close fully.

I stood back and kicked the door so hard I felt the impact in my wrists and at the top of my skull.

The door closed.

I stepped back, winded.

Something hit the door like a sledgehammer. It swung open and a man – short, bald – came through, left shoulder first, right arm coming around with a long-barrelled revolver held shoulder-high.

He was so close I could smell his breath: alcohol and garlic.

I brought the steel pipe I was holding around with all the force I had. It only had to travel about half a metre before it made contact with the side of the man's head.

He went over sideways, hitting the doorframe with his right shoulder and falling back into the stairwell.

I dropped the pipe, slammed the door shut again and rammed the pipe though the brackets.

When I turned, Linda was behind me.

'Jesus Christ,' she said. 'Come on. Cam's on the roof next door.'

For a moment, I was too winded to move. Then I staggered after her. When we got to the parapet wall to the left of the roof hatch, I saw Cam.

He was on the roof of the building across the lane, sitting on the parapet wall, smoking a cigarette. Next to him on the wall were Linda's laptop and bag. She must have thrown them to him.

'G'day,' he said. 'Shove that ladder over.'

I looked over the edge of our wall. Six floors below, light was reflected off wet cobblestones. I looked over at Cam. His building was about four or five metres higher than ours. The gap between us was about the same.

I went over and got the ladder. It seemed terribly flimsy. I got it upright and leaned it over until Cam could catch the top rung. He pulled it up until he could hold the sides standing up.

'Ladies first,' he said.

I looked at Linda. She smiled, a tight little smile. 'We used to do this at Girl Guides,' she said. 'Piece of cake.'

She scrambled across in seconds.

My turn. My knee was aching. I'd grazed my hip. I was having trouble breathing. I felt a hundred years old.

'I was happier doing conveyancing,' I said to no-one in particular.

Then I went across that inadequate bridge like a big monkey.

Cam had a ute this time, a battered Ford with a lashed-down tarpaulin over the tray. It was parked in a narrow blind lane off Little Bourke Street.

'What's the next stop?' he asked.

We were all leaning on parts of the ute, trying to control our breathing.

'Shoreham,' said Linda and caught her breath. 'On the Mornington Peninsula. I know a place there. It'll be empty.'

Cam straightened up. 'Country air,' he said. 'Let's go.' He started loosening the tray cover. When he had the back open, he looked at me and said, 'They're looking for two blokes, mate. Hop in.'

'In the back?'

'There's a mattress. And pillows. Lots of air gets in. You can have a kip.'

I climbed in and lay down. Cam lashed the cover down. It was pitch-black under the cover, dark and claustrophobic and smelling of engine oil. I had to fight the urge to try and break out.

We were reversing over cobblestones. The springs transmitted every bump. I found a pillow, dragged it under my head, closed my eyes and tried to think about sharpening the blade of a number 7 plane. I was trying to learn how to grind a hollow angle and then hone the blade on that angle with a circular motion the way the Japanese did. I was thinking about how to improve my honing action when I fell asleep.

I woke with a start, no idea where I was, tried to sit up, bounced off the taut nylon tray cover, fell back in fright.

Cam's voice said, 'Nice place. They'd have something to drink here, would they?'

I knew where I was. How had I managed to fall asleep? I lay still and listened to my heartbeat while Cam loosened the cover.

'Breathing?' he said. 'Relaxed?'

Inside ten minutes we were drinking whisky in front of a fire in the stone hearth of what seemed to be an enormous mudbrick and timber house. I went outside and stood on the terrace. There was a vineyard running away from the house.

I went back inside. Cam was on his haunches, fiddling with the fire.

'Were they cops?' I asked. I felt wide-awake. I'd slept for more than two hours.

'Moved like cops,' said Cam. 'Very efficient. I gather you decked one.'

'Tony Baker he calls himself,' I said. 'Came to the pub to scare me off. Made out he was a fed of some kind.'

'If he's a dead fed,' Cam said, 'we have other problems.' He stood up and yawned. 'That's enough Monday now. I'll find a bed.'

I looked at Linda. She was asleep, head fallen onto the arm of the sofa, hair fallen over her face. In the end, perfect exhaustion drives out fear.

'I'll just sit here,' I said. 'Reflect on how I got everybody into this shit.'

'That's the past,' Cam said. 'Think about the future. How to get everybody out of this shit.'

After a while, I got up and found a blanket to put over Linda. She didn't wake up when I swung her legs onto the sofa and arranged a pillow under her head.

I kissed her on the cheek, got some whisky, put some more wood on the fire. The future. But we weren't finished with the past yet. What had Paul Vane seen on the night Anne Jeppeson died? What was the evidence he knew about? And what was the evidence Father Gorman had told Ronnie to bring to Melbourne and where was it?

Time passed. I fed the fire, listened to the night sounds. It was after three before I felt tired enough to find a bed. Sleep eventually came.

Sunlight on my face woke me. It was after 9 a.m. My knee was stiff and sore and the skin around my hip was tender. I felt dirty. Looking for a shower, I went into the kitchen. Cam was sitting at the table, eating toast and jam, clean, hair slicked back.

He pointed with his thumb over his shoulder. I went that way. Linda was sitting at a big desk, looking at her laptop screen. She looked clean too.

'Does that thing work anywhere?' I said.

She looked up and smiled. 'I've written the whole fucking thing. All of it. The whole Yarrabank saga. And I'm plugged in to the world again. Through my trusty modem.'

I said, 'Modem's not a word you can love.'

She tapped the computer screen. 'There's a P. K. Vane in Breamlea,' she said. 'Must have moved from Beaumaris. We can take the car ferry.'

There wasn't a single thing to lose.

'I'll have a shower,' I said. 'See if you can find the departure times.'

The woman was tall and thin and her labrador was old and fat. She was wearing a big yellow sou'wester that ended at her knees. Her legs were bare and she was barefoot.

There was no-one else on the beach. Just Linda and I and the woman and the dog and the gulls. We saw her a long way off, walking on the hard wet sand, hands in pockets, head down, getting her feet wet when the tiny waves ran in. The dog walked up on the dry sand, stiff-legged, stopping every few yards for a hopeful inspection of something delivered by the tide.

When she was about a hundred metres away, I got up and went towards her. The labrador came out to meet me, friendly but watchful. I stopped and offered him my hand. He came over, nosed it, allowed me to rub his head.

When she was close enough to hear me, I said, 'Mrs Vane?'

She nodded. She had strong bones in her face, big streaks of grey in her hair, skin seen too much sun.

'Are you the widow of Paul Karl Vane of the Victoria Police?'

She nodded again, still walking.

'Mrs Vane, I'd like to talk to you about your husband and the deaths of Anne Jeppeson and Danny McKillop.'

She kept looking at me and didn't say anything until she was close, three or four metres away. The dog went to her.

She leant down and rubbed its head, eyes still on me. Her eyes were startlingly blue.

'I was hoping someone would come,' she said. 'I don't think I've had one happy day since they killed that girl.'

She put out a hand and I took it. We walked up the beach.

The shack was up in the hills behind Apollo Bay. We got lost once, retraced our route, found where we'd gone wrong. Cam was driving, the three of us crammed onto the bench seat, Linda in the middle.

On the way from Breamlea, keeping to the back roads, Cam said, 'How come she doesn't know what it is?'

'Paul Vane never told her,' I said. 'He woke her up on the night Anne was killed and told her he'd seen it happen. He was electric, sat drinking all night. The next day, when the television had the news of Danny's arrest, he told her Danny hadn't done it, that it was murder, that he knew who'd done it but couldn't tell anyone.'

'So she kept quiet too,' said Cam.

I moved my cramped arm from behind Linda's head. 'She says it haunted her. When she read about Danny's sentence, she was sick. Paul became morose, drank more, used to say he'd done the wrong thing but it was too late. Eventually he took early retirement. Then he got sick, bowel cancer. He kept telling her he was going to give her the evidence, that he was going to get a lot of money to provide for her after he was gone, that she should tell Danny that he was innocent and give him the evidence.'

'Money?' asked Cam. 'Did he get it?'

I shook my head. 'No. She thinks he tried to black-mail someone over Danny's death and that's why he was murdered. He told her where the evidence was the morning of the day he was shot.'

'And then she rang Danny?'

'Later. After Paul's murder, the house was broken into and searched from top to bottom. Then Paul's boat caught fire at its moorings at Sandringham and blew up. She says she was too scared to fetch the evidence. And then she was watching television and saw the news that Danny'd been shot. After that, there didn't seem to be any point.'

'That must be it up ahead,' Linda said. She'd fallen asleep a few times on the trip, head lolling on to my shoulder.

The shack was old, just a big room and a lean-to, probably a timber-getter's humble home. It was made of timber slabs, weathered to a light grey, but still solid. The whole place was leaning slightly, held up by a huge brick chimney.

We got out, stretching stiff limbs. The air was cold and moist. Far away, we could hear a vehicle changing gear on a hill, then silence. The birds were quiet at this time of day.

The front door was padlocked, no more than a gesture considering the condition of the door and its frame. I opened the lock with the key Judith Vane had given me.

Inside it was dark, almost no light coming through the dirty panes of the two small windows. To my right was the fireplace, a huge red brick structure, the front blackened almost to the roof by thousands of fires.

You couldn't light a fire in it now. The opening, about the size of two fridges side by side, had been closed in with fibreboard. Some kind of wooden frame had been built in the opening and the fibreboard nailed to it. This work was recent compared to the age of the shack.

'It's in there,' I said, pointing at the chimney.

'There's a crowbar in the ute,' Cam said. He went out to fetch it.

Linda and I looked at each other.

'So, Jack Irish,' she said. 'This is it.'

I nodded.

Cam was in the doorway, a weary little smile on his face. He didn't have the crowbar.

'No crowbar?' I said.

He took a step into the room.

There was a man behind him holding a pump-action shotgun. It was Tony Baker, with a big plaster on the side of his face where I'd hit him with the steel pipe.

'Move along, coon,' he said.

Cam came into the room. Baker came in too, a safe distance behind Cam. He'd done this kind of thing before.

Another man, in an expensive camelhair overcoat, came into the doorway. He was tall, somewhere beyond fifty, that was the only safe guess: full head of close-cropped silver hair, narrow tanned face with a strong jaw and deep lines down from a nose that had seen contact. He had a young man's full, slightly contemptuous mouth. In one hand, he held a short-barrelled .38. In the other, he had the crowbar.

'Jack Irish,' he said. 'I'm Martin Scullin. You're a fucking pain in the arse.' His voice was as flat and his diction as slow as Barry Tregear's. Country boys both, grown old in the city. Or maybe it was the standard issue voice in the old Consorting Squad.

'I've heard a lot about you,' I said. To my surprise, my voice sounded normal.

'Where's the stuff?' Scullin said. He didn't sound particularly interested.

'I don't know. We're just looking.'

Scullin looked at Tony Baker, no expression on his face.

Baker clubbed Cam across the jaw with the shotgun barrel. Cam went down like a suit slipping off a clothes hanger. He fell to his knees, tried to stand up.

Baker stepped over and hit him in the face with the barrel again. Twice.

Blood spurted out of Cam's nose, turning his shirt black.

Baker turned his bull-terrier head and looked at me. Even in that light, I could see the gold fleck in his eye.

'I'm going to kill this coon,' he said. 'Then I'm going to kill that bitch.'

He kicked Cam in the ribs, a short, stabbing movement, full of power. Cam shook his head like a swimmer trying to clear water from his ears.

Baker kicked him again, harder. Cam put his hands on the floor, got into a sitting position, looked up, eyes closed. His mouth was wide open, a cave streaming blood.

Baker hit him under the jaw with an upward movement of the shotgun butt. Cam fell over sideways.

Baker stepped back, readying himself to kick.

'Leave him,' I said. 'It's in the chimney.'

Baker looked at Scullin.

Scullin said to me, 'Get it.'

Baker pointed the shotgun at me. Scullin passed me the crowbar.

I looked at Linda. She was kneeling next to Cam, holding his head, blood all over her arms.

The fireplace cover came off easily, nails squeaking. In the fireplace was an old stove, a Dover, filthy with soot, stovepipe rusted.

'Get up there,' Scullin said.

There wasn't room for me and the stovepipe. I took it in both hands and worked it loose. It came off and fell behind the stove with a crash. I got on the stove awkwardly, kneeling, bent over, and looked up the chimney. Soot fell on my face. Dark. I couldn't see anything.

'Get up there,' Scullin said again.

I pressed my hands against the chimney sides, got on one leg, then the other. I was in the chimney from below my waist up.

I put my hands up and began to feel around.

Nothing. Just flaking soot. I reached higher. A ledge. The chimney had a jink.

My fingertips touched something. Smooth. Cold. I felt sideways, found an edge.

A box. A metal box. Felt up. A projection. The lid. Ran my fingers left and right.

'What the fuck you doing up there?' Scullin said. 'Is it there or what?'

There was something on top of the box.

'It's here,' I said. 'It's here.'

I bent my knees slowly, got the right one on the stove, turned my body to the left, arms above my head.

'Get a fucking move on,' Scullin said.

I ducked down, came out of the chimney, soot falling like a curtain, bringing my right arm down and around my body.

'Here,' Scullin said, 'give it to me.'

He was just a metre away.

I shot him in the chest, high, right under the collar-bone. He went over backwards.

Baker was looking at me, a little smile on his face.

I shot him in the stomach. He frowned and looked down at himself.

I got off the stove and shot Scullin again, in the chest.

Baker was bringing up his shotgun, slowly. He was looking at the floor.

'Steady on, Jack,' he said thickly, like a very drunk man.

I shot him again, in the chest. The impact knocked him up against the wall. Then he fell over sideways.

'Stop now,' Cam said. 'I think they understand.'

We were going through Royal Park, Linda driving Scullin's dove-grey Audi, Cam in the back, strapped up and stitched and plastered by the doctor in Geelong. I came out of my reverie. No-one had said anything for eighty kilometres.

Something flat, that's all. Ronnie's friend Charles's words. Ronnie had brought something small and flat to Melbourne.

'Ronnie's evidence,' I said.

Linda glanced at me. 'What?'

'I know where Ronnie's evidence is,' I said.

I gave her directions.

Mrs Bishop took a long time to open her door.

'Mr Irish,' she said. 'How nice to see you.' She inspected me. 'Have you been in mud?'

'Doing a dirty job,' I said. 'Should have changed. Can I come in if I don't touch anything?'

We went down the passage and into the sitting room. I looked around. On a bookshelf between the french doors was a small stereo outfit, no bigger than a stack of three Concise Oxfords. On top was the CD player.

The CDs, a modest collection, perhaps twenty, were on the shelf above in a plastic tray.

'Mrs Bishop,' I said. 'I wanted to come around and say how sorry I am about Ronnie. But I had to go away.'

She nodded, looked away, sniffed. 'Both my men,' she said. 'Both gone.'

I wanted to pat her but my hand was too dirty. I waited a while, then I said, 'You told me Ronnie put a new CD with your others.'

She cheered up. 'That's right. It's Mantovani's greatest hits.'

'Have you played it?' I said, and I held my breath.

She put out a hand and found a cleanish place to touch my arm. 'I haven't been able to bring myself to,' she said. 'It's the last thing Ronnie gave me.'

'Do you think we could put it on for a little listen? It might help me.'

Her look said that she thought all was not well with my thinking processes, but she switched the player on, found the CD in the tray and, holding it like a circle of spiderweb, put it in the drawer.

She pressed Play. The drawer slid in.

We waited.

The silken strings of Mantovani filled the room.

I expelled my breath loudly.

'Thank you, Mrs Bishop,' I said. 'I don't think it's going to help me after all.'

Her eyes were closed and she was moving her head with the music.

I got into the car and slammed the door. 'I don't know where Ronnie's evidence is,' I said. 'Shit.'

Cam started the motor. 'Let's think about a drink,' he said.

Doug always said Ronnie would make a good spy.

'Hang on,' I said. 'One more try.'

This time, Mrs Bishop opened her door in seconds.

'Sorry to be a nuisance,' I said.

'Not at all, Mr Irish.'

'Did you live in this house when Ronnie was a boy?'

She smiled. 'Oh yes. We've always had this house. It was Doug's mother's. Doug grew up here, too. I wanted to sell it when we went to Queensland, but Doug wouldn't have a bar of it. He was a very wise person, wasn't he.'

'Very. Mrs Bishop, did Ronnie have any special place in the house? A secret place?'

'Secret? Well, just the roof cubby. But that wasn't a secret.'

'The roof cubby?'

'Yes. It's a little hidey-hole in the roof. Doug's father made it for him when he was a boy.'

'Ronnie didn't by any chance go up there?'

She frowned. 'To the roof cubby? Why would he do that?'

'He didn't?'

'Well, I don't know. I wasn't here all the time, but—'

'Could I have a look at it?'

She didn't reply for a moment. Her eyes said she was now reasonably certain that I was deranged. Then she said, 'Are you any good at climbing trees, Mr Irish?'

The entrance to the roof cubby was the ventilation louvre in the back gable of the house. It was about six metres from the ground, brushed by the thick, bare branches of an ancient walnut.

I considered calling for Cam. But pride is a terrible thing.

'You wouldn't have a ladder?' I said.

Mrs Bishop shook her head. 'That's how you get up there. The tree.'

I took hold of the lowest branch of the tree. There was moss on it. I groaned.

It took five minutes to get up there. I almost fell out of the tree twice and a branch poked me in the groin before I got close enough to the small door to put out a hand and push it. It resisted. I put out a foot and pushed.

The door opened with a squeak, swinging inwards and pulling in a short length of nylon rope attached to a ringbolt in the bottom of the door. I puzzled over this for a moment before I realised that this was how you closed the door from the outside: you pulled the rope.

I clambered across from my branch, got my head and shoulders and one arm in and pulled myself across.

The floor of the hideaway was below the level of the doorway. I lowered myself tentatively into the gloom. About a metre down, my feet touched the floor. For a while I couldn't see anything, then gradually I made out the corners of the room. Light came from the door, now a window, from gaps between the bargeboards and the roof. It was a little box, perhaps three metres square, with a pitched ceiling, boarded off from the rest of the ceiling of the house. The floor was covered with flower-patterned linoleum.

It was empty.

Not even cobwebs.

Nowhere to hide anything.

There was no sign that anyone had ever used the room, had ever had a secret life up here.

I groaned again. Going down would be even harder than coming up.

I squeezed my upper body through the entrance, reached out and got a grip on a branch above my head. I pulled myself up to it, getting a knee on the sill, then standing up. As I did so, the jagged end of a short dead branch almost took out my left eye.

I pulled my head back.

The tip of the branch was just inches away. It was bone white, except for odd grey marks, almost like fingerprints, on the underside.

I wanted to put a bandaid on the scratch on his cheek but he didn't want me to.

That's what Mrs Bishop had said when we first talked about Ronnie's disappearance.

Ronnie had been here.

Standing just where I was standing. A scratch on his cheek bleeding.

Ronnie had scratched his cheek on the branch. He had put his left hand to his cheek and it had come away with blood on it. In anger, he had grabbed the branch and tried to break it.

But it wouldn't break. And he left his blood on it, dark marks now weathered to grey.

'Are you all right, Mr Irish?'

Mrs Bishop was looking up at me, eyes wide.

'I'm fine,' I said. 'I'll be down in a minute.'

I scrambled back through the small door.

Somewhere in here. Somewhere in this empty room was Ronnie's evidence.

I went around the walls carefully, feeling for a loose board, a door to a hiding place. It took about five minutes.

Nothing.

The floor. Perhaps there was a gap between the floor and the ceiling below. I knelt down and tried to lift the nearest corner of the linoleum.

It wouldn't come up. It was held down by tacks, one every few centimetres.

I went all round the lino edge under the doorway, trying to lift it with my nails. It was tacked down tight. Along the right-hand wall, it was the same.

In the right-hand corner, a small piece came up.

I tugged at it.

It was just one broken tack. The rest held.

Along the back wall, all hope gone, feeling the regular line of tackheads.

The tacks stopped.

I ran my fingertips into the corner, perhaps thirty centimetres away.

No tacks.

I ran them down the left-hand wall.

No tacks for the first thirty centimetres.

I felt in the dark corner. The lino curled back slightly. I pulled at it. A triangular piece peeled back stiffly. I felt beneath it with my right hand.

There was a small trapdoor, perhaps twenty centimetres by fifteen.

I pulled it up with my nails. It came away easily.

I put my hand into the cavity.

There was a box, a long narrow box, shallow, lidded.

I got my hand under it and took it out of the cavity. It was a nice box, pearwood perhaps, the kind that used to hold the accessories for sewing machines.

I got up and went to the entrance, to the light.

The lid had a small catch.

I opened it.

Cam's girlfriend's flat was the way we'd left it, apart from the battered front door. My malt whisky was still standing next to the telephone in the kitchen.

Cam was in the Barcelona chair, holding himself upright, drinking Cascade out of the bottle again. I was on the sofa, drinking nothing, nervous. Linda was at Channel 7.

'They'll run it you reckon?' asked Cam.

'Depends what's on Vane's film.'

We sat in silence in the gloom. After a while, I got up and drank some water. Cam finished his beer, got up painfully to get another one out of the fridge. When he came back, he said, 'That shooting today. Made me think of my German.'

'Your German?'

'Last bloke who shot at me. Before...when was it? Yesterday.' He lit a Gitane. 'Gary Hoffmeister. We were shooting roos out to buggery, out there in the Grey Range. I only met him the day before we went. Off his head. Had a whole trunk of guns. Rifles, handguns, shotguns. Never stopped shooting, shoot anything, trees, stones, anything. He was full of Nazi shit, too.

Kept asking me about my name, how come I was this colour. I just said, I'm a tanned Australian, mate. I thought, you'll keep. Wait till we're out of here.'

Cam drank some beer.

'Last night out,' he said, 'Gary was off his face, talking about Anglo-Saxon purity, Hitler was right, the coming Indonesian invasion. I went to take a piss round the back of the cooltruck. Came round the corner, .38 slug hits the truck next to my head. Into reverse, got to the cab to get my rifle, he fires about five shots, trying to hit me right through the driver's door.'

He appeared to lose interest in the story.

'What happened?' I said.

'Got the iron, off into the scrub. Took about half an hour to get a clear shot at the bastard. He was trying to stalk me like Rambo. I put him in with the roos, took him to the cops in Charleville. He was nice and cold. They knew fucking Gary there, handshakes all round, good bloody riddance.'

'They charge you?'

'Had to. Court found I acted in self-defence. Had to come back from WA. Took a little trip back to the scene while I was there. Near there, anyway.'

'What for?'

Cam smiled his rare smile. 'Dig up the ten grand Gary had in his gun crate. And that Ruger. No point in giving that kind of stuff to the cops. Spoils 'em.'

The phone rang. It was 6.25 p.m.

I went into the kitchen and picked it up.

'Put on the TV,' Linda said. 'Seven at six-thirty.'

I went back to the sitting room and switched on the set.

'Something's on,' I said. 'Six-thirty.'

The ads went on forever. We sat in silence.

The current affairs show began with its montage of news footage: bombs, riots, politicians talking.

Then the serious young woman came on, dark top, little scarf, air of barely controlled excitement.

'Tonight,' she said, 'this programme deals with allegations about the involvement of a Cabinet Minister, public servants, a clergyman, trade union leaders and others in an under-age sex ring. It also alleges police involvement in the death in 1984 of a social justice activist, and massive corruption surrounding Charis Corporation's six hundred million dollar Yarra Cove development.'

She paused.

'These are serious and dramatic allegations. And we believe they are fully substantiated.'

Another pause.

'First,' she said, 'we show you, exclusively, shocking photographs taken by a Special Branch detective on the night in 1984 when social justice activist Anne Jeppeson met her death.'

First, we saw some old footage of Anne Jeppeson leading a Save Hoagland march and answering questions at a news conference. A male voice-over gave a quick history of the Hoagland closure.

Then the woman said, 'On the night of 18 June 1984, Anne Jeppeson was leaving her terrace house in Ardenne Street, Richmond, at 11.40 p.m. Unbeknown to her a Special Branch officer, Paul Karl Vane, was watching her house from a vehicle parked across the street. He had a camera and began taking pictures as she left the house.'

I held my breath.

The first photograph came on, startlingly clear. It showed Anne Jeppeson, in a leather jacket and jeans, coming out of the front door of a terrace house. Her head was turned back, as if she was speaking to someone. It must have been Manuel Carvalho.

The next picture showed Anne stepping off the kerb. She was looking to her right, not alarmed.

The next one showed her almost in the middle of the road, still looking right. Now her mouth was open, her right hand was coming up, the whites of her eyes showing.

Then the camera turned its attention to where she was looking. The picture showed a car, a Kingswood, two figures in the front seat, faces just white blurs.

There was another shot, the car closer, the faces clearer.

In the next picture, Anne Jeppeson was lifted off the ground, top half of her body on the bonnet of the Kingswood, the lower half in the air.

Now you could see the faces of the driver and the passenger clearly.

The driver was Garth Bruce, Minister for Police. Younger but unmistakably Garth Bruce.

The passenger was Martin Scullin, now lying dead on the floor in the shack in the Otways.

'We have every reason to believe,' the presenter said, 'that the driver of the vehicle seen colliding with Anne Jeppeson is Garth Bruce, now Minister for Police, and that the passenger is Martin Scullin, then a Drug Squad detective and now owner of a security company, AdvanceGuard Security, the company started by Garth Bruce after leaving the Victoria police.'

Cam made a sound of triumph that could have been heard by low-flying aircraft.

Then they got on to Ronnie Bishop's videos, the ones I had found in the nice sewing machine box under the floor of the roof cubbyhouse. They did their fuzzy pixels to prevent us seeing exactly what was happening but it very clearly involved sexual acts with young people of both sexes who couldn't be said to be willing partners.

They did show us the faces of the adults.

Lance Pitman, Minister for Planning, was there.

Father Rafael Gorman was there.

So was a man the presenter identified as the late Malcolm Bleek, once the highest ranking public servant in the Planning Department.

Then there were two leaders of the trade union movement, a prominent financial entrepreneur now living abroad, and other men the presenter didn't identify. Someone would recognise them. Wives. Children. Colleagues.

There were a lot of close-ups. Ronnie had made sure everyone was identifiable.

'These shocking films,' the presenter said, 'are believed to have been taken by Ronald Bishop, an employee of the Safe Hands Foundation, an organisation founded by Father Rafael Gorman to help homeless young people. It is likely that the films were used to blackmail Mr Lance Pitman and others seen in them. It appears likely that Bishop kept a copy of the films, perhaps as some form of insurance.'

Then Linda came on, poised and professional, and told the full story of Yarrabank and Hoagland. Names, dates, everything. How Anne Jeppeson came close to torpedoing the whole thing and was murdered for it. How Detective-Sergeant Scullin probably provided the helpless Danny McKillop to take the rap and how Father Gorman probably provided Ronnie Bishop to seal Danny's fate.

The whole thing took half an hour. Much of the detail was conjecture, but it made a powerful case. When it was over, Cam got up, flexed his shoulders gingerly, and said, 'Shocking. Could undermine faith in grown-up people. There's some Krug around here. What about you?'

I looked at him and said, 'Give me a beer mug full to start.'

There is ice in the wind at Caulfield on a Saturday in late autumn. Long-legged Cynthia the head Commissioner and Cyril Wootton were both dressed for it: tweedy, scarves.

At 2.50 p.m., I was looking at Nancy Farmer, Tony Ericson, and Dakota Dreaming, aka Slim, in the mounting yard. Nancy was fidgety, patting the horse, tugging at her silks, pushing strands of hair into her cap. Tony was worse. He had the air of a man waiting for the jury to come back. But the horse was calm enough for the three of them. He looked at the ground mostly, like someone who knows about waiting.

Tony's children were at the rail, popeyed with excitement. The girl had been neglecting her grooming. Dakota didn't look as lustrous as when I'd last seen him. It was worth trying, but it wasn't going to fool anyone. The horse was right: rippling, tight behind the saddle, poverty lines on the rump.

The man next to me was looking at Dakota too.

'Nothin wrong with that bugger you can see,' he said, pointing at the horse with his rolled up copy of the *Herald Sun*. 'Shockin history though.'

'Shocking,' I said. Ron Pevsner in the *Age* thought so too. He assessed Dakota's price at 50-1. That was about tops for Ron. His colleague Bart Grantley rated the horse at two out of ten. No-one knew what a horse had to do to get a rating of one. Die in its previous race, perhaps. The form comment was: 'Comeback race. Lightly raced but injury prone and seems fully tested. Hard to have.' All the other form guides said much the same. The Wizard assessed his odds at 100-1 and said: 'Must improve.' It would be hard to argue with this daring judgment.

I'd driven Harry to the track. Cam was in Sydney, handling the plunge on the interstate ring at Randwick.

Harry was in a philosophical mood. 'Jack,' he said, 'pullin off a coup's a bit of a miracle, y'know. I've had a coup horse run last. Stone motherless last. Goodbye seventy grand.' He smiled. 'There's a number of worries. The horse, the weight, the jockey, the barrier draw, the track. Any one can sink you. And then there's another tiny matter. Today, thirteen other bloody cattle. Some of 'em even trying to win.'

Before we parted, he said, 'Lunch money in your pocket?'

I nodded.

He said, 'Jack, somethin extra I want you to do. Occurred to me.'

At 2.45 p.m., I went over to where Wootton was reading his race book. He looked every inch the bank manager at his leisure.

'Well, Cyril,' I said, 'I've been thinking about another one of your commissioners. Eddie Dollery. I hope your Cynthia doesn't have a taste for rooting men wearing uniforms and crotchless underwear.'

I gave him the small white card. He took it with the

lack of enthusiasm of a man being offered a business card by an encyclopedia salesman.

He turned it over and read: 'Six nine.' He looked at me for confirmation.

I nodded. 'Six nine.'

Then I gave him Harry's last-minute instruction. Cyril didn't blink, put his race book into a side pocket of his jacket and walked off. Cynthia was talking to a tall man with the hair of the young Elvis Presley and the face of peatbog man. She saw Wootton coming, cocked her head and said something.

Wootton walked straight up to her, gave her the card, said two words.

Cynthia said two words back, looked at Elvis Peatbog, walked off briskly.

Dakota Dreaming opened at 50-1. The favourite, Shining Officer, was at 4-1. The second favourite, Steel Beach, was 6-1.

I approached a bookmaker called Mark Whitecross, a large man, sour, a reputation for staying well ahead of the punters. Harry saw Mark as a challenge.

'I'll have $12,000 to $2000 on number four,' I said.

Number four was Steel Beach.

Whitecross looked at me without interest. It went into the computer.

When I had the ticket, I said, 'I'll have another twelve to two on number four.'

This time, Whitecross pushed out his cheek with his tongue.

I put the ticket in my top pocket and said, 'Twenty-four thousand to four thousand. Please.'

No interest. I got it. Then I said, 'Same again.'

Whitecross's offsider said something in his ear. He leaned forward to look across at another bookie. I looked too. Cyril Wootton was there. The bookie had just shortened Steel Beach to 2-1.

'It's 12 to 6 now,' said Whitecross.

Between us, Cyril and I pulled Steel Beach down to 9-4 before we stopped.

We also pushed Dakota out to 100-1, which was when Cynthia, Elvis Peatbog and the others went into action.

The 100s dropped to 66s. They shrank to 33s. Then the word came through from Randwick. Cam had struck. The price went to 20s, 14s, 7s. When Dakota and Nancy Farmer set out for the starting gate, the price was 9-4 and nobody was taking very much.

Wootton drifted over. 'Mission accomplished,' he said, your World War II RAF squadron leader back from holding off Jerry above the fields of Devon.

'Part one,' I said. 'Part one.'

'Tremendous interest in this race,' the race caller boomed. 'A big plunge on number ten, Dakota Dreaming. Very big plunge. Interstate too. Hammered in from 100-1 to 9-4. Not often you see that. Lots of excitement. A three-State plunge. Someone must think they know more than the form shows. If this horse gets up, there'll be a lot of bookies stopping off at the teller machines on the way home to get some Sunday collection money. Surprise of the century some would say. Longer than that. Lazarus gets gold in the marathon. This horse hasn't seen the track for two years and didn't exactly go out in a blaze of glory then. Money too for Steel

314

Beach in the early stages and it tightened for a while. Then the Dakota Dreaming avalanche hit the books.'

He went on like this until they were ready to go.

The interval between the time the light on the starting gate began flashing and the instant the horses lunged needed a calendar to measure.

Nancy Farmer missed the start. Badly. They were all on the way before Dakota Dreaming. That wasn't in the plan.

Dakota was coming out of barrier 10, which was not good news at Caulfield. Harry's instructions to Nancy were to get across onto the rails as quickly as possible.

'You don't need a Rhodes Scholar to tell you that,' he'd said to Nancy the night before, after we'd watched videos of all the main contenders racing. And a few Caulfield Cups for good measure. 'There's a heap of good horses never won from a wide gate at Caulfield.'

We'd watched videos of two of Steel Beach's races. 'Not much class,' Harry said, 'but he's the danger. One-pace stayer. Genuine stayer. If he gets the drop on you, out in front, settin the pace, in his stride, I don't know if you can catch him. Even five kilos to the better. Might be too big an ask for this fella Dakota. Too big for this Shining Officer, that's for sure.'

Six hundred metres from the start, Nancy found a gap and got onto the fence. Just in time. The long curve began after the first chute and to be trapped wide then meant covering many more metres than the rails horses.

The caller said, 'At the eighteen hundred, Steel

Beach's drawing away from Sir Haliberd, who's weakening, Shining Officer's coming up on the rails.' He rattled off a string of names before he got to Dakota Dreaming.

She was fourth or fifth last. This wasn't good.

I got my glasses on the field and picked out Nancy's black, white and green hoops. She had several horses outside her and a slowing one in front. I could see her looking around. Desperately.

At the 1200, the caller said, 'I don't know what the rest can do here. Bit of a procession. Steel Beach's looking good, Sir Haliberd's gone, Shining Officer's hanging on, third is Celeste's Bazaar, followed by Fear or Favour. Gap to Fashion Victim. Well back is the plunge horse, Dakota Dreaming. Deep sighs of relief from the books at this stage, I suggest.'

I had my glasses on Nancy. She was at least fifty metres behind Steel Beach, in a pocket and looking for a way out. A bad mistake had been made, I thought. I loved the Sisley drawings. Isabel had loved them. I'd hoped to give them to Claire one day. Now I'd lost them and $25,000.

I lowered the glasses and looked around. Harry was two rows back, a dozen metres along, anonymous-looking as usual. He had his glasses up.

The caller said, 'Signs of life from the plunge horse here. Farmer's taken her out wide at the turn. Don't know about that. And it could be too late now. It's eight hundred to go.'

Nancy had come off the rails, gone between two horses and moved Dakota wide, out towards the middle of the track. It was an act of desperation.

There were six horses between her and Steel Beach, strung out. The leader was fully extended, comfortable, ready to run all day. His jockey turned for a look. Nothing to alarm him.

Nancy was on Dakota's neck. They went up to horses number seven and six in what seemed like a dozen strides.

Then it was five's turn to be swept away. Next was Shining Officer. He appeared to lose heart, running out of pedigree, carrying five kilograms more weight than Dakota.

It was Celeste's Bazaar's turn. The horses ran stride for stride.

'Two-fifty to go,' shouted the caller. 'Celeste's Bazaar's gone. It's Steel Beach and Dakota Dreaming. Unbelievable. Come from near-last to challenge. They're at the two hundred. What a race. The plunge horse. Bookie's nightmare. Sayre looks back. Taken the whip to Steel Beach. Hundred to go. Can he hold?'

Nancy and Dakota. She seemed to be whispering in his laid-back right ear, all her weight on the horse's neck. Gradually, the gap closed.

They were at Steel Beach's rump.

Not enough track left for Dakota to win.

Nancy, only hands and heels, every fibre of her body urging Dakota to win.

The horse responded.

Dakota's stride seemed to lengthen by half a metre. They surged, seemed to drag Steel Beach back.

Level.

Metres to go.

Dakota stretched his neck and put his head in front.

'Dakota,' shouted the caller, 'Dakota! It's Dakota Dreaming! Steel Beach second, Celeste's Bazaar a miserable third. What a finish! What a disaster for the bookies!'

Nancy was standing in the stirrups, up above the horse. She raised her whip in triumph. That would cost her a fine. But she didn't care. She'd come from ten goals down at three-quarter time. Life would never be the same again.

We were home.

I looked for Harry. He was unscrewing the top of the little flask of Glenmorangie. He took a swig. I caught his eye. He gave me a nod.

Down below, I could see Tony Ericson and Rex Tie dancing together. The boy, Tom, had his sister on his shoulders.

'Dakota,' said Linda from behind me. 'That's the word you said in your sleep.'

I turned. She was in her leather jacket, windblown, full of life. 'Don't tell Harry Strang I talk in my sleep,' I said. 'Get here in time?'

'Only just. But I didn't know what I was looking for.'

'As long as you found me,' I said. 'That's the important thing.'

She leaned across and kissed me on the mouth. 'Yes. That's the important thing.'

We didn't stay for the rest of the day's racing. On the way back, I put the radio on. Fitzroy was leading Collingwood by two goals with eight minutes to go.

'Got anything on it?' Harry said.

I said, 'Just my whole life.'

'That's too much,' Harry said. 'It's only a game. Not like the horses. You and the lady free for dinner? Cam'll show up, gets out of Sydney alive.'